POPULAR PUBLICATIONS  FACSIMILE EDITIONS

The Pecos Kid Western #1
(July 1950)

The Pecos Kid Western featured Dan Cushman's unconventional Western hero in a dramatic, action-filled pulp. Published by Popular Publications, this series stood out for its unique approach to the genre, featuring gripping clashes and storytelling that broke from traditional Western norms.

Authors:

Dan Cushman, Lloyd Eric Reeve, James Shaffer, E.E. Halleran, Jhan Robbins, Giff Cheshire, Harry F. Olmsted

Illustrators:

Norman Saunders, Frederick Blakeslee, A. Leslie Ross, Charles Dye, Nick Eggenhofer

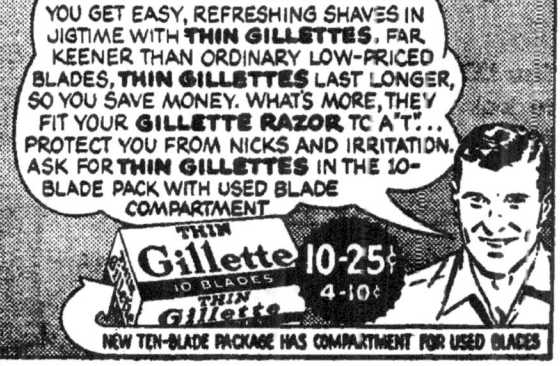

You can buy Lee work clothes
in more retail stores coast-to-coast
THAN ANY OTHER BRAND

Lee WORK CLOTHING DEPT.

Lee RIDERS

More Men wear work clothes bearing a Lee label
THAN ANY OTHER BRAND

The LEE Guarantee: Every Lee garment is guaranteed to look better, fit better and wear longer than any you have ever worn, or you can have a new pair free or your money back.

SANFORIZED FOR PERMANENT FIT

Buy Lee work clothes at leading stores coast-to-coast.

THE H. D. LEE COMPANY, INC.
Kansas City, Mo. ● San Francisco, Calif.
Minneapolis, Minn. ● South Bend, Ind. ● Trenton, N. J.

COPYRIGHT 1990
THE H. D. LEE CO., INC.

WORLD'S LARGEST MANUFACTURERS
OF UNION MADE WORK CLOTHES

25¢

THE Pecos Kid WESTERN

Vol. 1   **July, 1950**   **No. 1**

ALL STORIES NEW—NO REPRINTS   NEXT ISSUE ON SALE JULY 26

Published bi-monthly by Recreational Reading, Inc., an affiliate of Popular Publications, Inc., at 1125 E. Valle Ave., Kokomo, Indiana. Editorial and Executive Offices, 205 East 42nd Street, New York 17, N. Y., Henry Steeger, President and Secretary. Harold S. Goldsmith, Vice-President and Treasurer. Application for entry as second-class matter is pending at the Post Office at Kokomo, Indiana. Copyright, 1950, by Recreational Reading, Inc. This issue is published simultaneously in the Dominion of Canada. Copyright under International Copyright Convention and Pan-American Copyright Conventions. All rights reserved, including the right of reproduction, in whole or in part, in any form. Single copy, 25c. Annual subscription for U.S.A., its possessions and Canada, $1.50; other countries $.38 additional. All correspondence relating to this publication should be addressed to 1125 E. Valle Ave., Kokomo, Indiana, or 205 East 42nd Street, New York 17, N. Y. When submitting manuscripts, enclose stamped, self-addressed envelope for their return if found unavailable. The publishers will exercise care in the handling of unsolicited manuscripts, but assume no responsibility for their return. Printed in U.S.A.

Come and Get It!

A Department

MAYBE once in a blue moon an editor turns over the last page of a manuscript and notes with regret that there is nothing more to follow. With a thoughtful sigh, he gazes out the window and thinks, Too bad it had to stop there. I'd like to know more about this man.

Yes, once in a while real characters leap out of the pages of type—men who breathe the fire of life into the things they do, into the words they say—and it is then that the pages and the words disappear and we are alone with those men out on the Dakota plains, in the redstone canyons of Arizona, up the green draws of Montana.

So it was with the manuscript of the Pecos Kid, which we just finished. We liked it so much that we wanted to hear more about the Kid and his companions, and we think you will too. We started this magazine bearing the Pecos Kid's name, and commissioned Dan Cushman, its author, to do a story each month.

We think you're in for a pleasant surprise. The Pecos Kid is hardly a regulation Western character. For a long time now the Western story has been changing—in style, in slant, in theme. And today, we feel, it has finally grown up.

Writers have found that more true drama and real story value lies in the struggle of the frontiersmen for survival than in the incidental shootin' wars that broke out sporadically in the West—the conflicts which have long been the steady diet for Western fans.

These dramatic clashes did not always break forth in gunfire, but resulted rather in powerful human conflicts that split families up into warring factions, pitted cousin against cousin. Although no bullets may have flown, human emotions were bared in all their raw, naked fury by men struggling with these vital problems of survival.

Of course, Western stories will always have their sweeping movement, their dramatic impact, their stirring conflicts, and will always feature good lively, he-man brawls. And the lusty, hell-for-leather characters of the Old West will always be present, with their tough, vigorous ways and their crisp, salty talk. But the presentation has changed.

More and more the fundamental, basic struggles for life are finding their way into the fiction of the West; more and more the dramatic revelation of character and the evaluation of human worth. An epic figure who could turn a wilderness into a productive range has now found his place in the sun—ahead of the crazy gun-nut who would knock off a dozen Apaches every day to appease his gun-toting ego.

THE Western has come of age. It is no longer a ride-'em-cowboy treatise with a shoot-out per page and a carcass per paragraph. It is a realistic, living story of the true drama of frontier America. It is a credible, vital, true-to-life re-creation of the past, told in terms of the fight for human decency against insurmountable odds in a savage environment.

You can see these problems of human adjustment becoming more important in

(Continued on page 8)

Our new refrigerator had a new fur coat in it!

SMART WOMAN! She didn't have to go without either a fur coat or a new refrigerator. The money she saved by getting a modern air-conditioned ICE refrigerator bought a magnificent fur coat.

You can do the same! You, too, can have a new refrigerator *and* that new fur coat—or new furniture—or electric washer.

And when you have your new ICE refrigerator you'll enjoy the finest in complete, scientific food protection—in a beautiful, roomy refrigerator you'll be proud to own.

See your local Ice Company today. You'll be surprised to learn how much you'll save by buying a modern air-conditioned ICE refrigerator.

Genuine ICE

1850—ONE HUNDRED YEARS OF ICE PROGRESS—1950

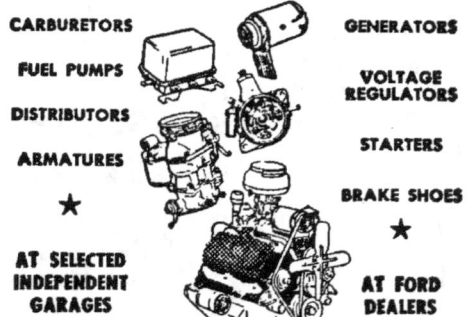
THE PECOS KID WESTERN

(Continued from page 6)

other forms of entertainment, too. Take the movies. In "Quicksand," a new United Artists picture starring Mickey Rooney, the theme is the struggle for riches against a hostile background of poverty. Rooney's fight against the "quicksand" of crime that pulls a fundamentally honest man down is fascinating drama for the audience, because of our growing interest in the whys and wherefores of crime and criminals.

In "D.O.A."—Dead on Arrival—a United Artists picture starring Edmond O'Brien, the theme is slightly different, but once again it emphasizes the battle a normal man must make for survival against a background of crime and evil. It is the theme and the problem of crime that dominates the picture—not the blood-and-thunder shoot-outs.

Entertainment in the U.S. has come of age, certainly. And so have our Westerns.

This is all in the way of an introduction to the Pecos Kid. Here you will meet real people and live with them at a time when all life seethed with the fires of political intrigue and social upheaval—the time of the building of the West. You will see the world as it was then—lusty, tough, raw—and you will see it, feel it, live it, with one of the most interesting gents of the frontier—Bill Warren, known otherwise as The Pecos Kid.

And by the way, this is the space where readers, writers, and editors have their say. We'd be delighted to hear from you on any topic concerning the Old West, or, if you'd like to tell us what you think of the Pecos Kid and his compadres, we'd be glad to hear about that, too. This space here belongs to you. Come and get it!

See you again in our second issue—on sale July 26.

Until then—*hasta la vista!*

I.C.S. training was <u>his</u>
"BRIDGE TO SUCCESS"

Hayden M. Hargett took his first I. C. S. course while he was still a student in high school.

He is now County Engineer of Franklin County, Alabama. Last year Mr. Hargett designed 27 homes, two theaters, a bus station and three bridges. He supervised fifty miles of highway construction and the paving of one hundred thousand square yards of city streets.

Mr. Hargett recently enrolled for another I. C. S. course

Listen to what he has to say about I. C. S. training: "It's more practical—more flexible than any training I've had. I can't speak highly enough of my I. C. S. training."

Mr. Hargett says his first I. C. S. course was his "bridge to success." "There might not have been much of a career," he said, "if it hadn't been for that first I. C. S. course."

I. C. S. training can be your "bridge to success." Mail the coupon today!

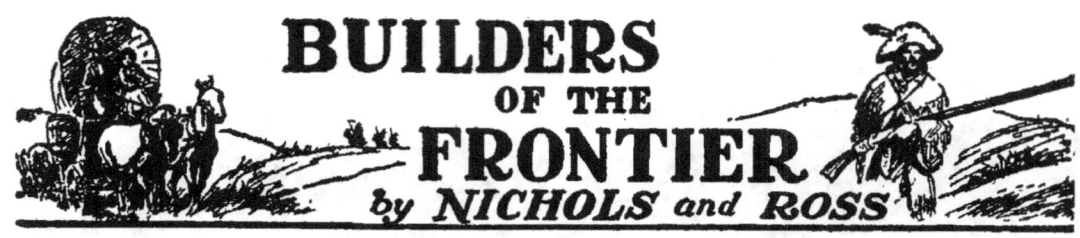

BUILDERS
OF THE
FRONTIER
by NICHOLS and ROSS

HERBERT WELLES

1 When little Herbert Welles arrived in San Francisco, the local populace held on tightly to their wallets and laughed at his queer accent. Herbert was one of the notorious Sydney Ducks, an ex-Australian convict. Although most of the other Sydney Ducks remained on the coast and practiced their specialized talents of robbery, mayhem and murder, Herbert headed south. He wanted to leave his past behind him.

2 In Ladenton, Texas, Welles took a job with Mel Porter's Bar-P Ranch. Porter found him a valuable hand. Once when Indians attacked the ranch, Welles assumed command and routed the redskins. Another time when Porter's young son came down with a mysterious malady, Welles stayed by his side for eight days and nights and nursed the youngster back to health.

3 The Australian was well on his way to amassing enough money to buy his own ranch when five of his former comrades arrived in Ladenton. They threatened that unless he helped them rustle the herd, they would reveal his past to Porter. Herbert's answer was his gun. Although he killed two of the Sydney Ducks and wounded the other three, he himself was badly shot up.

4 When Porter came to his side, Welles was near death. His last words were, "There's no room for such crooked blokes in our West." The cowboys from the Bar-P who attended the funeral said it was too bad that the little cowpoke died so far away from home. Porter knew better. Herbert Welles had died protecting his home.

Behind them, Hoss and his men were making a run for it.

Introducing Three Men You Can Ride the River With

By

DAN CUSHMAN

Riders of the Gunsmoke Rim

A more strangely assorted trio of saddle pardners you never met. Big Jim Swing met trouble like a starving man hitting a beef-steak .... Hernandez Flanagan, the irrepressible, laughed at it, then bet his last peso he could lick it one-handed .... While Bill Warren, the Pecos Kid, rider of mystery, carefully doped out the angles, and then hit with the sudden force of a lightning bolt .... Take that certain night when lawless Miles City was roaring for their blood....

CHAPTER ONE

Action at Night

HE RODE at a steady pace, slowly out-distancing his two companions and the four hundred head of Wyoming stocker cattle they were driving, and finally reined in on a rise of prairie overlooking the limitless badlands and mirage of the Yellowstone country.

He had the slouched and easy manner of one who spent as much time in the saddle as out of it. He seemed perfectly relaxed. His eyes had a slow thoughtfulness as they roved and picked out the tiny details of that vast, brown prairie.

He'd been there long enough to smoke his way slowly through a hand-rolled cigarette when his two companions quit their places by the herd and rode up, one on each side of him.

"So, Señor Keed," the smaller of the two said, with a handsome flash of teeth from his deeply browned face. "The Yellowstone. The end of the trail—no?"

"Sure, Butch, that's the Yellowstone." Then the Kid twisted the left side of his mouth and added, "The hell with it."

William Calhoun Warren, the Pecos Kid, had no particular reason for this condemnation. It was merely a statement of attitude, general in scope, including many things besides the muddy Yellowstone. It was thus his companions accepted it.

"Yes, Señor. Si. The hell weeth it. To hell with this hot country—the sun, the heat, the dust in the throat. Tonight the Two Bar and more of thees miserable salt pork and beans. But *tomorrow!* Tomorrow the bright light, the sparkle of wine, the laughing señorita. So?"

"So. So you get in any more jams and you'll shoot your way out of them by yourself."

The Pecos Kid could remember saying substantially the same thing to Hernandez Pedro Gonzales y Fuente Jesús Maria Flanagan in McCaffeyville, Arkansas City and Abilene, in Baker Town, Cheyenne and in a number of lesser places along the route without once exactly backing up his threat when the chips were down.

"And that goes for you, too, Jimmy my boy," he said to Big Jim Swing, a huge cowboy with pale eyes and a mass of burlap-colored hair only partly hidden by his California sombrero. "When we get to Miles, you can visit the fleshpots on your own. Oh, the hell with it. Why should I worry about an Irish-Spanish halfbreed and two hundred pounds of California saddle tramp?"

"And to hell weeth you, too, Señor!" Hernandez Flanagan said.

Bill Warren, the Pecos Kid, slouched around in the saddle. His eyes had come to rest on a rattlesnake that had just slid partly from view in a clump of sagebrush. His right hand came up in a movement that was apparently casual, and yet it was weighted with a .44 caliber Colt. It exploded and he shouted,

"Heads!"

THE SNAKE writhed into view. Hernandez Flanagan drew an instant later, hesitated half a second aiming across the saddlehorn and pulled the trigger.

"Tails!"

His slug, traveling with a fine degree of accuracy, had severed the snake's rattles.

Big Jim Swing bent over and picked them up. "Eight," he said.

Hernandez sadly drew a black leather notebook from a saddlebag, wet a stub pencil, and carefully inscribed a figure.

"Thees makes fifty thousand dollars I owe you for snakes alone, Señor."

"I'll settle for a dollar six bits."

"Ha! Would I be insulted by taking a reduction? Have I not told you? A debt of the Flanagans is never forgotten. These moneys will I go on owing you until the last day of time."

Bill Warren laughed. It relaxed the lean, dehydrated lines of his face and gave it a fleeting, boyish expression. A person seeing him at that second would have found it hard to believe he was the man whose guns had burned the reputation of the Pecos Kid from the Rio Grande to Montana.

He loaded up and said, "You boys go back and keep those cows drifting toward water. Springs yonder. I'll ride down to the Two Bar."

The Pecos Kid touched his blunt, star-roweled spurs and let his sorrel cayuse take an easy pace down descending benches toward the scattered buildings and corrals of the Two Bar. A slight breeze was coming from the badlands of the Yellowstone, so he slid back his Confederate cavalry hat to get the feel of it in his unruly red hair.

He noticed there were no horses in the corrals. No one around. His instincts, long trained in the anticipation of trouble, caused him to ease back on the bridle and take the last two hundred yards at a slow walk.

He noticed a window of stretched antelope skin punched by three round holes near the bottom. Here and there, fresh scars cut through the gray weathered surface of cottonwood logs. The house had taken a bullet-beating, and not long before.

He reined in, shouted, "Hey, in there!"

His voice had a flat sound in the late afternoon heat. He swung down, walked with a tinkle of spurs across the hard-beaten ground, paused at the door. His eyes, long used to sun, were blind for a while—then he made out the main room of the house.

It was a combined kitchen and living room with even a couple of bunks against one wall. A can of flapjack batter stood on the table. A bullet had smashed through near the bottom and most of its contents had run across the table and through its broad cracks. The batter was dry and wrinkled across the surface, but still sticky beneath. It had happened that morning, or the night before.

He walked to the next room. Even darker, there. He kicked an empty cartridge case that jingled across the floor. Empty cases lay everywhere. Forty-fours, for either a Colt or a Winchester.

The room seemed hot and suffocating. Actually it was cooler than outside, but the Pecos Kid, like many who spent most of their time outdoors, had an aversion and suspicion of houses.

HE WENT back to the yard. Everything seemed to be as it had been, and yet a taut expectancy held him. He stood quite still, his face thoughtful, his eyes narrowed to blue-gray slits. No movement. No sound. Only the dull fly-drone of afternoon. He walked across to the stock sheds—rude buildings of upright cottonwood posts with pole and hay roofs. There again—the glint of cartridges.

"Heads!"

He said the word unexpectedly. Perhaps it even surprised himself. He spun, drew, fired, all in one careless movement.

There was no snake. One of the empty cartridge cases leaped from the ground and buzzed for fifty feet, coming to rest against a clump of hoof-trampled sage.

He laughed easily to himself, blew smoke from the gun, and reloaded it quietly.

Shooting had snapped the tight feeling of repression that had settled over him. It effected him like whiskey might another man.

He no longer felt that someone was watching him. He walked in his spavined cowboy manner across the yard, remounted, and retraced his way back to the herd.

"Snake?" Big Jim asked, referring to the shot.

"No, just *bang*. I don't like quiet places."

Big Jim jerked his head in disgust. He could go for weeks on end without feeling compelled to burn a cartridge, while Hernandez and the Kid were blasting them by the boxful.

The Kid went on, speaking softly, "Shootin' seems to be in style here in Montana Territory, anyhow. If you're in doubt of that, my three-ton friend, just go down and see what they did to the poor old Two Bar."

Another search of the place revealed nothing. Only more empty cartridges out in the sagebrush. It looked as if somebody had put up an all-night stand.

The Pecos Kid rode off, musing, "You know, I heard that Dermott was having himself some trouble over this Mandan Springs country. And Carson down in Cheyenne said there was plenty of money due to grow out of this ground once the Northern Pacific Railroad pushed her rails in from Dakota Territory."

"*This* ground?" Big Jim asked, looking at the baked gumbo.

"It doesn't look anything extra as a cow country, does it? I wonder what in hell was worth shooting about down there."

The Pecos Kid was unusually thoughtful all the while they moved the herd to one of the springs that made a green splash of color along the descending benches.

Hernandez, noticing his preoccupation, said, "I theenk it is that girl across the tracks in Dodge. The girl who would have been mine had she not seen your pink hair, Señor. Is she the one you dream of, Keed?"

"No. I was thinking about Dermott, and the million-dollar proposition he's supposed to have for us. And I was just wondering how many bullets we'd end up by ducking ourselves."

"Bullets, *poof!* The lead bullet is the national flower of Chihuahua. The coat of arms of my family, Señor—one bullet hole rampant on the upside-down sombrero. And the motto, 'Shoot first and talk afterward.'"

Big Jim Swing grumbled, "I'll end up by buryin' both of you."

It was almost dark when their supper of salt pork and flapjacks had been cooked on a tiny fire amid box elder brush.

"You stand first watch as usual," Bill Warren said to Jim. "On foot. Just hunker in the brush with your Winchester. I don't want some bushwhacker knocking you off."

For a long time after lying down in his tarp and blanket, Bill Warren lay watching the sky overhead through the box elder leaves. He fell asleep without real-

izing it, and awakened suddenly as Big Jim prowled in at the end of his watch.

"Nothing?"

"Didn't hear a thing."

WARREN dressed, drew his Winchester from its scabbard, followed the hoof-punched mud along a tiny stream leading down from the springs. Away from brush shadow, things were sharply revealed by the moon's strong highlight and shadow.

He moved carefully beyond the bushes, climbed a low knoll, and sat in the shadow of a sagebrush cold-smoking a cigarette.

The cattle seemed a trifle restless. One cow, three or four hundred yards away, was up and bawling. He flipped the cigarette away.

Gunfire came in a concerted rattle, sending pencils of flame from the side of a dry wash.

Warren instinctively brought up the Winchester, but the shooting was far out of range. An instant later riders appeared, single file, racing from the dry wash. shouting and firing to stampede the cattle.

The rest happened with amazing rapidity. Instantly the herd was up and on the move. It was as though every animal had been crouched and waiting instead of bedded for the night.

For an instant they seemed headed for the camp, but they ran parallel with the creek straight for the maze of coulees and dry washes that make up the Yellowstone badlands. Dust rose, and here and there he could still glimpse the red flare of burning powder.

He ran down, past the springs. Big Jim was bellowing.

"It's me," Warren said, glimpsing gunshine.

"What in hell?"

The hoofs were a diminishing rumble. No shooting now. He located his hobbled horse. Too late, by the time he'd freed the animal. Night air that had been sharp and clean was now choking full of heavy dust.

"Keed!" Hernandez said.

"Here I am."

"Ha!" Hernandez' teeth showed in the dark. "At least I have the good fortune to be relieved of my morning watch. You theenk perhaps it is rustlers? There is nothing your dear Hernandez Pedro Gonzales y Fuente Jesús Maria Flanagan would rather do that go on the hunt for those two-legged wolves, the rustlers."

"Rustlers be damned! No rustler would be dull enough to drive cattle in the breaks where it'd take two weeks to round them up."

"Ah, so. Then you theenk it is the enemies of our dear employer that we have never met, thees Señor Moneybags whose dirty Gringo name I have forgotten?"

"Dermott? I don't know. I don't know whether he has any idea what's going on out here or not. But I intend to ride in to Miles Town tomorrow and find out."

CHAPTER TWO

Gunman's Town

DAYLIGHT. They followed the churned ground of the stampede and sat for a while, scanning intricately eroded country in the direction of the Yellowstone. Half an hour later Hernandez located the tracks of saddle horses heading across bench country to the east.

Six horsemen. Perhaps seven. They made no particular effort to make sure. After eight or nine miles one of the sets a tracks quit the rest and struck out cross-country toward Miles.

Bill Warren jerked his head indicating they'd follow the lone rider's tracks.

"Follow *one* of 'em?" Jim blurted.

"I'd rather swap bullets with one man than five," the Pecos Kid said with great seriousness. "It's safer."

For mile after mile the Pecos Kid rode in silence, watching the hoof marks of the lone horsemen as they disappeared and appeared again on the hard-baked gumbo of the prairie. He was thinking about this job he'd taken. There was something peculiar about it. He'd thought so from the first when Wallace Carson, the wholesale merchant in Cheyenne, had hired him in the name of Roger Dermott of Miles Town to drive a herd of cattle northward to the Yellowstone.

Three hundred dollars would have been generous enough pay for the three of them. Instead, Wallace Carson had paid over five hundred and promised him that Dermott would have an unusual proposition for him when the drive was completed.

"There are big things happening along the Yellowstone, what with the Northern Pacific on its way from Bismarck," Carson had said. "Dermott needs a man like you. He has a proposition that will make you one of the big men of the Northwest."

The idea of himself, Bill Warren, the Pecos Kid, late of the Confederate cavalry and later of more places than he could remember, being one of the *big men of the Northwest* amused him. He laughed about it now.

Hernandez was at one side, slightly behind. Something he did telegraphed his intention, and the Pecos Kid turned, drawing at the same instant. But Hernandez' cross-draw was ahead of him and the snake was left writhing and headless.

"Heads!"

Warren checked himself with his thumb hooked over the hammer. "Tails," he said sadly, taking a long bead to cut the rattles off.

"And now, Señor, I am pleased to tell you that I owe you only forty-nine thousand and nine hundred dollars '"

The sun had set when they reached Miles. Lights were burning here and there in a saloon or dance hall. The hoofs of countless saddle horses had pulverized the gumbo of Front Street until it was fine and grayish white, like unbleached flour. After the hard prairie it was like riding across a featherbed.

THEY reined in before the Apex Livery stable and sat for a while, stiff and tired from a day in the saddle. At last a halfbreed boy came from inside. Warren got down them, tossed him the reins, and limped around kicking the stiffness of long travel from his legs.

He started limping away and paused fifteen or twenty steps away on one of the platform sidewalks.

"I'm going to hunt out Dermott," he said, addressing Hernandez, "and you lay off the high wine till I get back. You just lost a herd of mighty fine stockers for the gentleman, and if he wants your story as well as mine, I'd like to have you sober enough to give it."

"You have ever seen me drunk, Señor? Me? Hernandez Pedro Gonzales—"

"I said to stay sober or so help me I'll part that wavy black hair of yours with the barrel of my .44." He pointed to Big Jim and said, "That goes for you, too. I'm sick of getting you out of jams. If you get in one tonight, you can go out feet first, and the hell with you!"

"And the hell weeth you, too, Señor!"

A batwing door flapped as he walked by, and the Kid caught the stale odor of beer. A grin broke the lines of his face when he thought maybe he'd have a hard enough time keeping himself clear of the whiskey dumps, let alone worry about anyone so eminently able to care for himself as Hernandez Flanagan.

It was growing dark, but there was still enough light to reveal a warehouse sign down by the river docks reading "Dermott & Co., Freight."

A jerkline mule outfit had been pulled up to the loading platform, and the driver directed him to some outside stairs that led to Dermott's office.

There was a short length of hall, a door. He rapped without getting an answer. No light. Dermott obviously wasn't there.

He cursed through his teeth. He was in a hurry to find Dermott. That lone horseman headed to Miles—it could mean nothing, but it troubled him.

He went outside, found the Carson Brothers store, asked for him there. They directed him to the express office. Dermott had not been there since late that afternoon.

He had no reason to suppose the lone horsemen had ridden in to kill Dermott. Yet the hunch was there, growing inside him.

He found the marshal—a long, lean man by the name of Wells. He shook his head at mention of Dermott's name. He didn't seem to care a damn whether Warren found him or not.

"Look for him tomorrow."

"What if he happens to get bushwhacked tonight?"

"Well, what if he does?"

Not everyone in Miles worried about Dermott's health.

He was passing a Chinese cafe. He stopped abruptly. A man sitting inside seemed familiar. He was lean and hunched with big hands dangling at the ends of skinny, long arms. He must have felt Warren's gaze, for he whirled around and stood with the thumb of his right hand hooked in his pants band just above the butt of a Colt revolver.

WARREN knew him by some mannerism of his movement, even before seeing his long, slack-jawed face. The gunman—Eldad Stark.

He carried two guns, low, and tied to his legs with bits of whang leather. The strings made his legs look skinny and his gray cotton pants too big for him.

"Well I'm damned," said Stark. "It's the Pecos Kid."

"Who you riding for these days, Stark?"

Stark lacked a well-rounded intelligence,

but there was a weasel quality about him, and he was sharp enough to catch the sarcasm in Warren's question.

"I take care of my business. And as far as that goes, you never was one to put many saddle boils on *your* rump, either. If you have an idea of ringing me in on that Arkansas River business, I'll tell you this—I was in Dodge that time, working for Sam Black."

Bill Warren had spent four months of the past year working for the Arkansas River Stockman's Federation running down a band of cattle raiders, whites and halfbreeds who's disguised themselves as Comanches.

"You're too quick for me." Warren watched him with eyes that were narrow and hard as slits of blue-gray quartz. "I never thought you had anything to do with it."

No, Stark would never fool with anything that involved so much work as cattle raiding, but the Kid didn't say so. Stark was afraid of him, but he'd go for those low-slung guns rather than take any abuse in public. He wanted no fight with the man right now.

Stark swaggered a little and said, "All right, then." He leaned against the building so he could see Warren and down the street both. By his attitude it was obvious he was waiting for someone. His right hand stayed nervous above his gun.

"Who you waiting to bushwhack, Eldad?" Warren asked.

"I don't bushwhack."

"You didn't just ride into town, did you?"

Stark was looking at him beneath droopy eyelashes. His slack jaw moved and he was smiling a little.

Warren went on, "You didn't ride in from Mandan Springs way on a lame horse to put a slug through Roger Dermott?"

Stark laughed, and it sounded genuine. "Why, Kid. Ain't you heard? I shouldn't tell you this, not yet, but it's too good to keep. Us, me and you, we're on the same side of this fence. Sure. I work for Dermott, too."

Warren stood for a while, thinking it over. "How did you know I was working for Dermott?"

"He told me. Right after you rode into town."

"He knows I'm here?"

"Dermott keeps pretty close tab on things in Miles. He knows you're here, all right."

"Where is he?"

Stark shrugged his loose shoulders. There was something down the street now occupying his attention. That nervous right hand had stopped. A woman had come from the front door of a two-story frame building called "Jonny's Round Tent" and was walking toward them along the platform sidewalks.

She was taking her time, apparently waiting for somebody to see her. Warren knew she was part of the play—part of Eldad Stark's play.

A third party took his place. This was a tall young man, a cowboy, who walked from the door of a general store and was looking across at her. The tall young man started to cross the street. Stark had gone lax, his arms long and loose.

"Stark!" Warren shouted.

Sound of the gunman's name made the young cowboy spin around. He saw Stark then by side light from the Chinese cafe. He realized instantly that the gunman had been placed there to kill him.

HE STEPPED back. For an instant it seemed that he was going to reach for the sixgun on his hip. He didn't. He got his hands high, hooked the door behind him with his spur, opened it, went back inside.

"Stark, you got a match for my cigarette?" Warren asked in soft amusement.

The woman had stopped and was looking across the street at them. She had a soft, dusky loveliness—no ordinary dance hall girl even though she had come from the Round Tent.

Stark said, "Do you know—"

"I know I don't like deadfalls."

Stark remained for a moment looking at him with savage eyes, then he turned and slouched down the street.

A couple of freighters came from the Chinese cafe picking their teeth. "Who was he?" Warren asked, jerking his head at the tall cowboy.

"One of them tough Barbour boys from Mandan Springs. He's in here chasing Lona Pearl again. Hoss Barbour would break his neck if he knew." He appraised the woman and muttered, "Not that I blame him."

Warren glanced at the woman again. So she was Lona Pearl! It was easy to see why men were still talking about her when they got as far away as Dodge. She had a round, full beauty that hit a man hard.

She was looking at Warren. Still watching him, smiling a little, she stepped down from the platform sidewalk and picked her way across the soft dust of the street.

"Hello, boy," she said.

Bill Warren was twenty-eight, with three years of the Civil War and ten years of frontier trails and boom towns behind him, but there was something that made those camp-following women grow wistful when they saw his face. That woman in San Saba had called him "boy," too, and there was that blonde girl across the tracks in Dodge.

Lona Pearl came close, and he was conscious of her subtle, New Orleans perfume.

"Boy, why don't you speak to women?"

Warren grinned and said, "Is it safe?"

She laughed, knowing he was referring to the deadfall that she and Stark had set for that tall Barbour fellow. She was the sort of woman who would enjoy seeing a man die for her.

"Why don't you see me at the Round Tent?" she asked, tilting her head at the two-story dance hall down the street.

"How about Johnny Malette?"

She was Johnny's girl—Johnny Malette, the riverboat gambler who had lighted in Miles and built the Round Tent.

"You're afraid of him, M'shu? I thought the Pecos Kid was afraid of nothing."

Everyone seemed to know him in Miles town. It's not easy to ride off and leave a reputation after once you've blazed it out.

She walked away, smiling over her shoulder. There was a swaying motion about her that was an invitation.

SO DERMOTT knew he was in town, and Dermott was able to take care of himself. The Pecos Kid decided to have that cold bottle of St. Louis beer.

A wrinkled old Chinese was blocking his way when he turned. He was holding a slip of paper covered with Chinese characters—a lottery ticket.

"Fifty cent? Win fifty dolla?"

A four-bit piece caught light from one of the windows as he flipped it over.

"Does Roger Dermott hang out at Johnny Malette's Round Tent?"

"Yah. Plenty much." He was at work on the ticket, dabbing saliva-ink over certain of the Chinese characters. He handed it over grinning harder than ever. "You lucky. Red hair lucky. Maybe you win hunna-dolla. Two hunna-dolla."

"Don't break yourself, John."

He put the lottery ticket away and clomped inside a bar. He was there when Big Jim Swing rushed in and said,

"You better come down to the Round Tent."

"Have a beer."

"No. Listen Kid, Butch has got hold of the tiger's tail for sure this time."

"That Spanish-Irish halfbreed can take

care of himself. Who's the woman—Lona Pearl?"

"You already heard?"

"No, I'm just a good guesser."

CHAPTER THREE

The Lone Rider

WARREN stopped at one end of the crowded bar in the Round Tent and asked for St. Louis beer. He looked around, studied the room. The saloon and gambling house were in one section of the building, there was a wide arch, and beyond a combination theatre and dance hall. Only a couple of lamps were burning. A fiddler was tuning up.

The ceiling of the dance hall was lower than the saloon and a balcony had been cut through with stairs that led directly from the saloon to its second story. A man was sitting up there, keeping to shadow, tilted against the wall.

After a time he moved, scratched. It was Eldad Stark.

Deadfall. The more he looked at things here in Miles, the less he like working for Roger Dermott.

"There's Tom Barbour!" a man said near him.

He whirled. Tom Barbour, the tall cowboy, had come in the room. Warren had his first good view of him as he stood looking flushed and sharp-eyed around the room. He was about twenty-one, and if a person didn't know, he'd have taken him to be one of those Easterners who came West to heal their diseased lungs.

Barbour saw Lona. He became eager, almost smiling. He pushed through, never taking his eyes from her.

A hushed expectancy settled over the room. Men edged away, wary for trouble.

Lona was smiling with a soft, feline quality. She moved with a slight sway of her body, half circled the table, stopped with her eyes on Tom Barbour's face.

Barbour reached as though expecting her to take his hand. She didn't.

"Lona. Come here."

She laughed. A dulcet sound.

"Lona. I want to talk to you."

"But do I want to talk to *you?*"

"But last week you said—"

"I have said many things. And I have changed my mind. Tonight I do not want to see you."

His face went hollow. He said something through his teeth. Perhaps he

Roger Dermott

cursed her. Warren wouldn't have blamed him. She was deliberately building the thing to a shoot-out.

Barbour started forward. She moved, but only a little.

"Don't touch me!" She flung herself against the wall, looked back at the table she had left. Warren started. Her companion there was Hernandez Flanagan. The Irish-Mexican's eyes were glittering with sardonic amusement. He smiled slowly. "You weel leave the girl alone, Señor!"

Barbour did not seem to hear him. He came another step, but Lona still avoided him. She pretended to be weeping. Barbour moved closer to her.

"Leave her alone!" Hernandez rapped out.

Barbour for the first time took notice of Hernandez. "You stay out o' this! I ain't takin' anything from any damned greaser."

Hernandez was smiling. There was a tense, glittering quality about it that Warren recognized.

"Butch!" Warren shouted.

Tom Barbour had turned to face Hernandez. His feet were spread, he'd rocked to a half-crouch, his right hand was poised and tense. It was a gunfighter's pose, but his Colt was too far back on his hip, its butt too flat with his body. He'd be no match for the deft, border cross-draw that those Chihuahua aristocrats start learning at the age of six.

THERE was a bare half-scond of hesitation. Then Barbour spun aside with his hand raking upward. Men stampeded. Warren was already hurling a heavy oak chair. The chair struck Hernandez shoulder high, its unexpected weight driving him to the wall.

His gun, already out, exploded, sending wild flame across the heads of the crowd.

Warren was diving forward even as he hurled the chair. He smashed Barbour's gun from his hand at the same instant it cleared the holster. Warren's weight carried the taller man to the wall.

Barbour's head snapped back and struck hard. Stunned, he fell forward. Warren wheeled to a crouch. His gun was drawn, angled toward Eldad Stark in the balcony.

"Drop it!" Warren said.

Stark was crouched, his left-hand pistol drawn. His face was slack and savage. He hated Warren—he'd always hated him. He'd been waiting up there to get Barbour in the back, but he'd gladly have blasted Bill Warren instead.

Stark looked for a few seconds down the black muzzle of Warren's .44. He shrugged and slid his own gun back in its holster.

"Johnny don't want trouble around her," Stark said lamely.

A man had picked up Tom Barbour's gun. Warren took it and punched out the cartridges. Barbour was up but groggy. He looked at Warren and snarled, "Damn you!"

"He just saved your life, cowboy," a short, middle-aged man said.

Warren gave him the gun. "Don't try to load it."

Barbour was still cursing, but he put the gun away as it was.

"You know him, Bolton," somebody said. "Get him his horse and start him out of town."

Bolton was a blond cowboy about Barbour's age. He said, "His horse is lame."

The words struck the Pecos Kid like a jolt to the face. He looked at Barbour and remembered what they'd said about "those tough Barbour boys from Mandan Springs."

Tom Barbour was the lone rider they'd been following. And he'd saved the man's life. He laughed and walked back to the bar.

CHAPTER FOUR

Dermott

BARBOUR was gone, and Warren was halfway through his second bottle of beer when a Negro man came up, touched the bill of his stiff-billed steamboat cap and said,

"Mist' Warren, seh. A gentman would like to see you. Upstairs."

"Who is he?"

"Mist' Dermott."

The name brought Warren up in a hurry. He clomped down the bottle and followed. At last he was to meet Roger Dermott face to face.

The Negro led him across the balcony, down a short hall, rapped at a gilded door.

"Come in!" said the voice of Lona Pearl.

She stepped back, silhouetted by lamplight, smiling at him. Warren went in. The room was luxurious. In the center stood a table of Caribbean mahogany, carved after the Cuban fashion. A chair had been placed for him. There were glasses and a decanter of something that looked like sherry.

"Drink, boy?" she asked.

It was Portuguese brandy with a sweetish taste—sickening after beer.

She said, "You're afraid of me, boy?"

"Leave him alone, Lona," a man said. He walked into the room. "I'm Johnny Malette."

Johnny Malette was medium in height and weight, about thirty-five years old, muscular, graceful. His skin was dark, hair almost black, thick and combed in a pompadour. Despite the warmth of the room he wore a coat and vest. No gun in sight. It would be carried gambler style in an armpit holster.

They shook hands and Malette said, "Well, it isn't often one finds a major of cavalry in this water hole of hell."

"I thought this was an army post." Warren was referring to Fort Keough across the river.

"Union army!"

"Why, yes. Isn't that the only army left? I'm sorry, Malette, but I stopped fighting the war eight or nine years ago."

"I suppose that's a good enough attitude—but I can't help hating the yellow guts of those Yankees who grab the range and let you Texas boys eat the dirt off the drag."

"Tom Barbour sounded like a Texas boy."

Johnny Malette's face went hard. "Why'd you say that?"

"I know you had a deadfall set. Maybe that's your business. But after this, fur-nish your own triggers, and don't drag my boy Hernandez in on it."

Mallette stood quite still. His fingers, long, manicured and dead looking, rested on the edge of the table.

"You're my guest," he said.

"That word only applies among gentlemen."

DERMOTT had a firm step. He came in and stood for a moment looking in Warren's face. He was powerful, about thirty-five, and his eyes, at that moment, seemed to have the power of seeing into a man's mind.

What he saw in Warren's seemed to please him. He said, "Warren, I'm damned glad to meet you."

"Not after you hear about those cattle at the Two Bar."

"I already heard, and I'm still glad to meet you. You don't need to tell me about the Two Bar. Those gunmen spent all night trying to get Prescott, but he was out in the coulees when they stampeded the cattle. In a way I'm glad they did it, because now you know what I'm up against." He lifted the brandy. "Have you ever heard of the Northern Pacific land grant?"

Warren nodded. There'd been much public attention centered on the Northern Pacific land since Black Friday, and the failure of Jay Cooke and Company, and the scandal recolving around the Credit Mobelier. The Credit Mobelier was a money-raising agency of the Union Pacific which had apparently insinuated itself a little too closely to the government moneybags. Although the N.P. had escaped scandal, there'd been considerable scrutiny of the forty-seven million acres of land which the railroad had been given on each side of its right-of-way.

Dermott went on. "I'm a businessman. I know what will happen to steamboat transportation when the Northern Pacific shoves its rails west from Bismarck. The

Dermott steamboat line will be through. Horse-drawn freight will hang on for a while. Maybe a dozen years, each year less profitable. I can't fight the railroad. It will develop the country, and if I make my investments wisely I'll develop along with it.

"It was with this in mind that I purchased my options on certain N.P. sections. Some of them happen to cover the area around Mandan Springs. The springs follow low ground roughly parallel with the Yellowstone, cropping up here and there on a flat valley floor. Naturally, they attracted settlers. The settlers have no title to the land, but they've built shanties, corrals, a few things like that, and they're running cattle.

"I have the right to put them off, but I don't care to get myself a bad reputation. I made an offer to purchase all the improvements. Offered to freight everything free of charge up north to the Musselshell. But the settlers got together and formed what they call the Mandan Springs Protective Association. They're fortified at Cap Coyne's ranch, now. Frankly, I think Cap would be willing to compromise, but the Barbour boys are shouting *damnyankee* and all the old Rebs want to fight Pea Ridge all over again."

Bill Warren said, "If it's only a long term investment, I'd sit tight."

ROGER Dermott laughed and stopped looking at his blunt fingers. "I've been sitting tight. Now they've taken to sniping at my steamboats. There's no way of patrolling the river, even if the army didn't have its hands full watching Sitting Bull.

"On its way up, the *Western Enterprise* was fired on and one of the bullets came within a single inch of striking Mrs. Thad Nolan of Bozeman. She was in her stateroom and it broke the water pitcher she'd just put back on the stand. The *Red Cloud* had three windows torn out of her pilot house while she was hung up on a sandbar at the Wilkes Crossing."

"Sure they weren't Indian bullets?"

"I'm not sure of anything. All I'm sure of is that I started having trouble with the Barbour boys and my steamboats started getting riddled at the same time."

Dermott got to his feet with a sudden movement and stood with hands thrust in pockets, fists doubled, drawing his cross-weave riding trousers tight. "Damn it, man, I've always believed in direct action. When a man shoots at me, it's been my policy to shoot back. Sitting still in the middle of this row is the hardest thing I've ever had to do."

"And so you sent for me," Warren said. "It's too bad that I'm not a traveling gun-hawk. When Carson talked to me in Cheyenne, he said you had some sort of a *business* proposition. I'm like you. I'd like to take root somewhere and grow. I have a couple of friends, too."

"I'm not interested in the gun at your hip."

"No?"

"Gunmen are thirteen to the dozen. I'm not gong to start shooting unless I have to."

"So what am I to do?"

"I want you to go out there for me. You're a Texan. You were once an officer under Johnston. Maybe they'll listen to you. It's as much for their good as it is for mine."

"Just *what* do you want me to do?"

"Tell them I'll pay for all the improvements they've put on the land."

"*Their* valuation?"

"Senator Reeves is coming out here next month—"

"Carpetbagger Reeves?" Warren said wrily.

"I don't intend to argue his qualifications for office. He's a United States senator, and he's coming here representing the Committee on Public Lands. I'm willing to let him arbitrate the price. If you can't get them to accept my offer, at least prevent them from attacking my boats. If they have anything drastic in mind, I'd like to know about it in time to fight it."

"And that business proposition you mentioned?"

"Carson and myself are incorporating under the title of Northwest Mercantile. It's inevitable, I suppose, that a concern like ours would get in the cattle business on a pretty far-flung basis. I can't think of anyone who could better manage it than yourself. You and those two friends you ride with.

"If you carry this thing through successfully, I'm willing to write you down for a five per cent share of our capital stock. I hope you realize how much that would amount to."

Dermott waited. "Well?"

"I'll tell you tomorrow."

CHAPTER FIVE

The J Bar O Boys

IT WAS evening when the Pecos Kid, Hernandez Flanagan and Big Jim Swing drew their horses to a halt on rim-rock overlooking the long valley which bore the name Mandan Springs. This was where the Barbour boys and Cap Coyne were forted up.

Streams wound here and there, their courses marked by dark lines of willow and box elder. Grass was good, but not exceptional. A log cabin and some corrals, built at one of the nearby springs, had apparently been abandoned. About three miles to the north they could see a larger accumulation of log buildings and corrals, and that, they knew, was Cap Coyne's place, the Double C.

They could see a man riding up from a pasture, driving half a dozen horses. Despite distance, the clear, rare atmos-

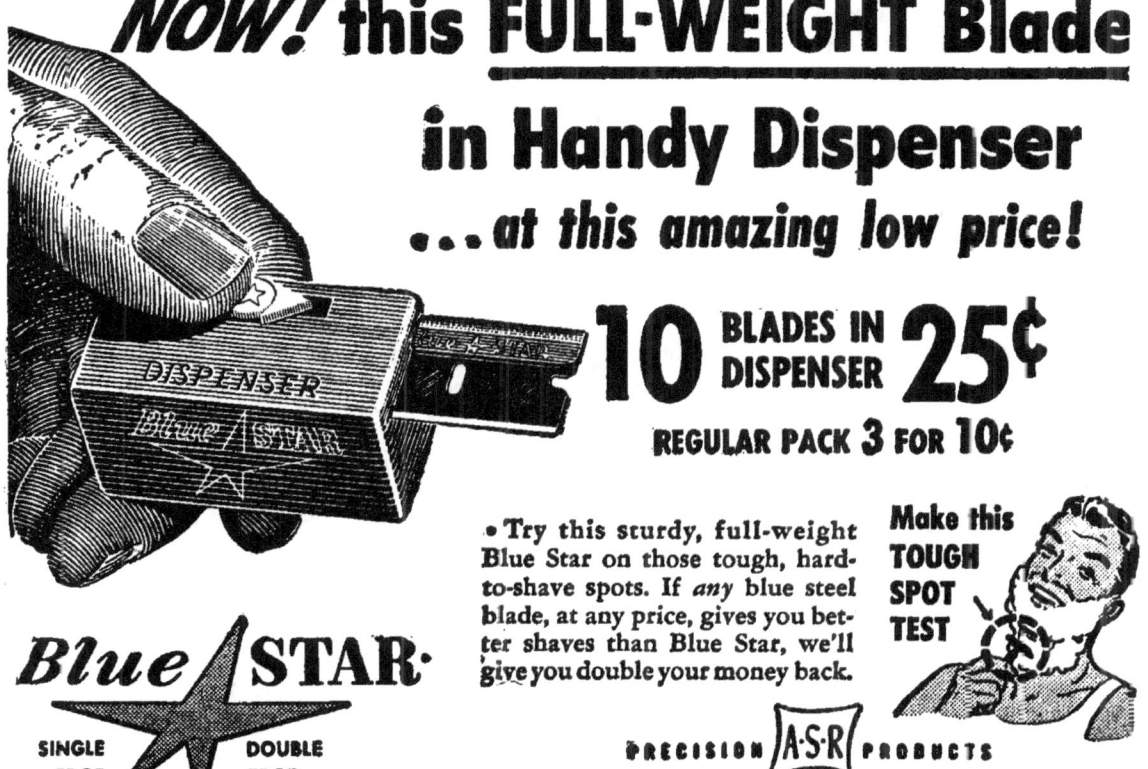

phere of the prairie allowed them to detect every move he made when he dismounted, lifted down some gate bars, and turned the horses loose in a corral.

"Peaceful enough," Warren grinned. "We shouldn't have anything to worry about, after saving young Barbour's hide. They'll probably butcher the fat cow when we get there."

"What ranch we supposed to have bought?" Jim asked.

"The J bar O. That was the Jaques and Oliver spread. But I'll do the talking."

Warren touched his spurs lightly, and his tired buckskin picked a zig-zag course through broken rimrock strata to the valley. The trail turned and followed along the side of a dry wash, but Warren avoided it, choosing instead a bulge of the country where their approach could be plainly marked from all directions.

A needlesharp reflection came from the side of a knoll, and Hernandez, seeing it, muttered, "Telescope."

"Sure, they have a lookout posted. Didn't Dermott say they'd turned this place into a fortress?"

A man walked into sight, leading a dark pony. He mounted and sat for a while. Other riders appeared from around one of the log bunkhouses. Eight altogether. They headed across the flats, fanning out, and light now and then caught reflections of gunshine from the Winchesters they carried across their saddles.

One of them spurred his horse to a lope and was a couple-hundred yards ahead when The Kid got close enough to see his face.

He was about forty, big, and raw-boned, with an unruly mass of rusty, bristly hair that hung below his collar. He reined in and sat back on his big chestnut horse, legs stiff, and the heels of his choke-bore boots thrust forward, one arm uplifted to shade his eyes against the sunset.

"What ye want?" he bellowed.

He might have been a trapper or moun-

tain man from the style of his greeting, but something in the twist of his words told Warren he was from Texas.

"You're one of the Barbour boys," he said.

The man had a chaw of tobacco in one cheek, and he took time to work it around for a while.

"So I be."

"Hoss Barbour." It was only a guess.

"I'm Hoss Barbour. But I don't remember you from nowhere."

"I'm Warren." Evidently the name meant nothing to him. "They call me the Pecos Kid."

HE MOVED then, and spat explosively. "I hear tell you saved that damn fool brother o' mine from a one-way trip to that Miles boothill."

"He was a little bit outnumbered."

"Anybody damn fool enough to walk inside a deadfall like Johnny's Round Tent deserves to get his lights shot out." Then he softened a little. "But he's the young 'un of us, and we try to look out for him. Anybody that saved his life is welcome to eat my grub and sleep in my bed and no questions asked." He nudged his pony forward and leaned to one side, shoving his Henry rifle in a scabbard. "You boys driftin' or stayin'?"

Obviously he'd fully expected them to say "driftin'," because he straightened suddenly and his blue-gray eyes became narrow when Warren answered,

"I guess we'll stay a year or three. We just bought up the J bar O place."

"Damnation!"

"What's wrong? Has somebody jumped the claim?"

"Squatter rights. Long as Jaques and Oliver ain't been gone more'n a year, they can sell to who they please, but I don't reckon you bought yourself more'n a potful of trouble." He motioned for the other men to come on, and in the meantime he poked more cutplug in the side of his cheek. "Maybe we *could* do with three more gun-whangers in case you have the stomach for suicide."

"Dermott?"

"They told you, then?"

"They told us."

"It ain't any of my business, but how much did you pay Jaques for that place?"

She was dressed in levis, boots, a blue shirt, and sombrero, like the rest. Warren might have mistaken her for a remarkably handsome boy were it not for her hair which had been braided, wrapped in close coils around her head, but still was so bountiful it escaped from beneath her sombrero.

"They got a lookout posted—see it?"

"Four hundred."

"Four hundred! Sweet land o' hell, if I had four hundred—"

"They said Dermott would pay more than that."

"I wouldn't sell to that damnyankee for four times four thousand." He proceeded to curse Dermott, naming him every vile term he'd picked up between the Brazos and the Missouri. Suddenly, noticing how close the riders were, he stopped. It seemed strange that a man like Hoss Barbour would not want them to hear his profanity —then Warren noticed the reason. One of them was a girl.

When Hoss stopped, Hernandez proceeded to add some south-of-the-border terms of his own before Warren stopped him.

"The girl," he said.

Hernandez' eyes became extremely wide. He smiled his pleasure, showing his excellent teeth. He touched his close, dark mustache and seemed to be sorry that his guitar was wrapped in his soogans and roped on the packhorse.

"Stay back!" Warren growled at him.

Hoss turned and said, "These are the boys that saved Tom's skin last night. Turns out they bought the J bar O. I reckon that makes 'em one of us if they want to stay."

A lank lean man, rusty complexioned, with a scar-disfigured cheek, rode closer and made a point of keeping his Winchester ready. He was obviously another of the Barbours.

"Where you hail from?" he asked, addressing Warren.

ALONG the frontier a man's backtrail was considered his own affair, and consequently this particular question was one reserved for lawmen and not often asked by them.

Hernandez turned suddenly, an angry motion, but Warren stopped him and said, "I'm the Pecos Kid."

The second Barbour jerked back, grunted. "So. Well, that's better'n being a damnyankee, but don't get the idea you can ride far on that business in the Round Tent last—"

"Zenis!" Hoss barked.

"What do we know about these?"

"I said they could stay!"

"All right," Zenis grumbled. "The Kid's a Texas man, and I don't object." He was looking at Henandez. "But I ain't bushin' up with any knife-throwin' greaser. He'd of kilt Tom last night—"

"Shut your mouth!" Hoss shouted. He held a short, coiled bullwhip in his hand. It was too long to be of much use as a quirt, so obviously it was carried as a weapon. He turned on Zenis with the thing shoulder high, but the threat only made his brother look more vicious than ever.

"No, I ain't closin' my trap!"

"You were speaking of me, Señor?" Hernandez said softly.

"Yes, I was speakin' of you!"

"Last night your brother called me this thing, and I let him live, for he was young, and a fool. I think you will die, for you are old, and a fool."

Zenis had the Winchester across the

pommel. It was a simple matter to lift it, cock the hammer, and fire. Hernandez' hand was already moving to his hip. He flung himself sidewise, spurring his horse with the same movement.

Hoss Barbour roared and came down with the bull whip. Its lash wrapped itself in quick coils around Henandez' wrist. He swung back. The gun flew high and thudded to the hard-baked prairie earth. The kid had drawn, but he kept his gun angled skyward, for Hoss Barbour had placed himself to block the Winchester.

Zenis cursed him and tried to get the gun clear. Hoss grabbed the barrel, and for a moment they struggled for possession. Then Hoss' superior weight made itself felt. He ripped it from Zenis' hand and swung it, stock forward, in a stabbing motion. Zenis caught part of its force with an upflung arm but it knocked him loose in the saddle. His horse reared, and Hoss finished the job of clubbing him to the ground.

"I told you before I wasn't takin' your lip!" Hoss yelled.

THE HORSE bucked and sprayed chunks of dirt over the fallen man. Hoss sat, looking down on him, breathing hard through his nostrils.

Zenis stood up, covered with dirt and fragments of dead grass, and commenced wiping blood from behind his left ear. He looked up at Hoss as though he hated his guts, but he didn't say another word.

Hoss Barbour jerked his head at Hernandez and said, "Tell him he better be peaceful, too. I don't like the gunfighter way he's got about him."

"Tell him yourself," Warren said.

The girl spoke, and the soft modulation of her voice was a shock after the raw voices of the men.

"It's you Barbours who are always starting the trouble, and there's no need of it."

Hoss laughed and twisted the bull whip

back in a tight coil. "I ain't goin' to argue with *you*, Miss Mary."

"I'll have you know you're not running this whole show."

"Reckon things would be a heap different if we were—a whole, heap different!"

The girl proved to be Mary Coyne, daughter of Cap Coyne, elected leader of the Mandan Springs ranchers. He was waiting on the back step of the ranch house, a squat and powerful man, with a broad face surrounded by hair that looked like white silk floss.

Dermott had told something of his history—a former Indian scout, captain of a band of Northern irregulars operating out of Fort Leavenworth during the Civil War. At one time in his life he'd carved out a reputation for drinking and gunplay, but the years had quieted him.

"I heard about you saving Tom's skin last night." Cap Coyne's handshake was strong, and there was directness and understanding in his bright blue eyes. "He's a wild kid, and he was on the prod because of that no-account woman, Lena Pearl. I want to thank you for all of us."

Zenis Barbour was listening, and it snapped his brittle temper once more, "Us Barbours can do our own fightin', and we can do our own thankin'—"

"Shut up!" roared Hoss.

Zenis clamped his lean jaw tight and strode on with his spavined, cowboy legs across the lean-to where he splashed water in a wash dish and commenced scrubbing blood and dirt from his face. It was twilight and quite dark beneath the cucumber vines that shaded the lean-to, but Warren was conscious of his eyes, hawklike and suspicious.

"Having a little trouble with your boys, aren't you?" Cap Coyne said to Hoss.

"*Fightin'* men are generally a little hard to handle."

There was a significance and bitterness in the remark that no one could miss. Those Texans under the leadership of Hoss Barbour were in the minority by twelve men to eighteen, but they were on the prod, looking for a showdown with Roger Dermott. It was a question whether Cap Coyne could go on handling them.

The division became more apparent as the night went on. They did not even have grub together—Cap Coyne and the Yankees eating in the ranch house kitchen while the Barbours and their Texans took food camp style from a wagon wheeled up to the door of a bunkhouse.

THAT night Warren sat in the big, roughly furnished front room of the ranch house with Cap Coyne. Neither man spoke for a while. Hernandez Flanagan had tuned his guitar and was singing one of the sad, rhythmical songs of the Chihuahua *caballeros*. He had a good voice, more Celtic than Latin, and Warren could sometimes spend hours with his eyes closed, listening to him.

"They didn't give you any bargain," Cap finally said, referring to the J bar O. "You'll have to fight for it to keep it. I don't know why this ground is so damned important to Dermott, what with free land reaching from Cheyenne to Milk River. Maybe you wonder why I just don't pull my picket pin and drag north like Jaques and Oliver did. I sometimes wonder myself."

Cap turned and watched as Mary came in the room carrying two thick pottery cups filled with black coffee. "I guess it's because this spread has took to looking like home."

Mary Coyne had changed from levis to a fringed, brown riding skirt. It buttoned tightly around her waist, accentuating her slimness, but making her look older than she had looked earlier in the evening. Warren guessed her age at about twenty.

He felt her eyes on him, but when he looked up she quickly diverted her gaze. "Canned milk?" she asked.

"No, ma'am."

There was something about her, something he hadn't found on Front Street in McKetrick nor across the tracks in Dodge. She was browned by wind and sun, lithe from hard riding. Her shirt sleeves were rolled up and he could tell by the supple fullness of her arms that she'd been raised to do the work of a man.

Cap Coyne was still talking, but Warren's thoughts had traveled far back, to Texas and that other girl, the girl who had promised to wait. It would have been easier if she hadn't *waited*, but she had. She was there for him to take, the day he rode back after the futile weeks of guerilla fighting that followed Appomattox—rode back ragged and dusty, his horse limping, his cutlass thrown away and one of Sam Colt's new .44 pistols strapped in its place.

He'd hired a rig and they'd driven out to the old ranch at Liveoaks the next morning. His mother had died during the first year of the war, and his father, lying about his age, had joined up and died of Yankee lead at Pea Ridge. And now the old home was in ruins, with cattle hunting shade in what had once been a drawing room, and everything valuable carted away by a lawless gang of former slaves who were encamped on Junction Creek. Nothing was left.

It was impossible, of course. The world that he knew had crumbled and could never be rebuilt again. He'd talked her into visiting relatives at New Orleans, and promised to come for her "when he got on his feet." She'd written, something about another man. He got to counting the years. Eight—nine of them.

"Your coffee!" he heard Mary Coyne say.

Warren took the cup and noticed that Cap Coyne was looking at him. "How was that again? I guess I was dreaming."

"I said you'd probably see eye to eye with Barbour and his crowd, seeing you're from Texas. All the other Texans have."

"I didn't ride up here to cut any Yankee notches in my pistols. What do they want to do, those Barbours?"

CAP COYNE didn't answer the question directly. "They're a rough crowd," he said. "I guess they've been shoved around too much. I feel like bushwhacking a fat money-grabber now and then myself."

"Dermott?"

"Sure. Dermott. And those Carson boys —if they ever got close enough."

"Why?"

The word seemed to touch Cap Coyne like a hot iron. "Why? I'll tell you. Because they have us against the wall and they're strangling us. We have cattle on the range. Grass-fat. Cattle aren't high but there's always a market for these northern grassers. We'd get by, but his boats won't carry them. 'Prior commitments,' he says—yet not one in five of his boats is loaded."

"You could drive to Deadwood."

"Through Sitting Bull's country? Our beef would end in a Sioux kettle and our hair on their *coup* sticks. That leaves Cheyenne on the U. P., and what would we have left after driving across Wyoming? Hide, bone, and tendons like the worst Texas grassers. We decided to sit tight.

"Now Carson's cut off our credit. Without cash we can't buy a sack of tobacco. It's not easy keeping the boys in line. Now it's not just Hoss and his Texas crowd. All the boys are getting ringy. They'll cut loose one of these days and maybe I'll be right in there beside 'em."

IN THE MORNING, Warren and his two companions saddled fresh mounts from their saddle string and set out down-valley for the old J bar O ranch. They found a one-room cabin of bleached cottonwood logs, a corral, a stock shed with a hay roof. Twenty-five or thirty longhorns wearing Barbour's brand ranged across the bottoms.

The ranch lay at the eastern end of Mandan Springs. Beyond were some low hills, and the descent toward the Powder River country. In the north, four or five miles of benches and badlands, and then the Yellowstone making intricate patterns through the mudbars of midsummer.

They looked around for an hour, saw little of interest, sprawled in the shade of a box elder tree through the direct sun of afternoon, returning to the Double C an hour past supper time.

"You'll have to take leavin's," old Jack Snow, the cook, told them.

They sat on the back steps and ate from tin plates. Through darkness men kept walking up from the bunkhouses and going in the front door of the big, log house. Little talking. Just a few low words, the thug of boots, jingle of spurs.

Warren put his tin plate aside and stood up, "There's a meeting yonder, and seeing I'm a landholder now . . ."

"You do not wait for the invitation?" Hernandez asked, smiling.

"It hasn't been my habit in the past."

"I don't like this," Big Jim said. His honest face looked troubled. "I don't like this sneakin' around. I'd like to know who in hell we're sidin' in this row. It it's Dermott, or if it's these Mandan Springs boys."

"We'll see which side will make us the most money," Warren grinned.

"That ain't been your style in the past."

"I've reformed."

Warren clomped through the kitchen. He stopped for a second by the closed door that led to the big, front room. He saw movement in the shadow. Mary Coyne was descending the stairs from the second story. She was looking at him in a certain way, and he knew she thought he was eavesdropping.

"You can't blame one man for listening when the other man whispers," Warren grinned.

He opened the door for her, but she shook her head and stayed part way up the stairs, so he went inside by himself. He stood with hands resting behind him, closing the door. The room was close from the heat of men, tobacco smoke. The grease dip burned low and reddish as though the press of their bodies tended to absorb the light and steal oxygen away from it.

A rugged man of twenty-five or so had been talking. He stooped. There were a few seconds of silence. Then Zenis Barbour stood up, looking tall and predatory,

"I didn't know anybody asked you to come here, Kid."

"Nobody asked me. We all make oversights. Don't apologize." He had an easy manner that asserted itself during taut moments like these. He kept smiling as though some thought in his own mind amused him. His hands were occupied in rolling a cigarette.

"Rode over and looked at my place today. The J bar O. Liked it first rate. Good grass and water, plenty fresh air, good view of the river. I don't reckon I'll have to drive more'n eight-ten miles once the N. P. lays steel through this country. Can't run much tallow off a critter in eight-ten miles. Lot better than driving clear to Cheyenne across most of hell and all of Wyoming."

"What are you getting at?" Zenis barked.

"Why, just that. The J bar O will be one of the finest spots north of Red River if I can hang and rattle till Mr. Villard gets that N. P. road built."

"And what'll you do until it does get built?"

"Why, I expect I'll plant a few spuds, and graze some cows, and maybe I'll vary my fare with a catfish now and then out of the Yellowstone. I've heard tell fishing is good down there, if a man has some patience."

"I got patience with fish, but I ain't got patience with wolves. The two-legged kind!"

"Who you mean?"

"Men like Dermott, and the Carson boys, and them that associates with 'em."

WARREN did not change expression. He leaned over the grease dip to light the cigarette, and again, as that night above the Round Tent, his face looked lean and coppery and hard. He was wondering how much Zenis knew and how much simply sprang from the bitter alkali in his system.

"If you think I came here for Dermott, the thing for you to do is say it. Right out. Your intestines ought to be strong enough for that, Zenis. I'm not hostile. And you got backing enough here even if I was."

Zenis spoke, "Sure, I'll say it. I think it was damned funny you'd be with Eldad Stark on Front Street to save Tom's hide the first time, and right handy in the Round Tent when the second play came up."

Warren inhaled and laughed cigarette smoke from his lungs. He sounded genuinely amused. "Now I'll be damned! And every time I ran into him, he was headed into trouble for himself." Tom Barbour was there, sitting against the wall, hunched forward. A big red welt lay across his face and it was only a guess that Hoss had put it on him with the bull whip. "Isn't that right, Tom?"

Tom Barbour met his eyes. They looked red and irritated, the way Indians' eyes sometimes become after long sitting in a smoke-filled tepee. He didn't answer.

Warren went on, "I saved your hide at least twice. It's been troubling me ever since. I'm not sure you're worth saving twice in a row. What do you think?"

Tom Barbour's legs uncoiled like twin springs, ramming him to his feet. Hoss told him to stay where he was, elbowed through and stopped a long stride from Warren, standing with his heavy, choke-bore boots set wide.

"It's like I told you last night. You saved him, and that makes you welcome to eat my grub, ride my horse, or flop in my soogans. But you ain't sitting in on this meeting."

"Why not?"

"You're a newcomer, that's why not."

"And you're afraid I'm a Dermott spy because I went to his office to visit him. Is that right?"

"If I thought you were playin' Dermott's game, I'd blast your insides out. It's a nice, moonlight night outside, Kid. There's a breeze from over the Yallerstone, and if you get on the right side of the corrals it smells fine."

Warren looked around. The faces were hostile and suspicious. He laughed, said, "All right, Hoss," and went outside.

CHAPTER SIX

On the Prod

A DARK, wiry man stood on the brush-roofed awning with a Winchester across the crook of his arm. He was Blakely, a cowboy from down in the Indian Nation. Warren spoke to him and walked around the house.

Hermandez and Big Jim were still seated on the back steps. Hernandez was talking softly, telling about something from his boyhood back in Chihuahua. Warren stood for a while, feeling the night breeze from across the Yellowstone. Hoss was right about it. It seemed like the farther north a man drifted, the finer those night breezes became.

He turned suddenly and noticed Mary Coyne standing by the corner.

"You didn't stay long," she said.

"I was taking Hoss Barbour's advice. Fresh air." He flipped his cigarette away and made a motion indicating the badlands and prairie that lay in early moonlight to the north.

"Every country has a different smell about it. That, for instance. The muddy Missouri. And maybe the lodge fires of the Blackfeet. I always had a hanker to see the Blackfeet. They must be fightin' men, those Blackfeet!"

"You meant you're getting ready to drift."

"It gets to be sort of a habit."

"What'll you do about the J bar O?"

"What'd Jaques do?"

"You don't even own it."

He looked at her. There was no use lying. He wondered how much she knew —or guessed. Her eyes were not hostile nor suspicious.

"I'm not playing Dermott's game," he said.

"I didn't think you were. I only knew you hadn't bought that place from Jaques." Then she asked softly, "Why *are* you here?"

"I don't know." He was being truthful when he said that. He wasn't certain why he'd left the Arkansas, or Dodge, or Mc-Ketrick, or all those other places where men of less ability took root and prospered. Money was an excuse. It no longer fooled Hernandez or Big Jim. It had even stopped fooling himself.

It's not so easy to take hold after a man's roots have been torn up. He gets to looking for something without knowing what it is, and pretty soon he's putting a thousand miles of grass under him and nothing smells good except the country over the horizon. And so, when the girl asked him, all he could say was that he didn't know.

Then he added, "There's some reason Dermott's so set on getting this Mandan strip. What is it?"

"I was going to ask you the same thing."

He noticed that Hernandez had stopped talking about Chihuahua and was listening to them. There was a creak of porch boards when he stood up.

"If you ask me, Señorita, there is gold beneath this earth."

Big Jim snorted. He was from the Mother Lode country of California, and anyone with the most rudimentary knowledge of gold would know that its presence in these flat prairie sediments would be preposterous.

Hernandez said, "Then, gems. Diamonds. Rubies. Perhaps the water in these springs will make the old man young. *Quien sabe?*"

HE SMILED on Mary Coyne. He looked handsome and debonaire despite the two-day growth of whiskers on his face, but a glance told him that she already preferred Bill Warren. Women always did, and Hernandez could never understand it.

"These Northern women," he said under his breath, moving back to sit by Big Jim. "They are cool, amigo. The cool blue eyes, the cold yellow hair. They do not have the fire of the women of Chihuahua." He fashioned a long, brown-paper cigarette filled with the strong Spanish tobacco he went to outlandish ends to secure. He inhaled, and the rich smoke seemed to mellow and console him.

"Sure and it's the truth, Jamie, me lad," he went on. His father had been an Irish dragoon, a deserter who ended in Mexico after some fantastic wanderings, and Hernandez could, when he chose, imitate his brogue to perfection. "In faith, Jamie, me bye, there are times when I am tempted to shave off me worthless mustache and burn me guitar for firewood."

"Trouble with you, you're *too* handsome."

Hernandez blew smoke explosively.

"No, it's the truth," Big Jim said. "Women don't like men to be too handsome. They like 'em like the Kid. Freckles and a hammered-up nose and some red hair that won't stay tamed."

"Too handsome!" Hernandez mused, returning to his Spanish accent. *"Si, mi amigo.* Perhaps you have sometheeng there."

The meeting lasted until almost midnight, with the men grim and brittle tempered when they came out. Next morning, Warren noticed there was a second pow wow inside the Texan's bunkhouse. He walked by and saw that young Bolton was standing near the door.

He was a Northerner, the son of a "Pike's Peaker" family who had traveled west during the Sixties to escape the ravages of Quantrell's raiders, and till that moment he'd considered him one of Cap Coyne's regulars. Evidently Cap's hold on them was slipping.

Big Jim Swing said, "Noticed Lem Barbour in there painting blue on his gun barrel."

"Sure," Warren said. He could guess what had taken place at the meeting. Dermott had pushed them to the spot where it meant fight or get out.

"What do you theenk?" Hernandez asked.

"You're always looking for excitement, and this time it looks like we came to the right spot."

AFTER breakfast, Cap Coyne called him to the front room. A hundred cigarettes were trodden on the floor in evidence of the meeting the night before.

"They're set to go for those steamboats, as you probably guessed already. A dozen snipers and some set-snags here and there could raise hell during low water."

"You sound like you'd go along with them."

"I'm not the king of this valley. They elected me captain, but when they swing against you four to one . . ."

"It'll be the end of you here. All of you."

"You got any better idea?"

"Yes."

The way he said it made Cap Coyne take interest.

"Dermott's not the only boat operator," Warren said.

"You mean the Block R? It operates from a separate warehouse, but Dermott owns it. He and the Carsons."

"I'm talking about Fort Benton. There's Baker Brothers, and Power, and the Gold Line. I delivered a herd to the Two Bar and the beef boss told me that they charter their own boat and bring it to Liver-Eatin' Johnson's wharf on the Musselshell. If they'll touch there, they'll make the turn at Fort Union and come back here."

"You think we can swing it?"

"I'll start Big Jim overland this morn-

ing. Give him that bay long-horse of yours to change off on and he'll sight Benton by night time, day after tomorrow."

"He can have the pick of my string. I'll go yonder to the bunkhouse and hold some more pow wow."

Warren expected trouble with the Barbours, but Hoss gave an ear to the proposition and asked for half an hour to talk it over. It didn't take that long. Inside of ten minutes he came from the bunkhouse with his heavy-legged stride and said,

"We'll give you eight days."

"Eight days isn't long enough."

"It's long enough for me. I doubt I could hold my boys longer'n that without hog-tyin' 'em."

CHAPTER SEVEN

Fire at Forty Fingers

JIM rode off, mounted on his big roan and leading a packhorse and two extra mounts, the pick of Cap Coyne's remuda. A couple of days passed uneventfully. The second night, Warren groped his way through the open-fronted blacksmith shop to the harness room they were using as sleeping quarters.

"Butch!" he said, but Hernandez was not there. It was past midnight by Warren's big silver watch when he walked in. There was mud drying on his boots.

"What'd you see down by the river?" he asked, guessing where Hernandez had been.

"They been sneaking off every night, so tonight I followed. They're fixing an ambush down where the river splits up at a place called the Forty Fingers. Narrow channel. They could raise plenty of hell there."

"Who was there? Zenis? Jib?"

"Sure. And Hoss, too."

"He'll keep them in line for his eight days."

"And after the eight days?"

"They aren't my steamboats," Warren shrugged.

"You would not even ride to Dermott with the warning?"

"I don't know what I'd do."

Warren lay awake, looking at the blackness of the ceiling for a long time after Hernandez was asleep. There was no clear-cut division between right and wrong here. He neither wanted to help Dermott nor betray the Mandan Springs ranchers, and yet blameless people might die if they tried to block the river.

Next night Hernandez went scouting again. One of the Territory's "dry rains" came up with wind and lightning. Warren walked down from the house and stood in the dark open front of the blacksmith shop. The wind had a feel of dampness and an odor of freshly wet dust. A man was moving near the corrals. He came up the path and Warren recognized Hernandez.

"You have seen Mary thees night?" he asked.

"Why, yes. I was just talking to her. What's wrong?"

"Wrong?" Hernandez sighed and kissed his fingers at the black sky. Lightning flashed far away briefly, illuminating his face.

"It was perhaps then a princess of the Blackfeet in love with your Hernandez."

"What the hell are you talking about?"

"That, Señor. A princess, beautiful as the stars of my own Chihuahua. I only glimpsed her for—so long." Hernandez snapped his fingers. "Horseback. A great, black horse, shining from the rain."

"There's been no rain," Warren said.

"Where she came from, there was rain. Did I not see the horse? I called to her and she rode to the bottom of a dry wash. I thought she would wait for me, but when I got there she was gone."

"Pick up her tracks?"

"In this darkness, do I have the eyes of a bobcat?"

Next morning they rode out together,

but there were the tracks of four horses, mingling, diverging, mixing together again. After a day of intense sun, the storm swung back and once more covered the western sky with cloud banks the color of bullet lead.

With darkness, Hernandez rode out again. Warren shaved, spent some time puttering with his saddle gear, and walked to the house for the ostensible purpose of securing a piece of beeswax. Mary Coyne was expecting him. He knew that by the starched calico dress she was wearing.

IT WAS a jolt to see her there, so small, and slim, and obviously eager to see him. She wasn't the kind for him. She wasn't a girl you kissed and said goodbye to. She was the sort you took home with you and kept for good.

But every time he saw her, there would be another vision in his mind, a vision of that girl back in Texas, so he was never quite looking at Mary Coyne. She wasn't the kind for him. His kind were the ones he'd met across the tracks in Dodge. They never brought foolish visions to his mind. They never made his insides turn over from regret.

He should have asked for the beeswax and left. But he didn't. He stood and talked about things, ordinary things, while he thought of something else.

Time went rapidly. He'd been there for more than an hour when the door was flung open unexpectedly and Hoss Barbour stood outside in a gentle drizzle of rain. He started to say something, checked himself.

Instead, he clomped inside, leaving blobs of mud, and touched her hair. The action was so unexpected that Mary and Warren only stared at him. He went back and was about to close the door. Then he said,

"You ain't been outside lately?"

"No."

He'd been seeing whether her hair was damp from rain.

"Now what the devil?" Warren said when he was gone.

"He's been having some trouble with Tom."

"Over you?"

"Of course not!"

"I'm sorry. I didn't mean that."

Cap Coyne came in a couple of minutes later. "Hear that shot?" he asked, without getting too excited about it. "Two or three miles. Winchester, I guess. Quarter-hour ago."

It was raining harder than he'd supposed. He stood for a while, hearing its soft hiss as it struck the brush-roofed awning. The dust of the ranch yard was wet to a depth of half an inch over its powder-dry base, and mud clung in clumsy masses to his boots as he crossed to the blacksmith shop. He stopped to listen. There was a commotion down by the corrals. A man raised his voice—Zenis Barbour.

Warren turned and cut diagonally across the shack-cluttered ranch yard, stopping by the roof of a root cellar. The bunkhouse used by the Texans was just beyond.

He could make out the big, rectangular outlines of buildings, but little else. Men were walking up from the corrals. Hoss Barbour said something and the voice of young Tom Barbour answered.

"You lay that on me again and I'll kill you, d'you hear?"

The response was sudden. Warren could hear the stamp of struggling men, the grunting exhalations of breath, the jolt of a fist striking bone and flesh.

Hoss panted, "Now maybe you'll tell why you was out there."

"Leave him be, Hoss," Jib said.

MEN commenced talking inside the bunkhouse. Someone lighted a lamp. It made an amber glow through the oiled antelope-skin window. Warren circled until he could see the open bunkhouse door fifty or sixty paces away. The Barbour boys came up through the lamplight, four of them, Zenis and Hoss dragging Tom who was wobbly-legged from a blow he'd taken across the jaw. Jib came behind.

"What the hell?" It was Eben Smith, a dark, heavy-shouldered Texan.

"Never mind us Barbours," Hoss said. "We take care of our own. Git a wash dish full of water."

They balanced Tom in the door and thrust him forward. Tow was erect for a moment with the crown of his Confederate ranger hat almost touching the door casing. Then he reeled forward and would have fallen flat but for a rough board table.

The others followed inside and left the door open. Warren could have gone closer without much fear of detection, but it would have been useless. The Barbours weren't giving out any information.

He turned and walked to the corral. Bob Guthrie, the night wrangler, was taking care of some horses.

"Now what in hell?" Guthrie said, peering through the gate bars.

"That my sorrel up ramming around?" Warren asked.

"He ain't even in this corral."

Bill Warren knew it. He wanted a glance at Tom's horse. He swung over the corral. It was easier walking through damp manure than through sticky gumbo.

"This Tom's bay horse?"

"Yeah." Guthrie had lined up with the Barbours. He answered the question reluctantly.

He ran his hand down the horse's flank. He'd been ridden hard. There were splashes of mud along his belly and thighs.

Warren climbed back over the corral, and walked to the blacksmith shop.

Darkness was solid inside the shop's smoke-blackened interior. He groped his way by habit around the forge, between the shoe rack and some bags of smithy coal. He stopped, listened. There had been no sound, yet he knew that someone was waiting in the black depths of the shop.

"Who is it?" he said.

There was a second or two of silence. He stepped back, one shoulder against the wall, his Colt lifted from its holster. "Who is it?" he repeated.

"Kid?"

He recognized the voice. It was Eldad Stark.

There were certain men that put Warren's nerves on edge, and Stark was one of them. Distaste and contempt and perhaps even a little fear were mixed up in it.

HE LIFTED the gun, depressed the trigger to hide the click-click sound, and cocked it. Then he answered, "Yes."

"You alone?"

"Yes."

"Better put your gun away."

Stark had heard the slight, metallic sound—that, or seen his silhouette against the dim glow from outside.

Stark went on, "Sure. Put the gun away. You know I could have killed you if I'd wanted to. That's a hell of a way to act to a man who's working for the same boss."

Warren lowered the hammer, dropped the gun lightly in its holster. "Who's with you?" he asked.

"How do you know I got anybody here with me?"

"You wouldn't have the guts to come alone."

Stark laughed. It wasn't a pleasant laugh. Darkness did not prevent Warren's knowing what his face looked like—the sideward twist of the slack jaw, the peeling back of his upper lip.

"I ain't a damned bit afraid of you, Warren, or of that knife-throwing greaser that sides you. What in hell's the matter with you anyhow? We're on the same side of the fence, aren't we? Or *are* we?"

"I made a deal with Dermott. If you'd had any part in it, I'd have told him to go to hell."

"Don't shove me too far, kid," Stark said.

"Why are you here?"

"Dermott sent us."

Warren laughed at the word "us." It was true then he wasn't alone.

"Who's with you?"

A new voice, guttural and low, said, "Me. The Cherokee Kid."

Warren remembered a heavy, bowlegged man of about thirty-five, dull enough to use his gun for anyone willing to pay him.

Eldad Stark moved forward a little, one boot grating against some iron on the floor. "He wants to know why Jim Swing headed cross-country the other day."

"Jim thinks there's no money in the business, and maybe he's right. What else did Dermott want to know?"

"He's got a hunch there's ambush being set up down by the river. Do you know anything about it?"

"If there's an ambush, I'll let him know in plenty of time," Warren said.

"You haven't found out anything, then?" The swagger in Stark's voice was indication enough that he was certain Warren was already a traitor to Dermott. When no answer came, he was bold enough to go on, "Maybe that girl at the house has more to offer than Dermott has."

Warren stepped forward, set his heels, and smashed a right toward Stark's jaw. In the dark it landed higher than he'd intended, between cheek and temple.

IT HAMMERED Stark back. His skull thudded the rough-board wall. He bounded forward, falling, and Warren met him with his other fist.

He was down, groping for his left-hand gun. Warren dropped, pinning him under

bent knees. He knew by Stark's movement that he was dragging on his left-hand pistol. He stamped hard, catching the man's wrist beneath the hard instep of his boot.

There was a crunching sound of twisting tendon and bone. Stark whinned from pain and his gun thudded on the dirt floor. Warren groped, picked it up, found

Hoss Barbour

Stark's second gun pinned in its holster beneath him and tore it free.

The Cherokee Kid was moving back and Bill Warren knew his guns were out, though darkness would not let him fire.

"Put 'em back, Cherokee," he said. "They'd just corner you here and kill you."

"What in hell did you do that for?" Stark whined. He was on his knees, clutching his injured wrist. "I came here peaceful. Risked my neck for the boss."

"Get up. If you have any more ideas about that girl, keep 'em in your own lousy mind." He punched the cartridges out on the floor and handed the guns back to him. "What was that shooting half an hour ago?"

"I don't know."

"Did Johnny send Lona Pearl out here to play the moonlight game with that Barbour kid?"

Warren knew by Stark's momentary pause that he'd hit on the truth.

"You go back and tell Dermott I'm going all right," Warren said. "Tell him I'd do a hell of a lot better if he'd lay the cards on the table."

"What d'you mean by that?" Stark asked.

"I mean about Lona."

"Maybe she did it on her own. Maybe she likes the—"

"Maybe she wants to marry him and settle down in a log shanty and raise kids. That *would* be Lona's style, wouldn't it?" Warren laughed shortly.

CHAPTER EIGHT

The Injun Sign

ON THE eighth day Big Jim Swing rode back from Benton with word that he'd chartered the Baker Company's old sternwheel boat, *Rosebud*. It would probably be as far as Fort Union that very day, and back to the landing at Woodhawk's Point by the mouth of the Powder in two more. In anticipation of its arrival most of the men left Cap Coyne's on a beef roundup, an easy job due to the fact that most of the four-year-old butcher stock had been brought in "on the grass" only five or six weeks before. Two days passed, but there was no sign of the boat. It didn't come on the third day, or the fourth.

The following afternoon was still and hot. From the east a column of smoke arose to great height and faded against the sky. There was another column, and another, the last broken into three separate puffs.

Big Jim Swing walked up from the corrals and saw Warren. "Sioux?" he asked.

"I suppose," Warren said. "I hear tell Sitting Bull and the Southern chiefs left the agency last month. He's got hell in his craw since that gold strike in the Black Hills."

"And Custer, drinking his wine in Bismarck!"

"Don't blame Custer. He can't fight without men. If the Blackfeet join up, we'll all wish we were in Texas."

Cap Coyne came in time to hear his words. "That's not Sioux smoke."

"Cheyenne?"

Cap shrugged. "It ain't Sioux."

A rider appeared from the northeast and approached, riding swiftly across the flats.

"Hope that ain't one of my horses," Cap said, referring to his speed through the heat of afternoon.

He proved to be Lee Pringle. Eben Smith's nephew. He hurried across to one of the horse sheds, and left a few minutes later accompanied by Zenis Barbour and Eben Smith.

"Maybe they're roundin' up stray cattle," Cap said. "It'd be a good idea with Injun sign in the sky."

Other unexplained arrivals and departures seemed suspicious too, so, as afternoon faded, Warren saddled and struck across in the approximate direction of the Forty Fingers.

The Yellowstone had dropped considerably through the last couple of weeks, leaving mudbars here and there, but its channel was still adequate for steamboat travel. A buffalo trail led across shelf land for a couple of miles, then the hills closed in and there was a slight climb.

The Pecos Kid drew just short of the low, sage-spotted crest and looked across a widening of the bottoms where the river split in intricate patterns, forming that pilot's perennial nightmare, the Forty Fingers.

He found tobacco and papers, twisted up a cigarette, lighted it, all without shifting his eyes from the flats below him. A herd of antelope moved across the flats, their tails like white tufts of cotton.

They stopped to drink at a backwater. Fresh man-scent would have kept them moving. There was no ambush at the Forty Fingers.

DARKNESS was settling when he unsaddled at the Double C corrals. He had supper, and then wandered down past the bunkhouses. Old Jack Snow, the Barbours' cook, and Guthrie, the horse wrangler, were sitting on a bench by the door.

"All alone, boys?" he asked.

Guthrie started to answer, but Snow made a movement that stopped him. "I reckon there might be some of the boys asleep inside."

He was lying, of course. Warren laughed in an easy manner, and walked on to the blacksmith shop.

He went inside and lighted the greasedip. Hernandez and Big Jim had ridden to a woodhawk's trade-shanty down toward the mouth of the Powder for tobacco or candy. Big Jim was extremely fond of candy.

Warren pulled off his boots and flopped on the bed which had been left out on the floor. The ranch was the quietest he'd ever known it. Through the glassless window he could hear the musical trickle of spring water flowing through the corrals. The heat of day had vanished, leaving the air cool, filled with the pure fragrance of sage and grasslands.

He dozed—then suddenly he was awake. Lona Pearl! The awareness of her presence was so strong he expected her to be standing there, in the yellow lamplight, looking down on him.

The room was empty. He got to one knee in his blankets. Then for the first time he realized what it was. It was the odor of that peculiar French perfume of hers.

Gone now. He tugged on his boots and stood up. A natural wariness kept him from revealing himself at the window with the light at his back. Instead, he moved along the wall and through the door to the blacksmith shop, closing it after him.

The shop was dark, with anvil and forge and grindstone making silhouettes against the moonlight outside. He breathed slowly, trying to recapture her perfume, but there was only the stale, ever-present blacksmith shop odor of dead coal and burnt hoofs and rusting iron. It seemed ridiculous, now that he was up and moving around.

He spoke, expecting no answer, "Hello!"

There was movement in the middle darkness, and again her perfume touched his nostrils.

"Yes, boy," she said. She was picking her way towards him in the dark. It seemed stifling in the airless end of the blacksmith shop. He started forward and drew up when he found her only an arm's reach away.

SHE WAS dressed in a blouse, riding skirt, boots. It made her seem smaller than in Miles. Smaller and younger. Her hair had been drawn back and covered by a black silk kerchief.

"Boy," she said. "Haven't you anything to say to me?"

"What do you want?"

"Why do you think I'd risk my life coming to see you? Don't you know Johnny would kill me if—"

"You've been here before," he said. "You were here seeing Tom Barbour."

"Yes. I was here seeing the young fool." It was too dark to make out her face, but he could imagine the momentary feline expression of distance. "It was nothing."

"Johnny's idea."

Her hands closed on his upper arms. They were soft and warm and surprisingly strong. "But I am not here to see him tonight. Tonight I am here to see *you.*"

It apparently had never occurred to

her that there existed a man anywhere who could resist her.

"Did Johnny send you to see *me*, too?" he asked.

Her hands tightened, and he could feel her fingernails burn through the fabric of his shirt. "Of course not. Did I not already say he would kill me if—"

"Sure."

She'd been expecting him to embrace her. He hadn't, and now his tone brought a sudden, catlike fury to the surface. She let go his arms and swung the back of of her hand at his cheek. One of her rings tore his flesh.

He stepped back, tossing up his hands to protect his eyes. The wall was there, jolting his shoulder. She kept coming. He seized her, and held her at arm's length. She writhed to get free.

It was futile against his strength. At last she stopped. He could sense the rapid rise and fall of her bosom. She spoke, controlling her voice, scarcely a whisper. "Perhaps you do not like Lona!"

"I didn't say that."

"Perhaps it is the girl at the big house. That pale thing with the hair like straw." She waited a second, and went on, "Tell me if you do. Tell me!"

HE WISHED Hernandez Flanagan could overhear their conversation. It would probably be enough to make him fulfill his threat about shaving his mustache and burning his guitar.

"Why do you laugh?" she said.

"Take it easy. I wasn't—"

"Do not think Lona is a fool! She knows what you are doing here. Perhaps I should return and tell Dermott it was *you* who sent for the steamboat! Perhaps I should tell him that you have taken to playing both sides in this business for your own profit. He would kill you! Do you hear? He would kill you. People do not cheat Dermott. Even though you rode ten hundred miles over the horizon he would send men after you to kill you."

"What made you think I was double-crossing Dermott?" Bill Warren asked.

"I, think? I do not think, I know! Johnny Malette, Eldad Stark, the Cherokee Kid—these are fools. They would believe anything. But I am a woman. I know when men lie. And you are here, lying to Dermott."

"All right, what are you going to do about it?"

"I lied for you. Listen how I lied for you!" She'd overcome her anger, and a vibrant eagerness filled her. "I learned things from that fool, Tom Barbour. About the steamboat, about the ambush they are planning tonight by the river."

His face went big-boned and hard, but darkness hid it. He waited, letting her go on.

"These things Lona found out. So easy, a kiss or two. But I did not say to Eldad Stark how I learned. I told him the information came from *you*. Otherwise Dermott would kill you when he learned of the steamboat—of the ambush at the Chalk Cliffs tonight. But instead you are now trusted as never before. And all because of Lona, after she held your fate like this." He could see the silhouette of her hand, cupped upward, slowly closing. "I could have. But I did not."

The woman was in love with him. He wondered why she'd chosen him from among all the thousands who had moved through Johnny Malette's, west on the great river, north on the long trail from Texas.

Tomorrow, it would be someone else. But today it was Bill Warren, the Pecos Kid.

"It wouldn't make any difference to me whether you saved my skin or not," he said.

"No?"

"No." His hands closed on her shoulders. He drew her hard against him. For a moment she was a bundle of taut muscle, then she laughed, her hands groped and closed on the front of his shirt, her head was tilted, her lips parted a trifle.

It was no great sacrifice to kiss her.

CHAPTER NINE

Hell at the Chalk Cliffs

WHEN Lona Pearl was gone, he started down for the corrals. Jim Swing and Hernandez Flanagan were just leading their horses through the gate.

"We'll have to saddle and ride," he said.

"Sometheeng is wrong?" Hernandez was looking at an extra gun Warren carried.

"Those Texas rawhiders have a deadfall set down by the Chalk Cliffs and Dermott knows about it."

"Ha! And that ees bad? So let the bushwhackers be themselves bushwhacked, Señor. I am very sleepy."

"We're riding down there."

"To save Zenis, maybe, and the rest of those *Señores Lobos?*"

"I'm not worried about the Barbours. This will give Dermott what he's been looking for. He won't stop with them. He'll keep coming. Cap will be next—and every poor squatter on these flats."

"Ah, so." Hernandez sighed and hitched his Colt pistol up. "But I would rather sleep in my good bed, Señor."

Warren went to rouse Cap Coyne and found the old man fully dressed, sitting in the kitchen waiting for Jack Snow to brew coffee.

"Sure," Cap said as soon as he saw Warren's face. "I knew they were up to some devilment. Where is it—down by the Forty Fingers?"

"The Chalk Cliffs."

Cap strapped on a second Colt revolver, stood on a chair to reach an upper shelf, brought down several cartons of cartridges—.44 Colts and 44-40 Winchesters.

There were only eight others left at the ranch. Apparently all the rest had joined the Barbours. That would give thm about twenty-four. Chances were that more had joined the Box R and the McCabe spread, and from the numbers of squatters and wolfers who had stuck to their cabins rather than hole up at the Double C. Forty men might not be a bad guess.

Mary Coyne climbed the corral, sprang to the ground, and walked across with a tinkle of spurs. She was dressed as she'd been when Warren first saw her, and a .32 calibre Smith and Wesson revolver was strapped high around her slim waist.

THEY set off, swiftly, thirteen of them, leaving Jack Snow alone at the ranch. It was not yet midnight when they reached an abandoned squatter's cabin called the Frome place and headed down a steep-sided coulee to the river.

Warren rode up abreast of Coyne and asked how far it was to the Chalk Cliffs. Cap told him it was a couple of miles.

"I been thinkin' about them smoke signals," Cap said. "I told you they weren't Sioux."

"You think Hoss had his lookouts down-river?"

"Sure. Maybe fifty, sixty mile down-river, signaling steamboat. He's no fool, that Hoss Barbour. Dermott better have plenty men because that Hoss'll give 'em one hell of a fight."

For half a mile they followed shelf land through belly-deep sage. There were no sounds except the river current, the soft thud of horses' hoofs.

A gun exploded somewhere up-river. A mile or two. There was the first sharp crack, the rapid clatter of echoes bounding back from hill faces, and a second of silence.

It set off a fury of shooting. Twenty guns—a hundred—it was impossible to tell with echoes rocketing from the hillsides. Someone spurred to a gallop, but Cap Coyne pulled his horse broadside and shouted, "Hold on. We ain't ridin' into any blind deadfall. We'd get kilt by either side. There's a considerable country down by the Chalk Cliffs. You follow me and do what I say until I get the lay of things."

He wheeled, spurred at a gallop. The shelf land ended and he swung inland from the river and put his horse up a steep climb. It was less than half a minute to the crest. More river flats lay beyond, and in the distance some cliffs that were white as porcelain by moonlight. They were the limestone formation known as the Chalk Cliffs.

"Steamboat!" Big Jim said.

Warren saw the craft a moment later. It was a huge, dark hulk which seemed to have run itself aground on the mud banks at the far side of the stream, perhaps a mile and a quarter away.

The hammer of guns was suddenly close. Here and there a flash and streak of burning powder cut the darkness from timber shadow along shore. No apparent plan or order, no telling who was the attacked and who the attacker. Apparently no one was shooting at the steamboat. It lay quietly, with black smoke climbing from its twin chimneys.

Cap paused only mometarily at the crest, then he rode on across a quarter-mile of flat ground, drawing up in the black-shadowed bottom of a coulee that ran down to the river.

"Here, dammit, you wait. I'll go yonder for a look." Cap started on by himself, then he glanced around and tried to pick Warren from the darkness. "Warren."

WARREN rode with him up a steep, crumbling bank. A stray bullet whipped close and rattled as it cut through the summer-dry chokecherry twigs. A second bullet cuffed dirt and hummed away.

Sound of shooting did something to Warren, lifting the sense of depression that had settled on him through a series of do-nothing days. He laughed, and Cap, hearing him, said,

"I'm damn glad this pleases somebody." He sat with his lips compressed, eyes rapidly knifing around the flats. "That's Talbott's Sharps," he was referring to one of the guns. "They got 'em pinned down, all right."

The Barbours had stretched a boom of anchored logs to block the river where sandbars thrust the channel close to shore. Ordinarily the pilot would send a skiff ahead to remove the obstruction, but a few men placed on shore would make their mission impossible.

But the boat had been warned, and an attack had come from the hills, pinning Barbour and his men against the river.

"Damn him," Coyne muttered. "Dermott's been waitin' for this."

They watched for half a minute, spotting the position of guns. It was a guess that Dermott had a force of sixty-five or seventy. There were no such numbers available in Miles, so it was probable he'd brought them up-river from Bismarck where hundreds lay out of work after the suspension of building on the N.P.

A new force of men was moving up along the opposite bank, and gunfire from that third direction would obviously make the ranchers' position untenable.

"Seen enough?" Cap asked, and without waiting for an answer, sent his pony crashing brush to the coulee bottom. Hernandez was there, and the others rode in sight a few seconds later.

"We'll take it up that side," Cap said. "Barbour and his boys seem to be pinned along that ten-foot bank upstream from the coulee mouth. Must be their horses are hid in the box elder grove. If we cut loose from behind. Hoss can make a run for it. Only be careful who you shoot at, and wait till I fire the first shot."

Hernandez was crouched in waist-high buckbrush, peering across the shelf land when Warren and Mary Coyne came up beside him.

Warren said, "Pick out one man. And Cap didn't mean Zenis Barbour."

An instant later Cap Coyne shouted, "Hi-ya!" and cut with his .44. The volley was sudden, and for a few seconds Dermott's men apparently did not realize the attack was centered on them. Then, when they did, most of them thought it was a mistake.

A man bellowed, "It's us, damn ye!"

He was visible for an instant, seventy-five paces across the flats. Warren fired, and the .44 slug made him fling himself aside. He lay on the ground and sent a return bullet that whipped the air by Warren's cheek.

Warren was on one knee, a Colt in each hand. Guns ripped from both sides. It was a baffling hell of fire and it seemed

to delight him. A bullet cuffed the earth and showered him with hard bits of clay. He aimed back at the flash and heard the responding thud of lead, the grunt of a man who was hit.

Feel of the guns, the rock and smash of their explosions, had an effect like alcohol on his system. He fired again, sending lead ripping into another nest of the attackers, and lifted his voice in a rebel yell.

A bullet tore past, so close it still held a sting of burning powder in its trail. Warren knew they'd spotted him. He pitched to one shoulder, rolled, came to a crouch, and both guns ripped again.

Two slugs coming close showered him with sagebrush twigs. He'd seen explosion less than thirty strides away with flame brownish-red through billows of drifting powdersmoke. Warren fired at the flash, fired again, and heard the hammers fall on empty cylinders.

NO TELLING whether one of the slugs had taken hold. There's always a ten to one chance against it in blind shooting like that. He bent down and poked out the smoking cartridge cases, thrust in fresh ones.

It gave him time to look around. Hernandez was no longer near him. A second later he saw the man crawling from sagebrush to sagebrush, evidently headed for a slight bulge of ground which, during some long-past high water period, had become heaped with drift logs.

"Come back, you damn greaser!" Warren hissed. "Our own boys will be sniping you."

Warren had reloaded. He moved a short distance, following Hernandez. The shooting had let up momentarily. Dermott's men seemed to have located the attack and withdrawn to form a more compact group.

Cap Coyne was shouting, "Hoss! Hoss!" over and over. At last an answer came from the beleaguered men by the river. Cap shouted, "Make a run for it. You hear me, Hoss?"

Hoss didn't answer. No telling what he intended to do.

Gunfire rose in fury. Bullets from unknown sources kept scorching across the earth, whipping dirt, fragments of sage. Cap Coyne, from the edge of the brush, was shouting at Hoss Barbour again, but nobody could distinguish a word he said.

Then, suddenly, there was movement and a rumble of hoofs upstream from the box elder grove. Hoss had his men mounted and was making a run for it.

One man was in the lead, bent low over the neck of his horse. The rest came in almost a solid mass, climbed a pitch from the river, galloped across the flats. Thirty horses would have been a reasonable guess, so they'd probably left some dead men back there.

Some of the riders fired as they rode, but they were useless bullets, as likely to strike a friend as an enemy. All of Cap Coyne's men were shooting to create a diversion. The noise was baffling. Powder-smoke, hanging in the still night air, looked like fog.

One of the riders was hit. He went down. There was a pile-up of horses, but they extricated themselves. One of the animals bolted directly towards the enemy guns. He bucked unexpectedly and threw his rider, who fell face first toward the ground. The man seemed to twist over in midair. His boot had hung up in the stirrup. He was down, being dragged, his arms tossed over his head. His boot must have come off. He lay huddled on the ground while his horse sunfished away with the stirrups whopping.

The man was stunned. He staggered to his feet. One of Dermott's men was only a dozen paces away. He fired, a deliberate bullet from that deadly range, killing him as he stood stunned and helpless.

It was a brutal act that wiped the elation of battle from Warren's lips.

Warren aimed and fired. The range was long, and his target uncertain through smoke and darkness, but he sensed, even as he pulled the trigger, that the bullet had gone home.

It smashed the man, spun him half way around. He took a step and his legs collapsed sending him face foremost to earth.

THE riders strung out more and more as their horses gained speed across the flats. Two more were hit but one stayed with his horse, clutching him around the neck. For a few seconds their course had taken them closer to Dermott's men.

Now precious distance was building between them and bullets made futile puffs of dirt at their heels. With three men hit, they'd got out of it better than they'd had a right to.

Warren's guns were empty again. He poked out the cases. They were beginning to stick from heat and fouling. He reloaded, tried to locate Big Jim and Hernandez.

The Spaniard still moved forward. Warren told him to come back.

"The Flanagans know not how to retreat, Señor!"

"Come back or I'll bullet-brand you in the rump. We have to get out of here." Warren mentally consigned Hernandez to the devil and turned to look for Mary Coyne.

He called her name without getting an answer. A sickness like nausea ran through him. He should have kept her out of sight beyond the edge of the coulee. He moved back, crouched, gun cocked and thumb hooked over the hammer.

"Mary!" he called.

"Here!" she said.

He'd never heard anything as welcome as her voice.

"Hurry."

"I can't." There was something like a tug of effort in her words. He thought she'd been hurt. He stood and hurried toward her voice. She was there in front of him, bent over the body of a man.

Warren saw it was Yergens, a nester whose place adjoined the Double C on the west.

"You'll have to help me." She was half crying, trying to lift the man's shoulders. "Don't you see I can't do it all by myself?"

Yergens had been struck high up on the chest and the bullet had traveled all the way through.

"He's dead," Warren said. There was no time to be subtle about it. "You can't help him now. Come along." He grabbed her, shook her back and forth as though awakening her. "Come along!"

She stopped crying suddenly. "All right," she whispered. "I'm sorry."

"This way."

Someone had been bellowing commands, and men on the far side of the coulee seemed to be executing a wheeling movement that was familiar enough to anyone who had fought through the War of the Southern Secession.

Cap Coyne, deep in brush up the coulee, was calling his daughter's name.

"I'm all right!" she shouted back. "Run for it!"

A man fired at the sound of her voice.

"Nice people, these Yankees." Warren said through his teeth. "Is this the way they always treat women up here?"

SHOOTING had almost stopped. A lull then an intense exchange about 150 yards up the coulee. And after ten seconds that leveled off.

The horses should be deep in brush at the coulee bottom, forty or fifty paces farther along. Big Jim led the way, with Mary after him and then Warren. A bank opened before them. There was soft earth, and waist-deep brush, and black shadow at the bottom.

"Jarvis!" The unfamiliar voice was close ahead in the dark. Alarm tightened the voice as he repeated, "Jarvis?"

The man lunged up and started back when he saw the huge shadow of Jim Swing beside him. There was a rifle in his hands. He started to bring it around, but Jim seized the rifle with one hand, his collar with the other.

The man writhed, helpless in Jim's tremendous grasp. He tried to scream for help, but the sound was pinched off in his throat. Then, with a quickness unsuspected in one of his bulk, Jim shifted his hold, lifted the man, and slammed him belly down across his bent knee. He let the man fall, writhing and helpless on the ground.

"Come along!" Warren said.

There was movement from the other coulee bank. A glow of gunshine. Warren was half turned. He spun and started to draw. Explosion and flame came from an unexpected direction, and the bullet smashed the man back, with his gun firing

wild and without any aim into the night.

The horses, spooky from gunfire, were tied a couple dozen steps farther on. Six of them. It was their first hint that someone besides Yergens had been killed. They mounted and commenced picking their way up the coulee.

It branched, and there was a wide area of brush. For a quarter-minute there had been no shooting. Little sounds commenced being audible—the clatter of pebbles underfoot, an occasional snap of dry brush, the drumming sound as a prairie chicken was frightened into flight.

So they covered a hundred yards, and another hundred. The trees played out, leaving only scattered rose thorn and sage. They rode up the side, and across open ground to the clay hills without drawing a shot.

CHAPTER TEN

Gun-Down

IT WAS graying off toward dawn when they struck Hoss Barbour's trail and followed it across the Mandan Springs area to the old Broken Arrow place.

Horses had been turned loose in the corrals and a light burned in the log house, but there was no sentry posted.

"Dermott's boys could still ride here and kill the bunch," Cap Coyne muttered, swinging to the ground.

He was too old for hard riding. It took him a while to limp a semblance of usefulness back in his legs.

He told Tab Mayberry to put his horse away and limped across the ranch yard. No one had lived at the Broken Arrow for more than a year, and cheat-grass was growing along the path that led to the cabin door. A man saw him and sprang out with a rifle in his hands while Cap cursed him.

"Sure," Cap said, "I'm Dermott in person. I got Wally and Tom Carson with

me. Left Eldad Stark back yonder in the corral."

Hoss Barbour limped to the door and peered out. He'd been wounded in the left thigh, and most of his pants leg had been cut away. "Lay off'n him, Cap," he growled.

Cap walked inside. Warren followed him, then Jim Swing, Hernandez Flanagan, and the rest, as many as could get inside the door.

The cabin was all one big room. Men filled it. Cap said, "Well, most of you made it. A damn sight more'n deserved to make it."

Cap stood and looked around the room, dimly revealed in the flame of a bacon-grease lamp. Most of the men were hunkered around the wall, looking tired and dusty. A couple were wounded, lying on saddle blankets in the bunks. One of them was Tom Barbour, the other a cowboy called Buck Boland.

"Jib got killed," Hoss said.

Zenis Barbour had been standing behind the table holding a tin cup over the lamp flame trying to make its contents boil. He banged it down and said,

"You hear him say Jib got killed?"

"Yes. I'm sorry about it," Cap said.

"You was a long time in saying so."

Eben Smith said, "We had enough fights for one night."

Zenis gestured with his left hand, meaning for him to keep still. He weaved around the table with men giving him room. Some of those along the wall sensed trouble and started to get to their feet. Hoss generally stopped Zenis, but this time he didn't say a word.

"Yes, my brother got killed. They was down there, ready for us. They knew what was up. Dermott's got a man planted here. A spy." He wasn't talking to Cap Coyne now. His eyes had traveled beyond Cap and were resting on Warren. And after him on Hernandez. "You hear that? A spy!"

Zenis was spun around. The gun exploded, driving splinters from the floor.

WARREN spoke in a voice that sounded dry and tired, "You mean it's me, or Flanagan, don't you? You've forgotten one thing. You planned that attack yonder without letting us know a thing about it, Zenis."

"You got ways of finding things out."

"You forgot something else. You'd all be wolf bait by this time if Cap and the rest of us hadn't saved your hides." He laughed without making it sound pleasant. "I did it because I like you, Zenis. You're such a nice fellow to have around."

"I ain't takin' your lip any more'n Hoss is."

"Zenis, you been looking for it a long time." Warren's voice sounded extremely quiet, and extremely deadly, and there was a stampede of men out of the way.

"Not here, boys," somebody cried.

Cap Coyne turned, grabbed Warren, wrestled him toward the wall. Warren twisted part way free. Zenis Barbour was all alone between the table and the wall. His hand came up, weighted by his .44 Colt. Coyne glimpsed the movement, let go and hurled himself against the wall.

No one had actually seen Warren draw his right-hand revolver, but it was there. It seemed to hesitate, poised and aimed for a fragment of time before it bucked his hand and lashed flame across the ill-lighted room.

Zenis was spun half way around. The gun in his hand exploded, driving splinters from the floor in front of his boot toes.

Bullet shock left him rammed between wall and table, propped erect. He went down with one leg folded and the other thrust out, with the spur leaving a line of tiny dots across the floor. The gun was still in his hand, but its barrel was pinned between his right hip and the floor.

Warren had moved back the instant he fired and now his shoulders were flat against the wall, and in that position he was momentarily safe from the other Barbour boys.

"He's not killed," Warren said. "I always like to waste one on your kind."

Hoss lurched to the middle of the room. He stood reared high, the bull whip clutched in his right hand, looking gorilla-huge beneath the low ceiling. He stared at Warren a second, at the gun, back at his face.

"You ain't got me turned yella-gutted. I'll cut your damn head off at your shoulders, gun or no."

He swung the whip up and around. It made a roaring sound through the air. Warren could have killed him. He didn't. He bent aside, but the lash did not reach him. Big Jim Swing had rammed his way forward, caught it with an up-flung arm, ripped back, jerking the stock free of Hoss Barbour's hand.

It took Hoss a second to realize what had taken place. Then he roared his rage and turned on Jim Swing.

He didn't try to draw. There was a heavy, three-legged stool beside him. He swept it up and charged. Big Jim let the stool strike his forearm and bound away. His right fist swung up in a short smash that connected with Hoss Barbour's jaw. Hoss didn't even see it coming. He snapped him back at the waist, and Hoss

sat down, his jaw sagging, eyes off focus.

Cap Coyne stopped a general battle by leaping to the center of the room and waving men back, "No. Dammit, let's not fight amongst ourselves."

Things finally quieted down. Zenis Barbour was not seriously wounded. The bullet had broken a rib or two near his right armpit, but the big artery that fed his arm was not severed. He let Eben Smith lay him on the table to swab it out.

One of the men brought sagebrush and started a fire in the fireplace. Afterward he packed a little pyramid of coal around it. The coal had come from a pit back of the house where the owners had once dug for well water.

Warren examined a piece of it. It was soft coal, but not the gray stuff, half shale, one often sees cropping out in those bad lands.

One of the Texas crowd said, "You strike that stuff all along the Springs. Now if we had it in Dodge City, it'd be worth a million."

Warren tossed it back in the fire. It was true there were uncounted millions in that country waiting for development. Cap Coyne came around and asked him to ride back toward the river and scout Dermott's men. Warren knew he wasn't so much concerned in scouting as in getting him out of the Barbours' way. As things stood, there'd probably be a shoot-out before nightfall.

CHAPTER ELEVEN

Beef at Miles Town

IT WAS sun-up when he led Hernandez and Big Jim away from the Broken Arrow, taking a short-cut trail through the little hills. Half an hour later they looked down on the far-flung flats of Mandan Springs.

It was still early, with purplish haze hanging in coulee shadows. Smoke rose from a point half a dozen miles away. It was too big for a cookfire.

Warren said, "That's Eben Smith's place. They burned it. Dermott's men."

They rode down several gentle benches, but there was no need of going closer. They could see all that was left—a few corrals, some charred rectangles of sill logs where the houses had been. Other traces of smoke rose from greater distance.

A gray streak ascended from the direction of Cap Coyne's Double C. The streak grew until it became a huge, black billow. An hour later, topping a bulge of the valley floor, they could see the smoldering remains of ranch house, bunkhouses, sheds. No one was in sight. Horses had been turned from the corrals and scattered.

"There's old Jinks," Jim said, pointing at a big bay. "We better round up our remuda, if we can find 'em."

Warren nodded. He kept on toward the smoking ruins. A man was lying face down about halfway between the creek and what was left of the house. One tuft of his fine grayish hair kept blowing in the morning breeze. It was the cook—Jack Snow. He'd been running and the bullet had taken him between the shoulders.

"We will keel the man who did that!" whispered Hernandez.

"I was thinking the same thing," Warren said softly.

They buried Snow, and Hernandez repeated a prayer in Spanish. Afterward they dug in the ruins of the blacksmith shop and rescued their scorched warbags that had been saved by a cave-in of the thick log walls. Then, after roping fresh horses, they rode on to Miles.

It took them till mid-afternoon. There was a great deal of beef along the way, trail stock, lean from hard travel. Miles Town presented a different aspect, too. It was spread over twice its former area by reason of several hundred canvas-topped Conestoga wagons, tents, and various lesser shelters that had been tossed up. The streets were so crowded they had trouble finding a hitch rack for their mounts.

Warren stopped a tall cowboy who had just clomped from the Carson Brothers store and asked if the N.P. was laying rails after all. It took the cowboy a moment to realize what he meant.

"You mean our new settlers? You can thank Sitting Bull for 'em."

There'd been stories all spring and summer about Sitting Bull leaving the Agency and fomenting trouble among the Western Chiefs. The cowboy went on,

"He's war-pathin', and he's got the whole Sioux nation behind him. Mandan, Arikara, Dakotah, Cheyenne—all of 'em. There's talk about High Eagle and the Blackfeet, too."

Warren went on down the street. All anyone talked about was Sitting Bull and the Sioux. Custer had sent two of his aides, Baker and Reno, to arbitrate, but Sitting Bull had demanded the expulsion of whites from the Black Hils, an area sacred to his people, as a condition of any settlement.

Already there were an estimated two thousand near the new town of Deadwood working the gold placers, and the demand was impossible. All that Reno could offer was an uncertain "readjustment" of the Minnesota Treaty lands dispute, and Sitting Bull's answer came in three weeks when he attacked Rockford, a settlement west of Deadwood, and massacred twenty men.

THE ATTACKS spread and now his warriors ranged the entire three hundred miles between the Middle Loup and the Belle Fourche, attacking wagon trains, trail herds, and all but the larger settlements. The Black Hills had been isolated now for almost a month with scarcely a freight wagon getting through the blockade, and a man who recently arrived from Deadwood told about jerked buffalo which sold at two dollars a pound, beans at a dollar, flour at seventy dollars a hundred.

Rumors of new Indian outrages continually swept through Miles, were altered in the telling, and then went the rounds again. Sitting Bull with eight hundred braves was sweeping up the Niobrara; Yellowtail had laid siege to Julesburg; Heavy Runner had attacked Densomore and killed a hundred whites, and men believed it even though not a soul in Miles had ever heard of a town by that name before.

And a steady succession of wagons, carts, even *travois,* lurched into town from the south and southeast, nesters mostly, who had abandoned their miserable holdings along the Belle Fourche, the Cheyenne, and the Little Missouri.

But while everyone talked of Sitting Bull, apparently there'd been no news of the fight at the Chalk Cliffs, though the steamboat that played a part in it was at that moment tied to the Dermott docks. The only news concerning the steamboat was that one of its passengers was Senator Wilton Reeves of Kansas.

A bartender at a saloon called "The Drag" expressed the opinion that Reeves would "pretty quick make those damned Union Generals wake up," and everyone within sound of his voice agreed, probably the same men who had recently been calling him "Carpetbagger Reeves" and wondering why in the hairy old hell he and his whole Washington gang weren't impeached and tossed into jail for their association with the Credit Mobelier scandal.

After a bath, haircut, and shave, Bill Warren started out to find Dermott. It was growing dark. There was a light in his office, but a black-whiskered man named Jack Bell sat just inside the hall, tilted back in his chair, a sawed-off shotgun across his knees.

"You're goin' no further, cowboy," Bell said.

"Tell Dermott the Pecos Kid wants to see him," Warren said loudly to Bell.

He said it with enough vigor to be heard through the closed door, and as he'd expected, Dermott came out.

"Warren!" He walked across with his hand thrust out eagerly, a smile showing on his strong teeth. "You've been gone a long time."

"Get my messages?"

"Certainly. I thought you'd know. After last night." He stepped back after shaking hands and the smile left his face. His jaw became prominent, eyes narrow. "They slipped away from us. I don't understand it. *Yet.*"

Warren didn't like the way he pronounced the word "yet." He kept watching Dermott's eyes. They weren't the kind that ever showed anything.

"I have a visitor," Dermott said, jerking his head at the door. "A rather important visitor."

"Senator Reeves?"

"You knew?"

"I guessed. Maybe you want me to come back."

"No. I think I'd like to have you meet the Senator." He smiled a trifle. "We're all in this together, aren't we?"

"The Senator, too?"

Dermott paused with his hand on the knob, "Senators are human, just like everybody else." He seemed to make a little grimace of distaste when he added, "In fact, *this* Senator is about the *most human* senator who ever went to Washington."

WARREN knew what he meant. He walked through the door that Dermott held open for him. Only a dim glow came through the big double windows that looked out across the roofs of warehouses, and the hanging lamp had been lighted. Two men were seated.

One was Wallace Carson, a pale, tall man of forty whose gray hair and stiff dignity made him seem older, and the other, evidently Senator Reeves, was short, soft looking, and fifty-five. He was pink and clean-shaven, and though the crown of his head was bald, he attained a senatorial elegance by allowing the hair to grow along the edges until he-could comb it back over his ears.

Warren already knew Carson, and shook hands with him. Then he was introduced to the Senator.

"Young man!" was all Senator Reeves said, but the stentorian nature of his voice gave the words a sound of importance.

Dermott said, "Mr. Warren is one of our associates."

"A cattleman, I dare say," Reeves said in his rich baritone.

"Yes seh," Warren answered in his soft Texas way.

"Tell me, how are you cattlemen progressing against those nester brigands out at Mandan Springs?" the senator asked. "A disgrace, sir, the thing that is happening to our public domain. These persons who insinuate themselves on another's property and defy him with force of arms!

"Yes, and even grow bolder. Attack the very steamboat that carries a member of the Congress of the United States! I'll have the army on these men. I'll not tolerate it, do you understand? We have troops, though sometimes a person would doubt it. I'll demand protection from Colonel Ludloe. I'll demand that he drive those

brigands into the river. And if he hasn't men enough, then by the gods I'll send a telegram to General Custer for reinforcements."

"You'll do no such thing," Dermott said. "I want no more men at Fort Keough than there are now. When the Colonel comes, I'd like to have as little importance as possible placed in that affair last night. The Army never insinuated itself into one of these matters yet without interfering with legitimate enterprise."

Warren knew that whatever kept Dermott interested in Mandan Springs lacked something of legitimate enterprise—otherwise he'd not hesitate to use the Army. There was something Dermott didn't want finding its way into the Army records.

Colonel Ludloe arrived about three drinks later. He was a small, erect man of about forty-five possessing the lean reserve that is typical of so many who have spent their lives in the profession of command.

He shook hands with Reeves, whom he'd met before, and then with Warren. He gave Warren a sharp scrutiny.

"You were Colonel Warren, serving under Price in Missouri?"

"That was my brother. He was killed. I was Major Warren under Johnston."

"Sorry—Major."

"Just the Pecos Kid," Warren said softly. "I'm afraid I didn't earn any such rank from a professional army man's view-

point. They weren't sifting their officers so carefully when I was made a major in '64."

"If you were Colonel Warren's brother, I dare say you measured up all right. He was a fine soldier. Sorry, I'd never heard he was killed."

He turned then to Senator Reeves. There was no deference in his manner, rather a meticulous courtesy. "Senator, I believe you were on the *Princess Jo* last night. I have learned there was some sort of an attack made on it."

REEVES spread his fat fingers deprecatingly. "These rumors! What haven't I heard since I arrived here? Sioux in solid phalanx all the way from Miles to Leavenworth. And yet we know that Sitting Bull could raise no more than a thousand warriors. Now a bit of nonsensical shooting from a half-dozen firebrands who have a pique against the 'big interests' and immediately this town of yours magnifies it to a scale of piracy unknown since the days of Elizabeth. I'm surprised at a hard-headed old army man like you giving any credence to it."

Reeves carried it off excellently, and yet there was a look in Ludloe's eyes that indicated something short of conviction.

"What was the cause of the shooting?" he asked Dermott.

"Everybody shoots at me," Dermott said. "During last year I lost a total of 113 freight wagons and almost five hundred head of stock to an assortment of cut-throats, white and red, here and there between Fort Benton and Cheyenne, and I can't recall any previous demonstration of concern on the part of the army."

"My forces are spread thin even when I try to cover my own parade ground, Dermott." He looked back to the Senator. "For a long time we've been trying to get reinforcements for Fort Keough. Lord knows, sitting here in the midst of Sioux territory, we need them worse than

they do to the east of the Mississippi."

Carpetbagger Reeves cleared his throat and assured Ludloe he would give the matter his scrutiny. "You must understand General Custer's difficulty, sir. I was dining with him at the cantonment in Fort Leavenworth only three weeks ago. He told me he'd had more than two hundred desertions since the discovery of gold in the Black Hills."

"I understand Custer's difficulty, but why should the army have more men stationed in Illinois than in Montana Territory?"

"I will give the matter my scrutiny, and I shall *insist* on the West receiving its just apportionment of the troops."

Colonel Ludloe thanked him, withdrew, and closed the door behind him. His absence seemed to leave the Senator a little less jittery. He poured another drink.

"I fail to see your position, Dermott," Reeves said. "If you want these nesters driven off the railroad sections, why not let me use pressure to bring Fort Keough up to strength? Let the Army do the job."

"I said I wanted the army kept out of it," Dermott said. "I don't care to give Ludloe the chance of poking into my affairs."

"Sir, you'll have a hard time preventing the reinforcement of Keough if this Indian business grows worse."

"I won't prevent it. *You'll* prevent it," Dermott said.

"Damn it, I have to think of my reputation."

"Beginning when?"

"The people, sir," Senator Reeves held up one finger. "I am governed by their opinions. No matter what you think, no senator, no matter how firmly established—"

"Can you keep Custer from reinforcing Keough for two more weeks?" Dermott asked.

"Not if Sitting Bull attacks along the Belle Fourche," the Senator mused.

"Then it's up to Sitting Bull, and not you," the steamboat owner said.

"I'm afraid that's the situation," the Senator nodded.

"IT WAS a mistake for me to bring you here," Dermott snapped. "Very well, we'll have to clean up the situation before then." Dermott did some cursing. "We should have finished it last night. Those limping fools should have wiped them out when they had them cornered along the river. Do you know how many men I brought down from Bismarck for that job?" he asked Warren. "One hundred and twenty-six! It'll cost me better than ten thousand dollars.

"I'll pick fifty from the lot and send the *Princess Jo* back with the rest in the morning. There aren't one in four of those railroad riff-raff who can handle a gun, and not one in ten knows enough to hold his tongue. If I could only have waited for my own freight crews to get in. There are fighting men for you!"

Warren said, "Mandan Springs will turn out to be the most expensive ranching land in the West."

"But bottomed by gold, sir," the Senator said. "Black gold."

Dermott turned on him with one of his sharp, exasperated movements. "And not one Senator in ten knows enough to hold his tongue, either!"

There was no more said concerning black gold. Dermott kept pacing the room. He usually reached his decisions rapidly, and his failure to come to one now seemed to upset him. At last he said,

"Sitting Bull is almost sure to attack toward the Belle Fourche. Maybe he'll try to burn Miles. That medicine man will try anything. If he does, there'll be five hundred soldiers tramping down the street as soon as a steamboat can haul them. We have to settle that business at Mandan or have it settled for us. Warren, they still trust you. Can you bring their leaders

in here for some kind of compromise?"

"What are you going to offer?"

"I'll pay railhead prices for their cattle. Every hoof. The rest we'll turn over to the senator's arbitration. You can go out there tomorrow morning. As a symbol of good faith, I'll send three thousand in gold as a down-payment. I dare say that's more

The Sioux

money than they've seen since they left Texas."

CHAPTER TWELVE

Powwow

WARREN went outside. Big Jim was seated on the loading platform, talking to a couple of freighters. He asked about Hernandez, and a moment later saw the Spanish-Irishman coming from across the street. He'd been atop one of the warehouse roofs looking into Dermott's window.

"I thought perhaps they would keel you," Hernandez said cheerfully. "I was never one to miss watching a man get keeled, Señor."

Hernandez already smelled of brandy, but he'd done a better-than-average job of keeping himself sober.

"It is that I am like a peon without money," he said bitterly when Warren commenced congratulating him. "You see me, Señor, broke and bankrupt, with my pockets empty. I have been watching from the roof to see if that king of the steamboats would give you money, for I would have my share."

"I didn't get a two-bit piece from him."

"Are you then a fool that—"

"We'll collect. With interest. This is one town we're not going to ride away from broke."

Warren had one drink with Hernandez and Big Jim at the Round Tent, then he walked to the docks where he hired a rowboat to take him across the river to Fort Keough.

He could tell at first glance that the place was ridiculously undermanned. Only one of the barracks buildings was inhabited. A Negro private led him through the gate and escorted him across the parade ground to Colonel Ludloe's house.

Ludloe seemed glad to see him. An orderly was just serving him coffee. He asked for an extra cup and proceeded to lace both with brandy.

"Why should Roger Dermott oppose the reinforcing of Fort Keough?" Warren asked.

"Dermott is like a busy blacksmith. He has many hot irons and he has to handle some of them fast to keep from getting burned. I don't engage in speculations that don't involve the military." The coffee was too hot to drink, but Ludloe sat and held the cup close to his nostrils, breathing the brandy fumes. "It seems to me that *I* am the one who should have asked *you* that question."

"I'm only one of his hot irons."

"Those Mandan Springs ranchers attacked the *Princess Jo* last night, didn't they?" Ludloe mused.

"And Dermott was ready for them."

"He was afraid I'd horn in and get it in an army report. He was wrong. The army is here for one purpose, and that's to keep the Indians under control."

"But you could get reinforcements if you had to," Warren said.

"I could. The Western department needs more troops—that's what I was talking about to the Senator. Custer will send more troops here if he decides Sitting Bull's main attack is aimed at Miles and the valley of the Yellowstone rather than at Deadwood, or Fort Pierre, or at the Union Pacific railroad. He has just so many men, and he'll have to deploy them the best he can."

"When will you know about the Sioux?"

"Tonight. Next week. Next month. No man can tell what an Indian will do. I have my scouts out, of course. Four of them are Poncas, so I don't know if they can be trusted. I'd rather have Crees to scout the Sioux. They hate them worse."

WARREN finally got around to the real point of his visit and asked what was so valuable about the Mandan Springs. Ludloe drank some of his brandied coffee and repeated what he'd already said about not engaging in speculations that did not involve the military.

"I have an idea this can damn well involve the military before it's finished. Do you know anything about coal deposits over there?"

"Any man can see coal cropping out in the badlands all the way through Dakota and Montana. I doubt that much of it will be valuable in our lifetime." He stood up and walked to a large map of the area. "By the way, the Geodetic Survey made some mention of coal strata in its report on that country near the Springs. Horizontal strata, pretty shallow."

"Where could I see their report?"

"In Washington. It was the *Geodetic,* not the geologic, survey. I doubt they'd much more than mention it."

"That's railroad land. They'd own all the minerals, wouldn't they?"

"If it's railroad land, they'd own it on alternate sections. The N.P. land isn't solid, you know. It's like a checkerboard."

"*If* they owned it?"

"Why, yes. If they own it."

"How could I find out *if* they own it?" Warren asked.

"Certainly not from me. But there's a land office in town—a man by the name of Wallace Gates keeps it open between drinks. The plats should be in his office."

Warren finished his drink, picked up his hat, and excused himself. Ludloe followed him outside. "Just who are you working for?" he asked.

"Why, lately I've decided to start working for a man by the name of Jim Swing. I need a considerable sum of money to keep him out of the sheep business." Warren grinned, and strolled off.

The Land Office was a narrow, low shanty with a bent-board roof. No light. Gates, who claimed the title of U. S. Commissioner, proved to be a tall, seedy, would-be lawyer of fifty, and, as Ludloe suggested, he was out for a drink.

"Closed at six, Government regulation," he protested, but Warren forced him through the swinging doors of the Longhorn Bar and down the sidewalks to his office. There Gates got the door unlocked and groped inside, falling over obstructions and finally lighting the lamp. The place was heaped with books, documents, and dirty dishes on table, chairs, the floor.

"What can I do for you, Sir?" he asked, getting himself seated beside a high secretary desk.

"I want to see the Government survey maps."

"What particular district?"

"Mandan Springs."

Gates had already started to reach for some rolled-up maps. His hand stopped and his eyes narrowed. The words had jolted him quite sober.

"They are not available."

"The Army has assured me that they were."

"You go tell the Army—"

Warren took a step forward, seized Gates by the collar and rammed him back in the chair. He tried to rise, but he was helpless against Warren's strength.

"Give me those maps!"

GATES shook his head back and forth and tried to answer, but the air was pinched from his vocal chords. Warren let up a little.

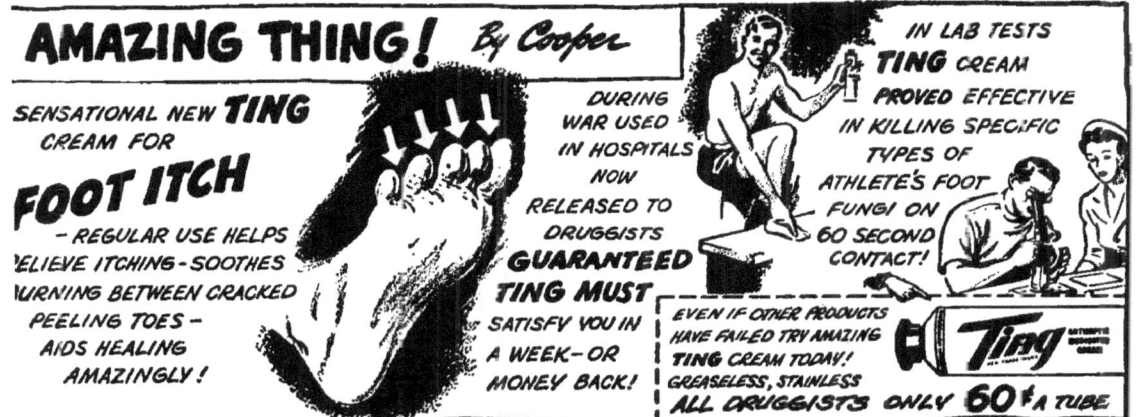

"They're—not here," Gates wheezed.
"Where are they?"

"In Bismarck. Railroad business—"

"You're lying." His fingers tightened again. "You're lying."

Gates' face was turning dark. Little drops of spittle showed at the corners of his mouth. His lips formed the words, "Yes."

Warren held him for a while anyway. "Where are they?"

"I loaned them. To—Dermott."

"When?"

"I forget. Damn it, I don't remember. Little things. Maybe—two months ago. Last spring."

Warren let him go. Gates got to his feet, leaned against the wall. He started forward, tripped and fell headlong across the floor. Warren watched him crawl to his knees, grope for a chair, pull himself to its seat.

"Just forget I came here," Warren said.

Gates nodded his head. He still breathed with a scraping sound. His eyeballs were sharp, distended. "Sure. I don't ever want to remember you."

Warren left him there. He walked up the street and looked inside the Round Tent. Hernandez was at his old place by the roulette wheel, but there weren't a great many chips in front of him.

The orchestra was playing, and the theater was jammed with dancing couples. Most of the men were refugees from Sioux country to the southeast, but they all seemed to have money to spend on the short-skirted dance hall girls.

Music stopped and the girls steered their partners to tables and the bar to collect percentage brass for the "house drink," and during the intermission a tenor on stage launched forth on "A Handful of Earth from Dear Old Mother's Grave." For some reason never fully explained, a man is always more generous in tears than in laughter.

A familiar figure was seated at a table on the balcony. It was Lona Pearl. He moved back to the sidewalk and walked to the steamboat docks.

The boilers of the *Princess Jo* breathed softly under a low head of steam, and somewhere a Negro crewman was singing,

> *"All night down in the engine deck*
> *I shovel in de coal,*
> *I'd rather be a gamblin' man*
> *And wear de ring o' gol' . . ."*

There was no light in Dermott's office, but the windows had been left open. He walked to the river side of the building. The eaves were low, and it was no great task getting to the roof.

From there he could see that the second story was merely a shack-like addition set atop the warehouse. He climbed to the second roof, crouched for a while watching for movement below, then lowered himself, clinging to the fancy molding along the front, until his feet touched the window sill. A few seconds later he was inside.

HE STOOD up in the inner darkness. The office seemed close and hot. He scratched a match, opened the drawers of Dermott's desk, moved on to some cases along the wall. Nothing that looked like maps. He finally found the map he was looking for inside a cluttered little storeroom.

There, with a lamp heating the close confines of the room, he spread the map on the floor and examined it.

It took him a while to orient himself, then he saw that the railroad sections barely touched Mandan Springs. Ludloe's hint had been correct. Neither the railroad nor Dermott owned the land.

Things started to clear up in his mind. He could see the situation that had confronted Dermott. There was coal across those broad flats—shallow layers of coal. It was worthless as dirt at the present time, but when the railroad came it could be worked by means of spur lines and steamshovels at a fraction of the cost entailed in underground methods. The resulting product could be shipped directly back to the new milling and manufacturing center at Minneapolis or on to Butte, where vast mineral deposits had been unearthed.

Dermott would have purchased the area, but he was prevented by land policy and the Homestead Act. He'd have laid claim to it under the Non-Metallic Minerals Act, but squatters occupied the ground, and squatter sovereignty was not a thing to be laughed at.

So he had decided to bluff. He knew that no man could follow the infrequent survey marks laid through that limitless country. He knew that no one, not even the moguls of the Northern Pacific themselves, quite knew where their vast land holdings were located. So he had bought options on railroad land which he claimed to cover Mandan Springs.

Warren put everything back as he'd found it, climbed from the window, dropped to the ground. There was no sign that anyone had seen him.

CHAPTER THIRTEEN

Confab

HE'D been a long time without sleep, so it was mid-morning before he got around to Dermott's office and picked up the three thousand in gold. At noon he headed out of town by himself, and that evening he reached the Broken Arrow.

Warren clomped inside and strewed gold pieces across the kitchen table.

"There's the down payment," he said as men gathered around, staring at the first real money they'd seen in months.

"Down payment on what?" Hoss Barbour asked.

"On your cattle. Dermott claims he's willing to buy every hoof at railhead prices. Maybe he'll do it. He wants to meet with you in town. Senator Reeves will be there to arbitrate. He doesn't know it yet, but Colonel Ludloe will be there, too."

"You think there's a chance of us getting a fair show for *that* damnyankee?" Hoss asked.

"*Ludloe* is honest. And I have a little surprise that'll knock Dermott right out of his chair," Warren added.

He let them argue it out among themselves, but even Zenis Barbour, wounded, with his arm in a sling, had his natural bitterness tempered by feel of the heavy gold coin. In the end, there was not a single dissenting vote against riding in for the meeting.

A committee was chosen—Zenis and Hoss Barbour, Cap Coyne, Eben Smith, and seven more. Mary Coyne, as usual, went with her father. They arrived in Miles shortly after nightfall.

No one took any special notice of them as they rode up the street, but there were lanterns burning along the front of Dermott's warehouse. If a man looked closely he could catch movement and flashes of gunshine here and there in the shadows, so Warren knew that they had been expected.

He swung down and jingled his spurs across the dusty yard. Big Jim came to meet him.

"Dermott isn't laying a deadfall, is he?" Warren asked.

"I doubt it. Not with seven men, and that's all he's got posted." Jim looked around at the Barbours and grinned. "By damn, I'd want a detail of cavalry if I went for them ornery Barbour boys."

Jim got Warren aside and went on in a lower voice. "There's something damn strange going on here, Kid. Couple trappers rode in yesterday noon and said the Sioux burned 'em out on Willow Creek. That's between here and the Belle Fourche. Fifty-five men under Calf Robe.

They laid out in the bushes and counted 'em.

"Same day a cowboy named Mader outran forty Sioux on the upper Lodgepole. You remember that Clawhammer outfit that was driving to the Sweetwater under Dad Slater? He rode with 'em. Anyhow, Mader's no damn Missouri punkin-roller that sees Sioux behind every sagebrush. It adds up that Sitting Bull is aimed right straight at the Yellowstone."

"Did you see Colonel Ludloe?"

"Saw him this afternoon. He said he'd have to get word on it from his own scouts. Couldn't believe all these stories."

"That's true, Jim," Warren said. "If the army believed all the stories that hit this town, they'd have troops scattered from Dodge to Fort Benton."

"Hold on! That ain't the all of it. Now comes the peculiar part. You know Hernandez—"

"Hernandez Pedro Gonzales y Fuente Jesus Maria Flanagan? You mean Butch?"

"This is no time to joke, Kid. What I was going to say was that Hernandez now and then gets snooted up on high wine and acts like he was locoed, but he ain't. He's only half crazy. The Irish half. That Mex half of him stays sharp and suspicious as the blade of that bowie he carries.

"Last night Lona Pearl got him to singing songs in her apartment, and next asking about you and little Mary. To make the story short, Butch staggered through the wrong door on purpose and guess what he found. A halfbreed Ponca asleep on Johnny Malette's couch with an empty bottle of Hennessey in his hand. Doesn't that seem sort of funny to you, Kid?"

"Did you tell Ludloe?" Warren asked.

"I ain't had a chance."

"Ride over there. Tell him to come up to Dermott's office. Tell him I said it was important. And tell him about the halfbreed, too."

DERMOTT wasn't in his office. They ate and returned, a heavily armed, suspicious group. This time Dermott was waiting on the loading platform.

"Glad to see you, boys," he said, with every appearance of sincerity.

Hoss Barbour was in the lead. He chawed for a while and looked at Dermott with narrow-eyed suspicion.

"You don't need to act any friendlier than you feel. I want you to know that I hate your Yankee guts and I'm willing to fight you down to the last cartridge." Then he tempered it by adding, "If that's the way you want it."

"That's not the way I want it. I want to start out from here, and to hell with what's past. This is no time to be fighting with the Sioux swarming around Deadwood."

"You're peaceful?"

"I'm peaceful," Dermott said.

"Then why you got them lads stationed by the river?"

"For the same reason you have Colts on your hips and Winchesters across your arms. You lighten that cargo of Hartford metal and I'll send my boys uptown for a drink."

"Let 'em go thirsty," Hoss muttered. "I ain't unbucklin' my guns."

They climbed to the office and Dermott sent one of his warehousemen out for more chairs. It took a while. The ranchers ranged the wall looking big, and rough, and truculent. Finally everyone was seated.

Dermott tapped at the door of an adjoining sitting room and said, "Would you care to come out now, Senator?"

Senator Reeves made his entrance carrying a legal volume and a thick folder of documents. He placed these things carefully on the edge of the desk and spoke:

"Gentlemen! May I say I have already conducted an independent investigation in the matter that brings us together, and

I see no reason why a settlement cannot be made that would be advantageous to both sides." He cleared his throat and looked at Hoss Barbour. "Most advantageous."

Hoss was not awed. He chewed and spurted a stream of tobacco juice across the floor.

"A carpetbagger if I ever seen one."

Dermott said, "Oh hell, Hoss, a senator has to use big words or else folks will find out he's human."

DERMOTT had lived a rough life, associating with aristocrats and buffalo hunters, spending one summer in fine hotels, the next sleeping on the ground in Indian country, and he'd developed a way of getting along with people, of speaking their language. One could see his personality working now. These ranchers were commencing to like him in spite of themselves.

Dermott called, "Joseph," but nobody came. He said something about "that damn boy," and got up to pull the cork from a bottle of whiskey himself. He didn't bother with glasses. He wiped the neck with his coat sleeve and started it on its rounds by handing it to Hoss.

It got back to him with a couple ounces left. He tilted it up, killed it, and threw it out the open window. By that time Joseph was there. He sent him out for more whiskey. Then he sat back and talked. He had an easy way with him.

He started by admitting that his fight for Mandan Springs had cost him twenty thousand dollars already, and that another twenty thousand was more than the country was worth. He talked for a long time, and it was not the speech of a man who had his opponents against the wall. It was the speech of a man admitting his defeat and resigned to be cheerful about it.

He dipped a pen and wrote the figure 3,000 in big letters across the top of a sheet of paper, and beneath it, "First payment."

"I'll pay gold coin for your cattle," he said. "At railhead prices. Do you hear that, Senator? Gold at railhead prices. See that I'm held to it."

"Indeed, sir! There is not a banker west of St. Louis that would not take those words as a bond."

The whiskey arrived and was passed around. After half an hour, Dermott's real purpose in bringing the ranchers there was still in no way discernible. It was almost as though he were on the level. Only he was too generous. These ranchers were about licked and they knew it.

It occurred to Warren that Big Jim had plenty of time to get Colonel Ludloe. He rolled a cigarette. He'd almost smoked it when he heard Colonel Ludloe's voice addressing Jack Bell outside.

Dermott recognized the voice and stopped talking. "Come in!" he called

without giving Ludloe a chance to knock.

Ludloe stood and gave the men a careful scrutiny. He nodded to Warren, Dermott, the Senator.

Dermott said, "Is there something you wanted, Colonel?"

"I was asked to sit in on your conference."

The words jolted Dermott, but he mastered any visible show of surprise. "There must be some mistake."

"I think not," the Pecos Kid said softly. "*I* asked the Colonel."

Dermott's jaw jutted more than usual, muscles knotted at its sides, and veins distended at his temples, all showing the fury he was trying to hold in check.

"Ridiculous! The Colonel has enough trouble of his own——"

"I'd like to sit in, if these men don't mind," Ludloe said, indicating the ranchers.

"Hell, no," said Hoss. "Grab yourself a piece of floor and squat."

"This does not concern the Army," Dermott said.

"Would you let me be the judge of that?" the Colonel said.

Ludloe preserved his scrupulous courtesy, and the words were more cutting because of it. He went on, talking to Dermott:

"It is my understanding that you have purchased options on certain grant lands of the Northern Pacific Railroad. As one of my duties is to protect such grants from unlawful seizure, would you mind letting me see those options?"

Dermott started to answer, but he couldn't trust himself. He reached for the whiskey bottle, and fury made it shake in his hand. He slammed the bottle back to the table with a force that made some of its contents jump from the open neck and spill across his hairy forearm. Then he said in a tight voice:

"They're in my vault. Downstairs. It will require some delay and——"

"Would you mind sending for them?"

"Joseph!" Dermott shouted savagely. He sat, still clutching the whiskey bottle, waiting for the Negro boy to come.

CHAPTER FOURTEEN

Hot Box

BIG JIM. Swing returned from Fort Keough and seated himself on the loading platform of Dermott's warehouse. Two Negroes were unloading a cargo of buffalo pelts from a jerkline freight outfit that had just rolled in from the southwest. Overhead, from the open window of Dermott's office, he could hear the steady sound of voices. He smoked his way through a cigarette.

A coyote had howled. It was such an ordinary sound he didn't think of its nearness. A violin was playing the Blue Velvet Polka up the street and he was enjoying its rhythm. It suddenly occurred to him how strange it was that a coyote should be howling there, in the midst of the settlement.

The sound came again. He crushed out his cigarette and walked around the freight wagons. He had a careless way about him that tended to minimize his frame and muscle which were on the scale of a percheron horse. He watched the rambling, shed-roofed buildings across the way. A twenty-foot passage between them lay deep in night shadow. He groped along it, heard movement, stopped. Hernandez Flanagan's voice came from above.

"Señor, if any women come looking for their Hernandez, you may tell them I have a good place to watch the stars." He was lying on the roof, head thrust over the edge, grinning down on him.

"Damn it all, Butch, this ain't any time for jokes," said Big Jim.

"To the Spaniard, love is not a joke. Love is the air he breathes, the wine he drinks. But tonight while I watched the stars, I saw many horsemen leaving this town. Perhaps Señor Dermott only keeps those men in his office so he can attack the others at the Broken Arrow. In my country, Señor, this is an old military maneuver known as the 'Keek With the Pants Down.' It would perhaps be wise to tell the Kid what strategy their General Yellow-Guts Dermott has planned for them."

Big Jim walked back, trying to appear casual about it, but his strides were half again as long as usual. The freight wagons were still being unloaded. He circled them, walked along the platform, climbed the outside stairs.

He stopped abruptly just inside the door. Jack Bell had rammed a sawed-off shotgun against his stomach.

"Where you been, cowboy?"

"That's none of your damn business."

"Don't get mouthy. Ever see a man get hit by an ounce of buck? It turns him inside out like an old feather tick. I asked where you been."

Big Jim could think of no good answer. He moved aside, hoping to get away, but the gun muzzle followed him. He found himself against the wall. His eyes kept moving to the gun and back to Bell's whiskered face. Bell rammed the muzzle and Big Jim retreated. There was a door at the far end of the hall, and a dark room beyond.

"Right through the door, cowboy," Bell said.

He noticed at the same instant that the shotgun was angled away from his abdomen. He started to turn, but something hit him. For a moment he seemed suspended while the world spun and an intense ringing rose in his ears.

Big Jim was down on hands and knees. He tried to lunge and grapple, but his arms and legs were heavy as though his veins flowed liquid lead. He was struck again, and again, each successive blow driving him deeper into a whirlpool of darkness. Finally he passed out cold.

DERMOTT had time to get control of himself while waiting for his bookkeeper to bring the railroad land options. He passed the bottle around and made some easy talk, but Warren knew that anger had settled cold and hard inside him.

The options proved to be conditional bills of sale, devised to become effective with the final payments three, four, and five years in the future. Naturally, he never intended to redeem them after the Mandan area once came into his hands.

Ludloe read through a couple of them.

"Satisfied?" Dermott asked.

Warren spoke, "Those aren't options on any land lying inside the limits of Mandan Springs."

Dermott must have been ready for something like that. He showed no surprise, no longer any visible sign of anger. He laughed, an easy, modulated sound. He seemed to be genuinely amused.

"Then I've been cheated. Just where are they if not in Mandan Springs?"

"Down in the badlands between Cap Coyne's Double C and the river," Warren said.

"No. I'm not that great a fool. They cover every alternate square mile of land from the old Block M cabin to within ten miles of Powder River."

The Senator was leafing through the papers.

"Sir, your allegation is preposterous," he said to Warren. "These options are obviously legal instruments covering the land specified. See, in each one the words 'Mandan Springs Quadrangle' is specifically—"

"Keep your yawp closed, you fat-gutted carpetbagger!" Hoss Barbour brayed. "That's the Pecos Kid you're talkin' to. He used to be an officer in the Army of the Confed'racy! He understands them things. What in hell do you know about surveyin'? How do you know about the Springs? You never been there."

"Sir, you will not address me in that manner."

"Keep still or I'll whop your teeth down your throat."

Hoss might have tried it, but Cap Coyne got hold of one arm and Colonel Ludloe was facing him. Dermott meanwhile moved a few things on his desk and kept smiling.

"Damnyankee," Hoss wheezed, sitting down.

"Hoss is right," Dermott said. "The words 'Mandan Springs Quadrangle' could mean lots of things besides the Mandan Spring *area*. The Quadrangle covers many miles. It means a folio of the atlas. But those options are still correct. They were okayed by the chief surveyor when he was in Bismarck."

He sounded so reasonable that the ranchers believed him in spite of themselves. Ludloe was looking at Warren.

"Well?"

"You want me to show proof? All right. I can produce it. It's right here in this office."

"Thoughtful of me to keep it handy, wasn't it?" Dermott said.

For the first time, suspicion knifed through Warren—suspicion that Dermott had been forewarned.

WARREN stood up and opened the closet expecting to find that the survey map had disappeared. It hadn't. It was still there, exactly as he'd left it. He carried it out, untied the string, unrolled it on Dermott's desk. He looked down and met Dermott's eyes. They were narrow, and hard as blue-gray flint. His lips were pulled tight showing his strong teeth. He was still smiling.

Led by Hoss, the ranchers had left their chairs to crowd around. The Senator, who'd had experience in such things, was already comparing the section numbers of options with corresponding squares on the map.

The map was not the same. Its township numbering had been changed, and the lightly shaded checkerboard of N. P. land now covered the entire Mandan area.

Warren could feel perspiration crawling along his hairline. Not once, in all their dealings, had Dermott been fooled.

"I shouldn't have underestimated you," Warren said.

"Never overestimate a friend or underestimate an enemy. I have followed that principle for some time," Dermott said.

"You have friends?"

"Why, no. I guess not. They're a prohibitive luxury for a man in my position."

Colonel Ludloe finished his inspection of papers and map. He looked at Warren. "Well? What do you have to say?"

"Nothing it would do any good to say."

"I see." He nodded to the ranchers, to the Senator, to Dermott. "Excuse me for intruding."

Ludloe went out the door. As he closed it, Warren had a glimpse of the hall. There were others besides Jack Bell there now. Someone was inside Dermott's sitting room, too. Dermott was talking again. He took up several things that had been covered before. He was killing time, probably waiting for Colonel Ludloe to get back across the river. The room was stifling. Finally Eben Smith said,

"Damn it, we've had enough talk. You say you'll pay our price for the places you burned. All right, let's settle it now. I was more'n a year putting up the house and sheds on my place. I wouldn't of sold it for five thousand, and that's my 'inventory' you was askin' for. I'll take the money now."

Dermott looked surprised and perhaps a little offended. "We'll have to draw up the papers. The Senator will be in town for a week or more, and it should all come under his scrutiny."

"To hell with the Senator," Hoss said.

"If you want to buy, I'll sell. The Barbour ranch is worth ten thousand dollars."

"I've already offered to take your cattle—"

"It's worth that *without* the cattle."

"It is my place without the cattle," Dermott laughed, pointing to the options.

Hoss started to shout back, but Dermott held up his hand for silence. "Hold on. Think it over till tomorrow morning. You've had a long ride and a tough night. Come back tomorrow at ten. If your offer is reasonable, I'll pay."

THEY got up and filed outside. Warren started with them, but there was a slight creak as the door to Dermott's sitting room swung a few inches farther open. Dark in there, but not too dark to see a dim shine of gunmetal, to make out the outline of tall, slouched Eldad Stark. He was aiming the gun quite steadily at Warren's temple.

"Yes, stay," Dermott said softly, keeping away from the line of fire. "I have a few things I'd like to discuss with you."

Cap Coyne started back from the hall when he saw that Warren was not following, but Dermott went to the door, smiling pleasantly, explaining that Warren would naturally want to take up a few of the technical points with Senator Reeves.

Cap was still suspicious. Warren said easily, "Go ahead, Cap. I'll handle things all right."

Dermott closed the door, bolted it. Then he turned and said, "You act confident of yourself."

"I have a way of squeezing through tight places."

"How old are you, Warren? Twenty-eight? That's old for a man with your reputation. Gunmen don't last long. Most of them don't last till they're twenty-two."

"Who ever told you I was a gunman? I'm an old rabble soldier in search of my fortune. Sometimes a man turns up and wants to shoot me. I have them buried all the way from here to San Saba."

"Don't reach for that gun on your hip."

"Why, no. I wouldn't do that. Not while Eldad Stark's in there with those sights notched down on my temple. I'd like to walk out of here alive."

Stark, hearing his name, had moved forward. He was standing in the door. He'd lowered the Colt a little and was holding it waist high. His jaw was loose, exposing his buck teeth. He'd always feared Warren and hated him. His hatred showed now.

His thumb rocked the hammer back. He held the trigger depressed.

Senator Reeves was staring at the gun. His eyes were like those of a man who wakes up and finds a coiled rattler beside his bed. Color had drained from his face, leaving it bilious yellow. He tried to speak, but only a dry hiss came from his throat. At last he said,

"That gun. Make him put that gun away."

"Why?" Dermott asked.

"He'll kill Warren."

"Why, sure. What did you think he was going to do? What else is there to do with a traitor than kill him?" Dermott said.

"No. Good God, Dermott. Not that. Why, *I'm* here. I can't associate with—murder."

DERMOTT laughed. He walked around the desk, approached Warren so as not to place himself in the line of fire, and plucked the Kid's gun from its holster. He dropped it in the top drawer of his desk. He'd let his own coat come open. He was carrying a Smith and Wesson rimfire .32, a custom-made gun with ivory stocks and engraved silver surfaces. Aside from the fancy work, it was the same gun Mary Coyne carried.

Senator Reeves was walking towards him saying, "No, Dermott. Not with me in here. You got to let me get out."

"Stay where you were," Dermott said. He meant it.

Reeves came on anyway and Dermott whirled, catching him with a sweeping, backhand blow. It sent him reeling half the length of the room. There he stood with one hand over his jaw, looking at Dermott with stunned eyes.

"You got yourself into this, Senator. You were the smart lad with plenty of ideas, but now that the going is a little cluttered up with dead men, you'd like to rise above the whole bothersome business. Well, you're in it and you're going to stay. You're going to stand there, and watch this traitor get shot, and you're going to keep your mouth shut."

Reeves kept wetting his lips. He was frightened. The thought of murder made him sick.

Eldad Stark kept edging inside the door. Warren started to elevate his hands, bringing them within the heat of the three-wick hanging lamp.

"Keep your hands down," Dermott said. "Well, Stark, you've been wanting this for a long time."

He stopped and listened. Someone had run up the stairs. No clump of boots, but the rhythm of moving weight vibrated across the flimsy structure. Colonel Ludloe's name was spoken. An unfamiliar voice. Dermott strode to the door, jerked it open. Men were scuffling.

"Stop it!" Dermott said.

Jack Bell and another man let the fellow go. He was a halfbreed, wearing a narrow-brimmed hat and fringed buckskins.

The breed's eyes fell on Dermott and he started to shout, "Colonel Ludloe! He's there—Ludloe? I want to see—"

"Sure, Steve. Of course he's here, Steve. Come in."

The halfbreed stopped just inside the door. His eyes roved the room. "You fool me again! Last time you said he would soon be there, at the saloon."

"You're a Ponca scout?" Warren asked.

"Yes. Steve, the Ponca scout. I had a message for Colonel Ludloe. It was stolen from me. Yesterday. A message that the Sioux would ride this way. Today, tomorrow. Heavy Runner, Yellowtail, maybe-so Sitting Bull himself, all with twelve hundred braves."

Dermott said, "Come on in, Steve. You can't go to Ludloe now. He'll shoot you when he finds out you've been drunk and lost your dispatch. I'll get you out of town."

The Senator came to life and shouted to the halfbreed, "You mean you're a dispatch rider for Ludloe and somebody got you drunk?"

"This man!" The breed pointed at Dermott. "And one other. They say that they would find Colonel Ludloe. But they gave me something to drink." He started to back through the door.

Dermott had drawn his gun. "No,

you're not going anywhere out of here."

Senator Reeves said, "Gad, sir, you can't do this. You can't interfere with a dispatch rider."

"No? I might even end up with a dead senator. Get back!"

THE PONCA whirled around and started for the stairs. Dermott's gun exploded, driving a pencil of flame across the room. The breed was hit but still on his feet. He got through the door, started to vault the rail of the landing.

Dermott had stepped to the hall. His gun was at arm's length. He could have shot a second before. He deliberately waited until the scout was at the crest of his leap, then he fired again.

This time the bullet found its mark and the scout crumpled, pitched head foremost to the ground.

Men had been shouting out in the hall, diving away from the line of fire, and suddenly it was quiet. "Get him out of sight," Dermott said.

He walked back inside the office, closed the door.

"That's the easy way to get it," Dermott observed. "On the run. Easier than standing there, like you. Waiting. But I couldn't deny Eldad the pleasure. I've been promising it to him for too long. Oh yes, by the way, who told you there was coal underlying the Mandan area?"

"How bad do you want to know?" Warrren asked.

"Not badly enough to bargain for it."

Stark showed his upper teeth in a weasel expression and said, "My arm's gettin' tired."

"All right. We've waited long enough. Ever see a man shot in the temple, Kid? One shudder, and that's the end of it. No more heat and alkali, no more forty below with the blizzard howling across these prairies. Lots of men would beat your head in for what you've done to me, but I'm not that sort. I always take the things I want the easiest way. All right, Eldad."

Warren had partly turned. His hand was against a chair. Stark was shifting his position a trifle. He wouldn't just let the hammer slip. It was too uncertain. He'd click it, and then pull the trigger. There was an outside chance.

Warren was ready to make his move. He stopped. Something whisked the air of the room. A bullet with the report rocking after it. Eldad Stark was hit. He spun, with the gun exploding in his hand. The bullet tore slivers from the floor close to the Senator's feet.

Stark was still up but his eyes were already flat-staring. Gunman's instinct made him cock and shoot again. The slug almost struck his own boots. He looked awkward and disjointed as he took one step over buckling knees and plunged forward to the floor.

Warren had caught the flash of a rifle on the roof across the street. Perhaps Dermott had, too. Both men started at the same instant.

Dermott had spun against the wall. His hand came up with a gleam of silvered steel from the .32 Smith and Wesson. Warren dived for him. His shoulder caught Dermott waist high, and slammed him to the wall. Dermott's elbow struck and the gun flew from his fingers, bounded to the middle of the room.

The door was open and Jack Bell charged inside, sawed-off shotgun in his hands. He stopped. Dermott tried to rip himself away. A big man in back of Bell picked up a chair and hurled it. It struck Warren across head and shoulders, drove him down against the wall. He went down, hidden by the desk.

Warren jerked the drawer open, grabbed his gun. Bell fired the sawed-off, but the shot only ripped furrows across the desk top and slugged deep in the wall above Warren's head.

"The light!" he heard Dermott say.

Bell's second load smashed the light from its moorings and sprayed the front half of the room with kerosene. Men were plunging away.

IT WAS dark for a moment. Dark, and and the air filled with the odors of burnt powder and kerosene. Then flame rose in a smoky red billow.

Warrren was on his feet.

"Dermott!" he shouted across the room. "Where's your fancy gun? Take your first shot, Dermott. I'll spot you this one."

A gun smashed from the midst of smoke and flame, and Warren fired back. He moved along the wall, pulling the trigger again, again. The hard buck of the gun felt good in his hand.

His voice rose in a shout, "Come and get it, lads. We're all fired up and ready for breakfast. Get your lead biscuits! One gutful guaranteed to last a lifetime!"

His eyes were blinded from flame and smoke. A shot came from somewhere amid the inferno, and his own gun answered it.

He heard Jim Swing's voice, "Kid!"

"Here, Jim."

He turned, groped, ran against another wall.

"Back this way," Jim's voice said.

He found his way inside the little sitting room. He was coughing and Big Jim was slapping his back. No flame there, but a blind layer of smoke filled it.

"I don't need any help. Get your hands loaded. We got to crowd out of here."

"I ain't got a gun."

"You're a hell of a fightin' man."

"I'm good enough to drag you out. Let's get down this hall. This whole dump will be a bonfire in two or three minutes."

Jim groped to a hall. It was dark there, but they could breathe. The blow on his head, the smoke and flame, had all combined to leave Warren unsure of himself. He kept running into the wall. They turned a corner and suddenly there were

men clustered around in front of them.

Someone realized who they were and shouted a warning. There were eight or nine men blocking the outside door. Warren sensed someone behind him and started to turn. He was slugged—down on hands and knees in the midst of charging, cursing men. He was blindly aware of the battle raging around him.

"Kid!" Big Jim bellowed hoarsely. He was in the midst of things, swinging a chair. It was knocked from his hands. Despite the wild mix-up, somebody fired. Big Jim seized a bench. It was massive plank, a dozen feet long. He lifted it high, flung it. Its weight swept a mass of men in front of it.

Three or four were down and others charging for the stairs. Big Jim lurched after them. A man stood up in front of him, a gun in his hands. Groggily, he tried to lift it. Jim batted it away, lifted him so high his shoulder rammed the ceiling, and hurled him into the stampeding press of men in the door.

"Kid!" Big Jim bellowed again.

"What the hell do you need me for?"

Dermott's men had smashed the stair rail down getting to the ground. Four or five were running across the freight yard. One had taken cover behind some platform steps. He rose, aimed, but a gun spoke from the warehouse roof across the way, sending him clawing for cover.

"Ha, Señors!" Hernandez shouted. "Thees was just like running my grandfather Guzman for the post of senator from Chihuahua!"

CHAPTER FIFTEEN

Hell-Town

FIRE raced quickly through the big, draughty warehouse and flame lighted the town, even bringing the far bluffs of the river to ruddy relief. A mob had formed along Front Street and was moving that way. Leading it was huge, black-whiskered Buffalo Bourke, a rancher from down in the Sundance country.

"Hunt your holes, you Injun-lovin' renegades!" he was bellowing. "Whar is he? Whar's the man that kilt the Ponca scout?" Someone must have told him it was Dermott, for the bellowed, "Come out here, you money-grubber, and we'll roast you in your own fire."

Warren was satisfied to lose himself in the crowd for a while. He reloaded his gun. His throat and nostrils were still raw from heat and flame.

"*There's* one hangin' I want to get in on." Big Jim said.

"Jim, you go over there and show them how to tie that California knot."

Dermott wouldn't be near the warehouse. He was too good at saving his own skin. Down by the river, Senator Reeves had mounted an empty hogshead and was orating. Now and then some of his words reached Warren over the hubbub of the mob. He was accusing Dermott of every perfidy known to man.

The upper end of the street was deserted when he got to the Round Tent. He stepped inside. The place was empty save for one derelict asleep in a chair by the wall. He climbed stairs to the balcony, found the door to Johnny Malette's apartment, stood outside for a while, listening. Tiny sounds came to his ears—someone moving across a padded floor.

He turned the knob, started the door swinging inward. The room was dimly illuminated by lamplight from an open door at the left. He saw Lona Pearl bent over, hurriedly stacking things in a suitcase.

She suddenly became aware of him and whirled around. "You!" she whispered. "You, boy!"

"Yes."

Her eyes darted to his holstered gun, and back to his face. He knew then that she was the one who'd squealed to Dermott, and that she thought he'd come to

kill her for it. Her dark eyes were wide. "Why'd you do it?" he asked softly.

"You did not come to see me! You were in town, and yet you rode back to that other woman. That pale thing with—"

"Never mind."

He stepped inside, closed the door. He looked at the suitcase. "Going someplace?"

She didn't answer. She was standing quite stiff, her eyes looking beyond him. A scream leaped from her lips, and he wheeled, drew, fired in the same ragged instant of time.

Johnny Malette had come from a drapery-hidden door. There was a gun in his hand. Warren's bullet had a shocking power that turned him half around. The gun slid from his fingers and made scarcely a sound as it struck the padded floor. He stumbled and fell, catching himself on one hand. He lay, looking up with baffled eyes, while bloodstain sponged through his embroidered vest.

"Lona. You remember—that day. In Cape Girardeau." He was speaking without expression, lips whispering the words. "I picked you up. Washed you. Taught you all you knew. I told you then, some day I'd kill you."

HIS HAND was in sight, dangling from the big sleeve of his coat, his long, dead-looking fingers just touching the rug. Lona must have known what was coming but she watched with the fascination of a bird charmed by a rattlesnake. Johnny's hand had not moved, yet gunmetal shone in it. He'd had a derringer in a spring-fed sleeve holster.

Warren's Colt mixed with the derringer, making a single crash of explosion. The bullet had finished Johnny Malette, but it hadn't quite saved Lona.

Lona was hit. She was holding the left side of her breast with both hands. It was accident that she found a chair to sit in. She was still clutching her side, with blood

"Come out here, you money-grubber," Buffalo Bourke roared, "and we'll roast you in your own fire."

running through her fingers. Johnny Malette was face down, and she was staring at him.

There'd been someone in the next room. Warren sensed the movement, the slight tremble of the floor. He stepped past Lona. The door was open, light streaming in. He didn't dare show himself.

Suddenly the light blinked out and he was in the midst of flickering blackness. He groped, touched the door casing. Gun-flame tore the blackness in front of him. He fired, aiming at the flash. For three seconds the exchange was rapid, deafening. Concussion in the small room had an effect not unlike bullet shock. Warren groped forward, stumbled, fell over a padded footstool.

He rose, collided with Dermott. They clinched and reeled across the room.

Instinctively they'd found each other's gun hands. Warren's gun had been forced high while he'd thrust Dermott's toward the floor.

Warren's gun was still high. He let it drop and twisted with a sudden motion that freed his right hand. Dermott cursed. He pulled the trigger, perhaps unintentionally. The charge flew wild across the room. For an instant Dermott was off balance, and Warren smashed a right uppercut to his jaw.

the stairs, tripped, fell the length of them.

HE GOT up from the saloon floor with cigarette butts and dirt in his hair. He found the front door, flung the batwings open, and fell again from the platform sidewalk. He got up, using a hitch rack to balance himself. He kept looking over his shoulder as he reeled on into the middle of the street. He did not even realize the mob was coming back from the flaming warehouse and that he was going directly toward it.

Hoss Barbour saw him and let out a bellow. "Thar he is! Thar's the damnyankee that kilt my brother!"

Dermott saw them then, turned, started to run. He got fifteen or eighteen steps.

The blow snapped Dermott's head back. He pulled the trigger again, but the hammer fell with a dead snap. He swung it like a bludgeon. Warren sensed the move and caught it with an upflung arm.

Dermott's head rocked under a left and right. He reeled, his shoulders struck the wall, he staggered forward.

"No!" he whispered. "No!"

Warren calmly smashed him to the floor.

There were unexpected resources of energy in Dermott's body. He staggered up, reeled through the door, lurched to

Someone fired. He was hit. He got up from the dirt. Half a dozen guns exploded. He was face down in dust that looked reddish by the shifting firelight.

Warren went back inside, climbed the stairs, lighted a lamp. Lona Pearl was still sitting in the chair, holding her breast as blood thickened between her fingers.

She looked up at the Pecos Kid.

"Damn you," she whispered. "Damn you, he was the only man alive that ever gave me anything but the dirt off his boots. And he's dead. Because I was a fool about your red hair."

"Let me see that shoulder."

Instead she reached and tangled her fingers in his hair. "You! I hate you! Kiss me on the lips before you go."

He held her against him for a long time, then he went out and spent a quarter-hour finding the doctor.

He heard that Mary Coyne had ridden in with the ranchers from the Broken Arrow. Hernandez had sent her to warn them, and she'd met them only a few miles out of town.

"They're camped down by the river," Big Jim said when he found Warren in front of the Antlers Saloon.

"Who?"

"You know who. Mary Coyne, her paw, and the rest of them. I imagine she'd like to see you."

"Why would she want to see *me?*"

"You know well enough. Because she's in love with you. You ain't ridin' off and leavin' her, Kid. She's too good, and sweet, and—"

"Sure. I know."

"I'm tellin' you, Kid, if you ride off and break that poor little gal's heart, there won't be enough blind canyons between here and the rimrocks of hell to hide you from Butch and me."

He looked up in Big Jim's eyes. It wasn't often Jim got steamed up like that. He wondered if Jim and Hernandez between them were men enough to do it, and the more he thought about it the more he decided that they were.

"Jim, if I'm fool enough to ride off and leave a girl like Mary Coyne, I hope you drag me back on the end of a lariat. And you can start looking for me up around the Musselshell."

THE YELLOWSTONE was falling with the drought of late summer and Bill Warren had no difficulty finding a place to cross. His buckskin saddlehorse, and the pack pony on its lead string, were belly-deep for a while, then they made the uncertain footing of mudbars and climbed to shelf land beyond. Warren kept on at an easy jog for half an hour, finally reining in atop the rimrocks.

He sat there with one knee hooked over the saddlehorn looking back at the lights of Miles. The prairie night had a rare purity, and he could hear little sounds, the slam of doors, an occasional shout of men, purified by distance.

He rolled a cigarette and lighted it, all without taking his eyes off the town. A campfire burned near the river. Even at that distance he imagined he could see Mary Coyne's shadow moving against it.

He'd be no good for her. He'd make a hell of a husband.

He idly felt in his shirt pocket and came across the lottery ticket. It had been washed with his shirt, but the Chinese characters were still there, and the faded smears of ink covering them. He could almost hear the Chinese say, "You lucky. Red hair lucky."

For some reason, it made him laugh. Perhaps the ticket had won. He'd never inquired. He wadded it, then reconsidered, smoothed it out, folded it, stuck it beneath the band of his hat. He'd always heard that a Chinese would pay off on a winning ticket until the end of time. Perhaps, someday, he'd come back to collect.

THE END

The Noose Hangs High

Harrow lifted a quirt to cut the horse out from under Lonnie.

By
LLOYD ERIC REEVE

When bigger and better hang-ropes were made, Lonnie Courtais' Johnny Reb neck seemed to fit 'em all!

A S BRAD COLTER rode up, Ellen Courtais came out of the sod house, having to stoop a little to get through the low doorway, as if she was emerging from a small and gloomy cave. He thought of the contrast it must be to the spacious plantation house where she had been born—the plantation which had been burned to the ground during the war.

She lifted an arm in greeting. He

swung from the saddle, tall and loose-jointed, the faint saber scar like a brand on one cheek. He looked across the space between them, at this lithe girl in the faded cotton dress, and saw what to him would always be all there was of woman's beauty.

"On my way into town," he said. "Thought maybe I could pick up something or other for you folks."

"Why, it's right nice of you, Brad," she said. "But Lonnie's already done our trading. That is, he meant to, but—" She hesitated, looking a little distraught, and just then Lonnie himself came around the corner of the sod house. He had overheard his sister, for he added, with a wry grin, "What she means, Brad, is I didn't do our trading. I only tried to."

"Oh, hush, Lonnie," Ellen said. "We'll get along, and anyway it isn't any of Brad's worry."

Brad got it then. "So Charley Travis cut off your credit."

Lonnie shrugged. "Until we pay our bill. He knows we can't do that without running cows this summer, not after last winter, and how can we run cows if we haven't supplies? Which is just the long way of saying Charley Travis has cut our throats."

Brad wasn't too surprised. "Hardly any cash anywhere this spring," he said. "But Charley has to pay cash for his goods. Not his fault if he can't carry us any longer."

"Us?" Lonnie looked thin and brown and the faint humor in his face was edged and bitter. "Don't worry. He'll carry you, Brad. He's a Yank and so are you. Me, I'm just another Reb that got licked. Let 'em starve, Charley figures, and good enough for them."

"Now, Lonnie," Ellen protested, "that's not true, and you know it. Mr. Travis has always been right decent. It's like Brad says, times are bad, and he has to think first of his own family and busi-

ness. It's a matter of making out."

"He's a damn' carpet-bagger," Lonnie said. "And what's more, I told him so, to his face."

"Now that was a fine thing to say," Brad said. "After the man's already given you a whole season of credit. Can't you get it through your head, Lonnie, the war's over. This isn't North or South. It's the West. And maybe we should thank God for it, that there was a new country like this waiting for us. All of us, no matter where we're from. Well, I'll have to talk with Charley. Maybe I can work something out."

"Work it out for yourself," Lonnie said. "But not for me. I want no favors from you or any other carpet-bagger."

"Lonnie!" Ellen said. "Brad's been as good a friend as any we've ever had."

"Any man who'd kill my father is no friend of mine," Lonnie said.

Ellen looked slightly startled. "Why, that's silly," she said. "Brad didn't kill father."

"Same as," Lonnie said. "Some Union soldier did, and Brad was one. Could be he even fired the shot."

"Oh, hush," Ellen said. "Out of the millions of bullets fired—that's crazy."

BUT she looked up at Brad, and suddenly her dark eyes were troubled. For an instant he could have kicked Lonnie clean around the sod house. Putting a fool notion like that in his sister's mind. She'd never have thought of it herself, but now that the idea had been planted . . .

He turned to his horse, his irritation growing, and swung into the saddle. Lonnie was grinning up at him.

"Work it out for yourself, then," Brad said, and rode off.

He hadn't meant it, of course. He'd still talk to Charley, do whatever he could. He wasn't sure it would be much, but still he had to keep trying. He had a sense of responsibility, almost guilt, forever fretting about them, worrying, wanting to help.

The sun was setting now, washing the illimitable prairies with mists of gold. Tender green touched the buffalo grass, smelling moistly of the vastly wakening earth, but already dust was rising from scattered patches of over-grazed range. Far to the left, along the winding cut-bank of Kansas Creek, gleamed an endless windrow of bleaching bones—the skulls and ribs and horns of countless cattle that had died during the blizzard months just past.

Sometimes Brad thought it would have been better for Lonnie if he'd actually been through the war. But he had been too young, even for the desperate Confederacy. Too young to fight, but not to forget the ravished splendor of the old plantation, or the legendary father who had fallen in battle, a Confederate hero. Every Union veteran, in Lonnie's eyes, had personally killed his father.

With Ellen it was different—sadness and regret, perhaps, for a vanished past that had ill equipped her for the frontier's raw struggle for existence. But no animosity. Unlike her brother she hadn't let resentment gnaw into a dark and festering sore. Yet she knew how helplessly Lonnie suffered, and it was not in her to rub salt in that wound. Least of all to give herself to any Union veteran.

It was twilight when Brad reached town. He stopped at the Longhorn Saloon before going on to the store, leaving his horse at the hitch rack in the warmly purpling dusk. At this supper hour only a few idlers were inside, Tod Beldon, the bartender, who had left a hand at Gettysburg, a couple of bearded freighters, and big Joe Niles and two cow-hands playing poker with a tinhorn known locally as Windy Harrow.

Brad lifted a hand to the card players as he went up to the bar, thinking that the boys couldn't find a quicker way to get rid of their winter wages than by playing with the slick-fingered Windy. Tod Beldon put a bottle and glass on the bar, at the same time gesturing briefly with his stump.

"What's the password?" Brad said, filling and lifting his glass to Tod.

"Same as always," the bartender said. "Misery. In this damn' country."

"It's a living," Brad grinned.

"For the buzzards," Tod said. "They been eating nothing but beef all spring. Hear a lot of big cattle companies are folding."

"Could be a good thing," Brad said. "Absentee owners. Those big outfits been grazing the range to the bone. Enough clear out and the grass will come back in a year or two, give some of us two-bit cowmen a chance. Let us build up the country, instead of just taking everything out while the getting's good."

"Charley Travis is having to take up his belt a notch of two," Tod said. "Cut off Lonnie Courtais' credit today. Lonnie was in here after, shooting off his face about it."

BRAD nodded. "I stopped by. He was still lathering a little. But you know Lonnie. Didn't get a chance in the war, so he's trying to fight it now, two thousand miles away, five years too late."

"Just the same," Tod said, "he carries it a little far sometimes. Called Charley a carpet-bagger. That's no way to talk about a man that's been carrying half the countryside on his shoulders for nigh a year now."

"We ought to lynch him," Windy Harrow called out from the poker table. Tod glanced up, and Brad swung half around, both looking in faint surprise at the tinhorn, unaware he had even been listening to them. Windy added, vehemently, "Hang him to a sour apple tree."

"Ain't no sour apple trees," Tod said. He grinned. "Ain't no trees. Anyway, you're mixed up, the sour apple tree was for Jeff Davis. Lonnie's just a kid, still smarting a little because he thinks he got a spanking."

"One of these days," Windy said, "you'll talk different, after he's killed somebody."

"Lonnie Courtais isn't going to kill anybody," Brad said. "A mite hot-headed is all, mostly just to prove he's a Southerner."

"You carry a musket in the war, Windy?" Tod asked mildly.

"I was at Vicksburg," Windy boasted, "and Wilderness Creek, too."

"The hell," Tod said. He looked in amazement at Brad, who was grinning a little now. "Man must have sprouted wings. Seeing as how those two battles were three hundred miles apart and both fought the same day."

Brad said, no longer with much humor, "It's men like you, Windy, that get decent ones like Charley Travis called carpet-baggers." He turned back to Tod. "Which reminds me, speaking of Charley, I got to get down to the store. Same password?"

Tod grinned. "Misery," he said.

"Misery," Brad repeated, and strolled out of the saloon.

Only a few pools of window-light splashed the darkness. A slow wind rolled through the town, talking fretfully to itself, warm and restless with the wild night scent of the Great Plains.

Brad went into the store, idling around while Charley finished waiting on a couple of townsmen. The cavernous place, lit dimly by two swinging oil lamps, was heaped with frontier merchandise—clothing, food, home remedies, saddles, cooking utensils, sun bonnets, boiled shirts, gaudy Indian blankets. He noted that Charley still had quite a lot of surplus stocks, army blankets, pup tents, canteens, hard-tack. If he never broke a tooth on hard-tack again, Brad thought wryly, it would be too soon. Or beans.

The two women left, and Charley in his splotched white store-keeper's apron, leaned against the counter, and said, "What's it for you, Brad?"

BRAD sauntered over, pointed with his chin at the hard-tack. "I ever tell you, Charley," he said, "the best way to fix that stuff? First you soak it for three days in water, and then put it in a skillet with some sow belly and start it slow cooking. Meanwhile you go out and dig a hole about a foot across and three feet deep. After the hard-tack's cooked for eight hours, you wrap it up in some buffalo grass and take it out and put it in this hole. Then fill in the hole, pack the dirt down tight, and pile some rocks on top. It's good that way."

Travis grinned. "None of you veterans ever buy it. Or beans hardly ever either. You're all beef eaters."

"Not this year, we won't be," Brad said. "The buzzards got there first. I still got credit here, Charley?"

"Long as I got stock," Travis said.

"Hear you had to cut off Lonnie Courtais."

"That's right. I'm a carpet-bagger now, Brad."

"He shouldn't have said that, Charley. I told him so."

Travis shrugged. "Ah, it didn't mean anything. The kid's got that burr under his saddle, makes him think we're all against him. Only thing, a man has to draw a line somewhere. Lonnie's trying to carry on his private war and run cows at the same time. It won't work. With him, I've known for a year now I was just throwing good money after bad. That was all right, so long as I had it to throw. But with the way things are now—Brad, you know yourself that if I go bust so will this whole damn' countryside. I had to draw a line."

"Sure you did," Brad said. "That's plain enough."

"Country like this, times like now," Charley said, "folks got to pull together. Man sets himself against the rest of humanity and he's finished. Hell, Brad, they talk about reconstruction in the South. Any reconstruction there is, it's right here west of the Mississippi. New country, veterans from both sides flooding in, they got to forget their grudges and pull together just to eat. But Lonnie don't see that."

"The whole trouble," Brad said, "Lonnie never had a chance to fight. Father got killed, lost their home, sees Ellen in rags. He's trying to make up for something he thinks he should have done five years ago."

"I used to figure he might grow out of it," Charley said. "If I still thought it I'd go on carrying him. But I don't. It's too late and he's got himself too mixed up inside."

Brad was silent an instant. Then he said, "I got no right to ask this, Charley, but how about giving him another year and charging it to me? We'd have to keep it under our hats, because he'll have no favors from me."

CHARLEY shook his head, "It's not that I'd figure to lose, Brad. You'd make it good, if it took the rest of your life. But that boy isn't going to change. Next year it would just be the same thing all over again. So why saddle yourself with it?" He looked up suddenly. "Or does that sister of his come into it?"

Brad shrugged. "Some. I don't want to see her go hungry. But she'll never have me, if that's what you're thinking, not with the way Lonnie feels. Latest thing, he's telling her maybe I'm the Yank that killed their father."

"What a damn' fool notion," Charley said. "And still you try to give him a hand."

"Well, maybe I did kill his father." Brad grinned. "He's damn' near got me

believing it now. No, but what I mean, Charley, we won the war, and the way I figure, that gives us all a kind of responsibility—particularly toward kids like Lonnie and Ellen. It's the way old Abe would have wanted it."

"But Abe's dead," Charley said. "Johnson made a mess of it, and now Grant's in the White House, with his whiskey bottle right there beside him. Well, hell, one more bad debt can't make much difference now. I'll send Lonnie word he can have his credit back, and you don't have to stand behind it either. I'll take a little of that responsibility myself." He grinned. "But Lonnie's not going to like it. He'll figure it's no decent way for any carpet-bagger like me to be acting."

Brad stopped in for a night-cap with Tod Beldon, and then headed for home. He had ridden only about a quarter mile into the prairie when he heard the shot. It echoed dimly, somwhere back in town. Some drunk, he thought, or someone taking a pot-shot at a prairie-wolf, or maybe just firing a gun for the fun of hearing the blame thing go off.

He thought nothing more of it then— not until the next morning when Tod Beldon, hammering up on a lathered horse, shouted him out of his bunk. Running to the door, he saw Tod, a wild figure against the dawn sky, reining down a rearing horse with his good hand, with the stump of his other clamping his bartender's sawed-off shotgun to his chest.

"Charley Travis was shot last night," Tod yelled. "Now a cotton-wood party's built up and are nigh halfway to Lonnie Courtais'."

"Lonnie?" Brad said. "Shot Charley? I don't believe it."

"Neither do I," Tod said. "I wouldn't be here if I did. But that wolf pack believes it—or wants to, anyway. Throw some clothes on while I catch you up a horse, and I'll tell you about it on the way."

Brad ducked back into the sod dug-out, jumping into his clothes, buckling on a six-shooter as he ran back outside. By then Tod had a horse saddled, and he had it going while he was still swinging astride. They hit across the prairie, into the vast crimson splash of the rising sun.

"Charley ain't dead yet," Tod shouted. "Or wasn't anyway when I left town. But that won't keep them from hanging Lonnie. I heard the shot, but didn't think anything of it until Windy Harrow came bellowing into the saloon, saying Charley had been held up and shot."

"Held up?" Brad said.

"Yeah, whoever it was took Charley's cash."

"Lonnie wouldn't do that."

TOD nodded. "Hot-headed young fool still dripping behind the ears, but no thief. Another good reason why he didn't do it is that Charley was shot in the back. But the best thing Windy Harrow does is talk. You'd think Charley was Abe Lincoln himself, and Lonnie—Windy even said it—just another assassin like Booth.

"He claims to have seen Lonnie running away from the store. Of course, the way Lonnie shot off his face yesterday and called Charley a carpet-bagger—that's bad. Anyway, Windy had a crowd in the saloon all night. They got liquored up— I refused them the stuff when I saw what was building, but it was too late then—and after a lot more jabbering Windy finally gets a bunch together and lights out to hang Lonnie. I cut ahead of them, Brad, but still we're playing it close. They should be at Lonnie's any minute now."

"Ellen can likely tell them Lonnie was home all night," Brad said.

Tod shook his head. "Who'd believe his sister? Even if they wanted to, which they don't. All they want right now is to hang somebody. None of it adds up to Lonnie, Brad, but just the same we got a bear by the tail."

"None of it adds up to Lonnie," Brad repeated. "But all of it sure as hell adds up to somebody else."

"Just what I been thinking," Tod said. "But how could you ever prove it? In time to keep Lonnie from hanging?"

"We can try," Brad said.

The sun, a great red globe of fire, swelled over the far rim of the world. All the vast sweep of the plains was washed suddenly in clear translucent daylight. Far ahead, as though afloat, Lonnie's and Ellen's sod hut stood out sharply, darkly etched, but still small with distance. Off to the left, boiling toward it, was a cloud of trail dust moving swiftly along the plains.

Tod said, watching the swirl of dust, "Close—they'll be there in just a few minutes now. Good thing a hanging takes a little time."

"If they don't just shoot him," Brad said.

Tod shook his head. "Got their hearts set on a hanging. For once I'm downright thankful the good Lord forgot the trees in making this country. They'll have to take him down to the creek to find one. Unless they rig up something at the barn, and that would take longer."

"Maybe," Brad said. "But we're still shaving it thin."

As they drew closer they saw the dust cloud swirl up to the sod house, thinning and separating into its milling core of riders. Several midget figures dismounted and swarmed inside. A moment later they came roiling back out, dragging a struggling shape. They hoisted it astride a horse, mounted again, and, just as Tod had predicted, swept off toward the willows and cottonwoods of Kansas Creek, a scant half mile away.

Following them, afoot and running blindly, was Ellen. Even at this distance, through that magnifying transparency of the plains, Lonnie's figure bobbed in that awkward way of a rider on a led horse, clinging to saddle-horn with his wrists bound, ankles tied beneath the animal's belly.

As Brad and Tod swept past the sod house, they saw the bunched riders ahead already herding their victim into the creek thickets. In another instant they overtook Ellen, and as they raced past, Brad shouted, "Ellen, go back. Stay out of this. We'll try to stop it."

Not until they were a couple of hundred yards from the creek did they glimpse Lonnie again, under a tall cottonwood, hemmed in by that tight circle of riders—astride the horse, ankles untied now, but with his wrists still bound together, and with a rope around his neck.

Tossed over a low limb of the tree, the rope was tied to the trunk below. As they reached the trees, Windy Harrow wheeled his mount. He lifted a quirt, to cut the horse out from under Lonnie.

AT THIS instant—it was that close— Brad and Tod bolted their blowing mounts through the hemming circle of riders, slammed them almost back on their haunches in a rearing halt. Brad grabbed the bridle of Lonnie's horse, and Tod, reins hooked over his stump, slapped aside Windy's quirt with the barrel of his sawed-off shotgun, holding and wielding it with his good hand like a pistol.

He rested it across his stump, leveled on Harrow, and urged softly, "Just give me an excuse, Windy. That's all I ask. Just one little excuse."

Brad was glancing over the crowd. They looked ugly, starting to mutter, but momentarily confused with their leader pinned by the black-mouthed hunger of Tod's scatter-gun. All of them a little drunk, Brad thought, not a veteran among them. There almost never was, in these vindictive little mobs that had kept flaring up throughout the country ever since the war.

He said, "Where you fellows going to find your fun after you've killed off all the kids and old men? Start in on the women and babies?"

Some of them shifted uneasily, their hot-eyed glares glancing away from Brad's faintly contemptuous grin. Windy Harrow spoke up hurriedly, sensing the quenching effect of Brad's manner.

"Don't listen to him," he cut in. "Him, and Beldon, too, they're just as much traitors as this damn' Johnny Reb. Trying to keep him from justice."

"Traitors we are now," Tod said. He lifted his stump and waggled it at the staring faces. "See?"

"Besides," Windy shouted. "Courtais is a murderer. Killed poor Charley Travis in cold blood. Hanging's too good for him, even if he wasn't a Reb."

"Keep it up, Windy," Tod urged, "you're doing fine giving me that excuse I asked for. Any minute now."

Brad said suddenly, looking back at the crowd, "What you doing here, Frank? I heard your wife was sick abed."

Frank Bailey looked a little flustered.

Brad's gaze shifted. "Could you spare a minute, Joe," he asked, "after you finish up here?"

"Why sure, Brad," big Joe Niles said. "We got no quarrel with you—that is— what the hell?"

"Just thought you could stop in and thank Ellen Courtais," Brad said, "for those mittens she made for your little girl last winter."

"Get on with it," Windy urged suddenly. "He's trying to talk you out of it."

"No," Brad said. "Just trying to talk you into hanging the right man. Lonnie didn't shoot Charley. Charley was shot in the back and his cash lifted. Lonnie's hot-headed and a fool kid, but do any of you who know him think he'd do that? Sure, he called Charley a carpet-bagger yesterday, and shot off his mouth in the saloon. But that was just dealing a full house to anyone who might have any ideas about holding up Charley. Lonnie would be sure to get the blame. Can't you think of anybody better than Lonnie for that?"

HE WAITED, seeing a little thought come into some of the angry faces. Then one of the bearded freighters he had seen in the saloon last night spoke up.

"Such as who?" he asked. "Not that it's much business of mine. I only came along for the ride. Ain't been to a good hanging for months."

"Such as who?" Brad repeated. He turned then, and grinned at Windy, "Who would you say, Windy?"

Harrow was beginning to have a badgered look. His gaze shifted from Tod's scatter-gun to Brad and back again to Tod. Tod said, "Cat got your tongue?"

"Last night in the saloon," Brad said, "you were hollering around that Lonnie should be lynched. You even said he was going to kill somebody. How'd you know?"

"I heard that," Joe Niles said suddenly. "I was playing draw with Windy. Losing, too."

"Lost a lot of money to Windy myself," Frank Bailey added. "Might be him after all we should be hanging. Do more good than hanging Lonnie."

Brad grinned. "Maybe it would have worked better, Windy," he said, "if you'd played it straight. Except you don't know how. Maybe now you've just talked up a lynch mob into hanging yourself."

Somebody laughed. The temper of the whole crowd was changing. The freighter said, "Damn-it-to-hell-myself, but that could be a good one, when he even brung the rope!"

Windy said, "You're crazy, all of you. You can't hang an innocent man."

"Haw," Tod said. "Can't we? You thought you could, didn't you? Still, I'd a sight sooner you save your worthless neck than for Lonnie to lose his. Tell you what, we might make a deal—prove to us

you did it, and might be we won't hang you. Maybe just ear-mark you instead."

Windy's eyes went a little wild. His hand swept his gambler's frock coat aside, dropping against his holstered gun. "Ah, take it away," Tod said. "This scatter-gun, this close, will blow a hole in you a foot square."

Harrow's hand fell away from the gun. His sallow face looked muddy, and his eyes skittered about the crowd and back to Tod.

He said suddenly, "I shot Charley just as he was closing the store. I took his cash."

Tod shook his head. "Have to do better than that. Just the say-so of a liar like you, that ain't no proof."

"But I can't prove it," Windy said. "I did it, I tell you, but you just got to take my word for it. I can't prove nothing."

"Sure you can," Tod encouraged. "What about Charley's money? Tell us where that is and then maybe we'll believe you."

ANOTHER instant the gambler hesitated, and then, with a confused look, dug suddenly in the side pocket of his long coat. He pulled out a buckskin pouch, on which Charley Travis' name had been lettered with a hot iron. He tossed it to Brad, and the bearded freighter, with a whoop, reined over beside him. A bowie knife was suddenly in his hand.

"Let me," he said, and grabbed Windy's right ear and sliced off the lobe. Windy screamed, and Brad said, "That's enough. Let him go now."

"Here now," the freighter protested, "I want 'em both."

Brad shook his head. "A deal's a deal," he said. "Even though he needs a hanging. Get going, Windy, and keep going. There'll be a rope waiting, if you ever show your face around here again."

Windy gave him a bleak look. Then he rode out of the cottonwoods and headed across the prairie. He kept going, not looking back, his hand clamped bitterly to his bleeding ear.

Brad freed Lonnie. With Tod they headed back toward the sod hut, while the others swerved toward town, riding slowly now, a little sheepishly, in that weariness of passions spent too suddenly and too blindly.

"Lonnie," Brad said, "Charley changed his mind about stopping your credit. He was going to send you word about it this morning."

Lonnie looked sick. "After I called him a carpet-bagger," he said. "Even killed him."

"You didn't shoot him," Tod said. "Windy did. Ain't you been around here the last few minutes? Didn't you hear what he said?"

"I killed him," Lonnie said. "If I hadn't shot off my mouth about him Windy would never have thought of trying it. Same as I told Ellen you could have killed our father, Brad. I got into a lot of crooked thinking. Maybe I needed something like this, only it's pretty late now, just to see it."

"Happy birthday," Tod said.

Lonnie glanced up at him with a surprised question in his eyes.

"You just came of age," Tod explained. "Say, there's Doc Alton, talking with Ellen."

As they swung out of their saddles, the chubby doctor waddled up hurriedly. He squinted at Lonnie. "Neck seems all right," he decided. "Afraid it might be pulled all out of shape. So was Charley Travis. Sent me hightailing out here, soon as he came to and heard what Windy was up to."

"He did that," Lonnie said, "when he thought I'd shot him? Is he going to live?"

"He didn't think you'd shot him, said he damn' well knew you wouldn't do a

thing like that. He was afraid of what Windy might make others believe. Sure he's going to live—take a sight moren' one bullet to kill a tough old bird like Charley Travis."

Brad had drifted over to Ellen. Now they walked around the sod house. "Could be the best thing ever happened to Lonnie," Brad said. "At least it seems to have taken a lot of poison out of his craw."

"I know. I think he's going to be all right now." She hesitated. "Brad, that crazy thing Lonnie said to you yesterday—"

"That I could have killed your father?" He shrugged. "I suppose so. Though the odds against a thing like that are a million to one."

"But I'd be just like Lonnie was, if I tried to shut my eyes to it. Father was a soldier, Brad. Just as you were. All that would seem important to him would be what you did today. Saving Lonnie's life from a mob."

"Ellen," Brad said, "what are you trying to tell me?"

"Don't you know?"

"There might be nothing but struggle and work for years to come," he said. "Everyone in the West is gambling. I might not win. A new country isn't built overnight."

"If it was," Ellen said, "it wouldn't be worth much. Brad, I'm through with remembering. Only the old look to the past. Here, everything is young and growing. We're young. New country, young country, but one we can grow up with, which we can belong to, which will belong to us—"

He reached for her suddenly and took hold of her arm.

"And to our children," she finished breathlessly, in that sweetness of surrender that was suddenly for her the shining victory.

Lilly's hand shot into the drawer and flashed back in sight, gripping a derringer.

By

JAMES

SHAFFER

Whipsawed!

When you're playing both ends against the middle in a quick-death game, let Brannan give you this advice: Never get whipsawed between the guns of a cold-deck gambler, and the claws of a two-timing hellcat. . . .

S AM BRANNAN was standing with his back to the bar when the surrey pulled up in front of the place. The surrey was a fancy rig. It had a fringed top, thickly padded seats and was pulled by a team of prancing, spirited blacks. He caught only a glimpse of the driver, but

in that glance he could tell it was his brother.

The driver helped the woman to the sidewalk. Their heads were close together for a brief moment as they said their good-byes, and then the surrey rolled away. The woman came up the steps into the saloon and went through the length of it to the stairs in the back.

Even without the help of clothes or makeup, she would have been an eye catcher. But with the clothes she wore— her dress low cut in front and clinging to the curves of her body as if plastered to her figure, and the makeup on her face enhancing the coppery sheen of the coiled mass of hair on her head—she was a stunning sight.

She looked neither right nor left as she passed through the nearly deserted saloon, but as she passed near Sam, he thought he saw a quick smile cross her mobile features.

For a moment he wondered if she'd seen him. Then he shook off his uncertainty with a mocking grin at his innocence. She'd seen him all right. He turned around, sliding his shot glass toward the bartender for a refill.

"That," he said, jerking his head toward the stairway, "was Lilly Golden, wasn't it? *The* Lilly Golden?"

The bartender was filling his glass, and the emphasis he'd placed on her name caused the man to spill a few drops on the polished mahogany. He flicked a glance down the bar, from whence a cold voice spoke up.

"And just what was meant by that, stranger?"

The bartender pushed the shot glass over, and Sam lifted it carefully, bringing it face level before he looked at the speaker. The man wore the garb of a professional gambler, and his white face and soft, well-kept hands were in keeping with his dress.

"No offense was meant, if that's what's worrying you," he told the gambler quietly. "Miss Golden's fame as a beauty has spread. There are not many like her."

"No," the gambler said in a flat voice, "there aren't."

"Sight of her also confirmed what I'd been thinking since I'd hear of her," Sam went on. "That we'd met before. I wanted to make sure."

"And now you're sure?" There was the barest hint of menace in the man's tone. His white fingers stirred in the pockets of his brocade vest, fondling the little Derringers that nestled there.

"I'm sure," he replied. "Fact is, Miss Golden and I are old friends." He turned to the bartender. "Would you send a message to Miss Golden's room? Tell her an old friend would like to have a drink with her. Tell her the name is Sam Brannan."

The bartender hesitated, glancing at the gambler. Sam looked too. Twin spots of anger showed on the gambler's face, and his lips thinned down in an angry line. For a moment Sam was surprised. Then, remembering Lilly, he was not surprised. Lilly was the type to have more than one iron in the fire—and more than one man dangling on the string.

He didn't want trouble. Not now, anyway. Not any time, for that matter, if he could avoid it. So Sam knuckled under a little.

"You seem to be looking for an excuse to take offense, friend," Sam said. He grinned a little. "You're acting like a jealous husband, and I was under the impression that Lilly Golden was still single. If you're her husband, and I've overstepped—"

"I'm her manager," the gambler said. "Jake," he said to the bartender without turning his head. "Take his message to Lilly."

The barkeep nodded, clumped across the sawdust floor and went up the stairs. The gambler poured himself a drink, then hesitated a moment before lifting the glass.

"Known Lilly long?" the gambler asked as he set his glass down.

"We got pretty well acquainted a couple of years ago in Dodge City," Sam said cautiously. "Lilly was singing in Barney Roscoe's place, and I was out to see the sights."

THE bartender came down and walked behind the bar without speaking. He lifted a dusty bottle of wine to the bar and wiped it with a towel before sliding it to Sam.

"She said bring that up with you."

Sam looked at the label. "Sherry. Yeah, I remember now. That's Lilly's drink."

"Second door on your left at the top of the landing," Jake said as Sam moved off. He went up, knocked and heard the rustle of silk on the inside. Then the door swung open and there was Lilly. Her eyelashes fluttered quickly, her full lips parted in a smile. She didn't ask him in. She took him by the arm and led him inside. He grinned. Lilly knew how to please a man. She knew how to make any man feel like the most important gent on earth.

"Sam!" She had a trick of making her voice flutter with excited pleasure, even though she spoke only one word. "It's good to see you, Sam."

She'd already slipped out of the dress she'd worn on the surrey ride, and she had a heavy silk wrapper wound tightly around her body. It fell open at the neckline. It was an expensive piece of clothing. A far contrast, he thought, from the tawdry clothes she'd worn at Barney's. He set the bottle on the table and slid into a chair.

"It's like old times, Sam."

"No, it ain't," he said with a laugh. "Last time we met, it was me that had money—and you were broke. Also," he added drily, "last time it was me you wanted to marry. Now it's my kid brother."

The soft green of her eyes turned jade hard. Those lips that could look so inviting, now turned down at the corners, revealing their natural, cruel set. And the tilt went out of her voice. It carried a sting.

"And so you rode two hundred miles to put a stop to it. You figure you can tell Danny what kind of a woman he's getting mixed up with, and break it up, huh?"

Sam grinned back at her, ignoring the warning lights that flashed in her eyes. "Danny's my younger brother. Half brother, that is. When I heard he was aiming to get married, I naturally wanted to come to the wedding."

His mildness disarmed her for a moment, and he saw the look of bewilderment in her eyes. But it was gone in an instant, replaced by that look of cunning he knew so well.

"Don't try to throw me off the track, Sam Brannan. You're here to break up this marriage. Think I've forgotten how you treated me, back in Dodge?"

Sam knew she'd never forgotten what happened in Dodge City. And he was remembering that old phrase that "Hell hath no fury like a woman scorned." But was that the reason she was marrying Danny?

Had her pride demanded that she trap Danny into marriage, to salve the blow he'd given her back in Dodge? It was a trick a lot of women would pull, but somehow Sam didn't figure that for Lilly's reason.

Oh, there were plenty of girls that would have considered Danny Curran a good catch. He was young, good looking, and had enough spirit in him to keep a marriage from becoming dull. Also Danny still had his share of the ranch they'd fallen heir to. It made enough money for a man to raise a family on.

Yes, Danny was a good catch—for some rancher's daughter. But not for Lilly. Danny wasn't her kind. That ranch of his wouldn't keep Lilly in the style she wanted.

He thought of another possibility. Some girls get swept off their feet by men. Danny could do that too—to some girls. But not to Lilly. Lilly couldn't be swept worth a darn. Lilly knew what she wanted out of this life, and she moved toward her goal with the surefootedness of a stalking puma. She'd get her stake, too.

"You don't figure I'd try to break up a couple of love birds, do you, Lilly?" he asked with a grin.

"Don't try to get smart with me, Sam," Lilly told him flatly. "You heard that your kid brother got himself engaged to Lilly Golden, and you come hotfooting it down here to break it up. Because we both know you'd rather see Danny dead than married to me."

"That's laying it on the line, Lilly," Sam said with a raspy chuckle. "And if Danny could see you right now, he'd break the engagement in two shakes."

Lilly laughed. "And wouldn't you like for him to see me like this—showing my claws! Don't worry, Sam. Danny thinks of me as a—"

"Just like I thought of you, the first few days in Dodge," Sam finished.

"And he'll keep on thinking that way—at least till we're married, Sam. And there's nothing you can do to break it up."

KNOWING Danny as he did, Sam was inclined to agree with her. Danny had a mind of his own. He was stubborn as a mule to start with—and he got more stubborn when Sam tried to influence him. Sam sighed. He reckoned all younger brothers hated for their elders to give them advice. And Lilly knew it too.

"Okay," Sam grunted. "We'll let that ride—whether I can break it up or not. What I'm wondering is why you're doing it, Lilly? How come?"

"Maybe I'm in love with Danny," she said archly.

Sam guffawed. "You ain't and never will be in love with nobody but Lilly Golden. So let's not be playful. What is it, Lilly? Danny's not your kind."

"Not good enough for him, I suppose?" Lilly snapped.

"Shades of Dodge City," Sam chuckled. "You know what I mean. You'd like Danny's life—ranching. And after a few

months he'd get sick of being cooped up in a saloon. He's not rich enough to attract you. So what is it?"

"Keep wondering about it, Sam. Maybe you'll get the answer."

She broke off abruptly, her head swivelling like a cat toward the door. It had swung open noiselessly, and the gambling man stood on the threshold—fingers still probing his vest pockets.

"What is it, Kyle?" Lilly demanded.

The gambler looked uncomfortable. His tongue darted over his lips a couple of times. He shot a cold glance at Sam, and again Sam was struck by the venom in the man's glance.

"Just wanted to know if you were all right," Kyle said lamely.

"You mean you were snooping again," Lilly snapped. "Get out. No, wait a minute, Kyle. Have a drink with me and my old friend, Sam Brannan."

Kyle looked as if he wanted to back out of the room, but Lilly went over and closed the door. She poured three small glasses and handed them around.

"Sam and I were good friends back in Dodge, Kyle," Lilly said. She set her glass down and pulled open the drawer of a small marble-topped table, rummaged around in it. "Got a picture somewhere me and Sam had taken in Dodge. I keep it as a souvenir."

Sam watched Kyle's face. Lilly was deliberately tormenting the man, working up his rage and hate. Sam remembered the picture. He'd had his arm around her shoulders, and she was smiling up at him. There was no point in showing the picture to Kyle, except to drive him mad with jealousy.

Sam knew how Kyle must feel. Hadn't Sam felt the same way back in Dodge, before the madness had worn off?

Lilly was having trouble finding the picture. She made a gesture of impatience and flung some of the contents of the drawer on the floor, muttering something about having thrown some of the junk away. Sam idly stirred the heap of knick-knacks Lilly had thrown on the floor.

A faded clipping from a newspaper caught his eye. Sam moved a piece of ribbon with the toe of his boot and read the headline. BANK PRESIDENT WOUNDED IN HOLDUP. CASHIER MISSING.

"Here it is," Lilly exclaimed. She swung around and handed the tintype to Kyle. "That was taken a few months before you met me, Kyle," she rattled on. "I did my hair different. I thought you'd like to see how it looked done different."

Sam abruptly set his glass down on the table and stood up. "Got to get going, Lilly. It was nice seeing you again."

"Going to be in town for a few days, Sam?" Lilly asked sweetly.

"Long enough to finish my business," Sam said with a tight grin. "Don't know just how long that'll take."

"Maybe we'll see each other again—while you're tending to your business," Lilly said with a smile. Sam went through the door. "I'll look forward to it," she went on.

Sam decided he'd like to know a little more about how things shaped up, so he stopped at the bar and ordered another whiskey. While he sipped it, he tried to pump the bartender. The man wasn't much of a talker—about things Sam wanted to know. About all Sam learned was that the gambler's name was Jack Kyle, that he looked after Lilly's interests as if they were his own, and that there was a young fellow in town who thought he was going to marry Lilly Golden.

"And that's a foolish thing for him to think," the bartender finished.

"Foolish?" Sam asked. "Why?"

But the bartender had said all he was going to say.

SAM went down to the Drover's Hotel, asked the clerk for Danny Curran's room number, then went up and knocked on the door. He heard footsteps inside.

Danny jerked the door open. The smile died on his face, and an angry red flush took its place. Danny was four years younger than Sam, two inches shorter. He had red hair. Sam could never see any resemblance between them, but some folks claimed they both had their mother's eyes.

"Did you bring the money?" Danny asked.

Sam dug a fat roll of bills out of his pocket and tossed it to Danny. "A thousand iron men. Had to sell some of your best horses to raise it."

"A man only gets married once," Danny muttered. He started to count the money, thought better of it and shoved it in his pocket. "I told you to mail it. You needn't have brought it."

"Like you said, a man only gets married once," Sam said. "You're the closest kin I got. I want to go to your wedding."

"I—uh—don't think we're gonna git married here," Danny muttered. "Li—that is, my future wife wants to go to Cheyenne."

"Just forget it, kid," Sam said. "I've already seen her and talked to her."

"Then don't try to stop me from marrying her!" Danny flared. "I guess that's why you come, to stop it. But just because she wouldn't have you back in Dodge—that ain't no reason why I shouldn't marry her." Danny balled his fists up and jammed them on his hips. "Don't try to horn in, savvy?"

"Whose horning in? Whose trying to break it up?" Sam asked wearily. "You wrote home for a thousand bucks to get married on. I raised the money and brought it. I want to go to your wedding. Anything wrong with that?"

"No." Sam saw Danny had expected fireworks from him, and was a little puzzled not to get any. But he was still suspicious. "Lilly told me the way you gambled away everything you had in

Dodge, and how you might try to keep me from marrying her on account of it. So I'm just warning you—"

Sam laughed and waved a hand. "Stop and take a breath, Danny. I don't blame nobody for what I did in Dodge. Nobody, that is, but Sam Brannan. Simmer down and quit fighting the bit. Lilly Golden is one beautiful gal, and she's a good business woman."

"She's had to be, Sam," Danny said in a dreamy sort of way. "She told me about the struggle she had when her folks died and left her stranded in Dodge."

Sam nodded gravely. It wasn't, he remembered, till after he'd left Dodge that he'd learned that Lilly had two live and healthy parents back East somewhere.

"It's a credit to Lilly that when she was forced to take a job in a honky-tonk, she didn't let it lick her. She watched her chance and bought a place of her own."

"Saved what little money she could out of the little she made," Sam agreed.

"She had to become a saloon owner whether she liked it or not," Danny went on. "She's just been waiting for a chance to quit. She hates the business."

Sam didn't quite remember it that way. The way he remembered it, it was the other way around. He'd lost all his money trying to run it into a stake big enough to buy Lilly a saloon. Sam kept drawing deuces when he should have drawn jacks.

Sam knew better than try to tell Danny any of that. Danny had it bad. He was, Sam thought, even worse off than Sam had been back in Dodge. Sam knew what he would have done to anybody who had tried to head him off. Danny was even worse, because he had Curran blood in him. Red hair went with Curran blood, and stubbornness and temper went with red hair.

"Well, it's nice that she's getting a fellow like you, Danny, if she really hates the saloon business," Sam said conversationally. "She can give it up and the two

of you can live on the ranch. The old house could do with a woman's touch since Ma's gone."

"I'm glad to hear you talk like that, Sam," Danny said. "Lilly was afraid you'd try to talk me out of it. And that," he stated darkly, "would have caused one big fight between the two of us."

"Ain't no use trying to fight fate, Danny," Sam said. "And besides, this thing might work out all right for me. Maybe Lilly will let me take over the saloon. Since I lost my share of the ranch in Dodge—"

"I reckon Jack Kyle will git the saloon," Danny said. Then he added, "That is, if he's still alive."

"Now what do you mean by that?" Sam asked mildly.

D ANNY shrugged. "Jack Kyle got drunk and did some talking last week, when word got around that me'n Lilly aimed to get married. Kyle claimed Lilly was his woman—and that he'd gun down the gent that tried to marry her."

Sam jumped. He knew now why he'd been dragged into the thing. Up till now, it had been a mystery to him.

Danny had written him to raise a thousand dollars cash and send it to him care of the Drover's Hotel, Buffalo Springs. He stated casually in the letter that he aimed to get married, and that he needed the thousand for a honeymoon.

Sam was foreman of Danny's ranch, having lost his own inheritance over the gambling tables in Dodge. He hadn't thought much about raising the thousand when the letter first came. Danny knew the condition of his bank account, and knew that Sam would have to sell some horses to get the money. A thousand dollars seemed like a lot to spend on a honeymoon. But then, a man only got married once.

Sam got busy collecting the cash, not giving a second thought to the girl that

Danny was going to marry. He figured that whoever she was, they'd squabble and make up like all married folks, till the kids came and made them settle down.

Then a drifter rode through town and spread the word that Danny Curran aimed to marry a slick looking gal in Buffalo Springs by the name of Lilly Golden. Sam heard the story. The thousand was ready for the mail, but he decided against mailing it. He saddled up and started for Buffalo Springs.

He'd been hoping that maybe that drifter had his tale crossed, that maybe it wasn't the same Lilly Golden that Sam had known back in Dodge. Or that maybe Danny had got drunk, made some wild talk about marrying Lilly, then forgot all about it.

His talk with Lilly had knocked all those hopes into a cocked hat. The drifter had the story straight. And somehow Sam was sure that Lilly had sent the man north to make sure Sam would find out Danny was going to marry.

It wasn't mere drunken talk on Danny's part. No. Lilly had her hooks into him good and solid. Danny aimed to marry her, and not even Sam could talk him out of it.

But he did know one thing. Sam knew now why Lilly had roped him into the deal. It was time to talk to Lilly again. But one more question to Danny.

"When does the wedding come off, Danny?"

"In the morning," Danny said. "Lilly made up her mind today. She'd been putting me off—kinda hesitating. She's kinda shy."

"Yeah, I know," Sam said drily.

"But today—just when we pulled up in front of the Golden," Danny went on, his voice growing soft with remembrance, "she made up her mind. Said she wanted to get married right away. In the morning."

Sam nodded gravely. That meant that Lilly's sharp eyes had spotted him through the windows of the Golden Saloon.

"I got to go git my fancy duds altered to fit," Danny explained. "Want to come?"

"I wouldn't git no kick out of watching you try on britches," Sam said. "But I'll see you later."

He walked back to the Golden. It was late afternoon, and the first few straggling customers were beginning to get to town. The place had more life in it than when he'd first seen it.

LILLY was over in a corner talking to Jack Kyle when Sam went in. The gambling man's face was a little flushed.

Lilly came over as Sam found a chair by a card table and slid into it. There was no expression on Lilly's face as she took a chair on the other side of the table. She was ready for anything. A fight—or a smile.

"Seen Danny?"

Sam nodded. "Ain't seen him so excited since he was seven. He roped his first steer that day. Dang near broke his neck."

Lilly smiled. "And did you give this marriage your blessing, Sam?"

Sam was getting a little tired of being nice by now. "Let's quit grinning at one another like we was old friends, and face the fact that we hate each other's guts. I know now why you brought me down here."

Lilly shot a glance at Jack Kyle. The gambling man was staring moodily into an empty glass. "Uh huh. I saw Danny shoot a gun once—at a rattlesnake. Molasses in January is quicker."

"And you saw me put a bullet in a gambler's shoulder back in Dodge," Sam said bitterly.

"That's right," Lilly said evenly. "You're plenty fast with a gun. And you hit what you aim at."

Sam rolled a smoke and blew a cloud of smoke toward the ceiling. "Off with the old and on with the new. Only in this case the old—Jack Kyle—don't like being put off. He goes loco, gits drunk, and shoots off his yap that he'll gun down the gent that tries to take you away from him. You've seen Danny shoot, and you've seen me shoot."

Lilly was still watching Jack Kyle. Now she turned to Sam. "You won't have any trouble with him, Sam. He's tricky with those Derringers when he's sober, but even if he's sober in the morning, he'll have the shakes. You ain't worried are you, Sam?"

"A good way to get killed in a gunfight is to worry about it beforehand," Sam said. "You'll get all nervous and tense. Throws you off."

"I figured I could count on you, Sam," Lilly said with a dazzling smile. "So don't worry."

"Who's worried?" Sam chuckled. "This could work out swell for me." He glanced at Lilly and saw the quick quiver as her eyes narrowed for an instant. "Since that trip to Dodge, I been broke. Lost my inheritance. Just got the salary that Danny pays me as foreman of his ranch."

"Don't blame me about what happened in Dodge." A suspicion, faint at first, then hot and glaring, suddenly flared in Lilly's eyes.

"Yep," Sam said, "I'm Danny's closest kin. If he got killed, I'd get that ranch of his. I'd be back in the chips—like I was before Dodge City."

A murderous rage flared in Lilly's eyes. Her lips didn't smile any more. They peeled back from her teeth. The diamonds flashed on her fingers as her hands worked helplessly in her lap.

Maybe it'll work, Sam thought, watching her. Maybe I can choke this thing off right here, have Danny in the saddle heading for home within an hour. He tried to keep grinning at Lilly, tried to keep up the pretense.

But he wasn't very good at it. He saw the fire die out of her eyes, and mocking laughter take its place.

"Some man might be able to do it, Sam," she lilted, "but not you. Remember, I know you pretty well. I know how much you think of Danny."

"All right," Sam exploded. "But I still want to know why you're doing it. Why are you marrying Danny? All he'll talk about is cows, and that'll drive you crazy inside a month. He don't make enough in a year to keep you in clothes for a month."

Lilly got up. There was a tantalizing smile on her face. She was in full command of the situation now. She had him where she wanted him, and they both knew it. There wasn't any way he could wriggle out of this. There wasn't any way he could stop Danny from going through with the marriage. And there was no way to stop Jack Kyle from gunning after Danny.

LILLY had planned the whole thing. Lilly was up to her old tricks, moving men around like pieces on a checker board. She'd set this thing up. Now she'd sit back and watch things happen the way she's planned them.

"Jack Kyle doesn't know you're Danny's half brother," Lilly told him. "And if I were you, Sam, I wouldn't let him know it. That is—don't let him know until he starts for Danny. That's time enough for Kyle to know who you are. It won't give him any time to worry about it—or to try any tricks."

Sam tried to eat a steak, but it tasted like sawdust in his mouth. So he tried to fill up on french fries and pie—but they all tasted the same. Finally he drifted down to the Drover's, but Danny was busy putting on his glad rags, polishing his boots.

"Me'n Lilly's going for a ride tonight. Gonna make final plans for our honeymoon," Danny said. "Reckon you can find some things to amuse yourself with."

"Yeah," Sam said. "Buffalo Springs is an amusing place."

He wondered how effective a poke in the jaw would be. Sam could knock him out, load him in a buckboard and start for home. But he knew that wouldn't work. He couldn't keep Danny locked up for the rest of his life.

Sam walked up to the livery with Danny and then watched Danny and Lilly roll out of town in the fancy surrey with the fringed top. Then, having nothing better to do, he strolled back to the Golden.

He found a table, got a bottle and was pouring a drink, when Jack Kyle came over. Lilly had been right about one thing. Kyle would have the shakes in the morning. He was at the limber stage of being drunk, and he fell into the chair opposite Sam and reached for the bottle.

"Your face seems fam'lar, Brannan," he muttered. "Ain't I seen you before?"

Maybe, Sam thought, there was something to that saying that he and Danny looked alike around the eyes. Maybe Kyle was noticing the likeness and couldn't place it. He remembered that Lilly had said Kyle didn't know he and Danny were half brothers. And maybe, he thought, it was smart not to let Kyle know that— just yet.

"I cut a wide swath in Dodge a couple years ago," Sam said quietly. "Maybe you saw me there. That's where you met Lilly, ain't it?"

Kyle nodded. "S'right. Met Lilly in Dodge. We moved west with the railroad. Set up the Golden when Buffalo Springs was end of steel. Lilly's pretty, ain't she?"

Sam admitted that.

"Gets in a man's blood like fire, she does," Kyle said. "And then you can't put out the fire." He peered at Sam with drunken gravity. "Say! Ain't I seen you somewhere before?"

"I think we decided that you'd seen me in Dodge," Sam said.

"S'right. Back in Dodge. Thass where I met Lilly. Was working in a bank."

"This is a lot different from working in a bank," Sam said, a faint excitement stirring within him.

"Funny what a man'll do for a woman," Kyle said. "Looka me. I gave up a good job in a bank. Back East it was. Give it up to come to this wild, crazy country, and run this stinking place. S'funny what a man'll—"

"Shore is," Sam agreed. "Me, I knowed a man once that lost everything he had. All his money, his ranch—even his saddle. Lost it gambling, trying to git a stake so's a girl friend of his could open up a saloon. Later on, he called himself a durned fool. But at the time, it seemed like a swell thing to do. Girl was kinda helpless, and this gent figured it would be a fine, noble thing to set her up in business."

"Know something?" Kyle asked, poking a finger into Sam's chest. "Some men will even rob a woman."

"So I've heard," Sam said. "Some women could make a man lose his head to do things like that."

"And if a man robbed and broke the law in the first place to git a woman," Kyle went on, "he'd sure be justified in killing to keep her, wouldn't he?"

"I reckon," Sam agreed, "that if he broke the law to git her in the first place, he wouldn't stop at nothing to keep her."

"You know, you're a smart fellow, and I like you," Kyle muttered thickly. "You'n me see things exactly alike. There's a lot of folks that wouldn't feel like a man had a right to kill to keep a woman like that."

"But I agree with you," Sam said. Kyle kept on talking, but Sam didn't listen. He was thinking of a cabin he'd passed a few miles out of town. Old and tumbledown it was. He doubted if anybody went near the place from one year to the next. Nice place to hide a man for a few hours.

Overnight, say.

He looked at Kyle, wondering how to get him out of the Golden. Then he heard the whistle of a train far down the tracks. He perked his ears up.

"Here comes my train," he told Kyle.

"Oh—leaving town so soon?" Kyle asked. "Sorry to see y' go. Me'n you'd git along fine, Brannan. We look at things the same way."

"Hate to be leaving," Sam said. "Why don't you walk down to the station with me?"

"Fine!" Kyle said heartily and staggered to his feet. He protested that they were going the wrong way when Sam cut away from the main street and started down a dark alley. But Sam told him it was a short cut and hurried Kyle along. Then, when he was out of sight of the street, he stopped, jerked Kyle around and swung hard for the man's chin.

NEXT morning Danny was with him when Sam knocked on Lilly's door. Danny was about to choke in his high collar, and he didn't know where to put his hands.

"Who is it?" Lilly yelled through the door.

"Me'n Danny. Open up."

"You're early," Lilly muttered, without opening the door. "The preacher won't be here for half an hour."

"Figured it best to get Danny over early," Sam said. "Before anybody got to stirring on the streets."

"I reckon you're right," Lilly said, swinging the door open. "Although I've heard it's bad luck for the bride and groom to see each other before the wedding."

"Just a silly superstition," Sam said, as he pushed Danny inside. "Better to git here early, than not git here at all, don't you think, Lilly?"

Lilly understood that, all right. And she understood the way Sam's holster was tied against his thigh with a rawhide thong. Danny hadn't even noticed that Sam was wearing a gun, let alone one tied for a quick draw.

"Yeah," Lilly said. "Better get Danny over here before that fool Jack Kyle wakes up."

"Say, I forgot about him," Danny grunted. "Reckon he aims to carry out his threat?"

"If he does, he won't get far," Lilly said, throwing a glance at Sam. "You don't think your big brother would let him do a thing like that, do you, Danny?"

"Listen here! I ain't asking Sam to fight my battles for me."

"Don't worry," Sam said guilelessly. "Jack Kyle ain't gonna try nothing. Your wedding will go off smooth as silk."

"Just the same," Danny said nervously. "I better git myself some kind of shooting iron. A Derringer, maybe."

"You couldn't hit the broad side of a barn with a Derringer, Danny," Sam said with a chuckle. "Besides, Kyle ain't gonna bother you. You see—" Sam's face assumed a look of angelic innocence—"I won't untie him till your train is gone."

"What was that?"

Sam looked at Lilly. He'd suspected all along that Lilly was a good five years older than Danny. Now he didn't know. It looked more like fifteen.

"I fixed things up for you two," Sam boasted. He stuck his chest out. "I fixed Mister Jack Kyle so he ain't gonna interfere with no wedding."

"How'd you do that?" Lilly asked. There wasn't any lilt in her voice now.

"I poked him in the jaw last night," Sam went on in his innocent, bragging manner. "I knocked him out, then carried him off to an old shack a few miles from town. He's tied up out there, and he'll stay tied 'till after you two are on the train."

"There wasn't no need for you to go to that trouble," Danny said, "but then, it was a smart thing to do."

"Yeah, it was smart, all right!" Lilly's voice was a harsh croak. Her jewelled hand slid into the drawer of the table and flashed back in sight, loaded with a Derringer.

"Lilly!" Danny yelped. "What's the matter?"

"Shut up!" Lilly said. Then to Sam, "Jack the live loads out of your gun, Sam. Then leather it again. We'll go out the back door."

"What's all this?" Danny muttered. "What's busted loose here?"

LILLY kept the gun out of sight, but ready for action, while Sam got the fancy surrey. Lilly sat in the back seat and told Sam to drive. She said he knew where to go. Danny just stared ahead.

"Took me a long time to get it through my thick skull," Sam said finally. "Lilly was killing two birds with one stone. She's been mad at me since I told her what kind of tramp she was, back there in Dodge. She figured marrying you—and ruining you—would fix that up. The other bird was Jack Kyle. Lilly was through with him. Kyle had served his purpose, and she wanted to be rid of him. Kyle wanted to stick around.

"Kyle robbed a bank back in Dodge, to get the stake to open Lilly's saloon. Lilly helped in the robbery. When Lilly got through with Kyle, she wanted him to let her alone. He hung on tighter."

"I hired a killer one time," Lilly said, matter-of-factly. "Kyle knew what the man was there for. He told me the minute he died that a letter would start East, implicating me in the robbery."

"So you see," Sam said. "It had to be somebody that Kyle didn't suspect. Kyle figured to gun you down, Danny, and he wasn't worried about doing that, so he didn't have that letter ready to mail. But I was the gent that he'd actually face, and he'd be dead with no letter mailed."

"How'd you find out all this?" Danny asked.

"Remember," Sam said softly, "I knew Lilly back East. Then I saw a clipping up in her room. I guessed a lot of it. Then Kyle talked, after he was tied up."

"You yap too much, Sam," Lilly said tightly. "Whip that team up."

Sam grinned and obeyed. With Lilly's little gun prodding him, he swung off the main road and up the lane to the old cabin. They went outside and Lilly untied Kyle.

"You drunken fool!" she raged. "Blabbing everything to Sam Brannan!"

Kyle just laughed. "It was a neat frame-up, Lilly. Brannan is fast with a gun, and he's Danny's half brother. I jump Danny, and wind up gunning it out with Brannan."

"Never mind that now," Lilly said in a cold rage.

She handed Kyle the little Derringer. He took it, turned it over in his hand.

"Get on with it!" Lilly screamed. "If these two get loose—"

Sam shifted uneasily as Jack Kyle lifted the gun. He scratched his left wrist vigorously as he stared into Kyle's eyes. The gambling man licked his lips, once more tried to level the Derringer. Then he swore softly.

"Nothing doing, Lilly. I broke the law to get you. I won't break it again. I don't have to break it any more—to keep you. C'mon, we're leaving in the surrey. We can be on the train before these two walk back to town."

Sam and Danny stood in the sagging doorway of the cabin as the surrey rolled down the lane. Sam sighed and scratched his left wrist again. A little gun dropped into his hand from his left shirtsleeve.

"Why didn't you plug the two of 'em, Sam?"

"Sometimes," Sam said, "people don't have to go to jail to pay for their crimes. I think this is one of the times."

Law of the Claw and Fang

By TOM ROAN

LELOO swung left and came around the bend, the dawn light now full in her face. She stopped noiselessly in the snow, her coppery eyes brightening. One forefoot lifted, she stood listening, her ears cocked, her shining black coat tipped from muzzle to tail with tiny gems of frost. With the long hind legs of two big jackrabbits gripped in her mouth and the rabbits slung back over her shoulder, she was as still as the wall of the cliff itself, waiting, watching, poised tensely.

Only fighting mettle tempered in the devil's crucible could send a lone black wolf against three hunger-maddened Rocky Mountain lynxes. . . .

One-Eye made a wild rush, filling the gorge with a blood-chilling lynx-squall.

Below the dangerous shelf of the ledge the floor of the gorge was a straight drop of three hundred feet. Up the east side of the gorge a mile from here was her den where two cubs were waiting, always hungry and probably whimpering in the manner of a black timber wolf's whelp.

She had been gone most of the night, ever since just before the little moon had come soaring up over the high and wild Montana Rockies. The hunting had been far and poor until long after midnight. Miles away she had come upon one of her most splendid opportunities in a winter-long of nightly going and prowling.

In a little glade surrounded by tall dark timber, seven fat rabbits had been playing around a clump of brush and rocks in the center of the clearing, their heels kicking up small spurts of snow. Never had Leloo stalked so painstakingly and tirelessly.

Rolling herself in deeper snow until her black coat was white with it, she had crept closer and closer to the frolic, hiding behind every available rock, drift or white-mantled brush. Once in position no attack had been swifter, more direct or positive.

There had been only a few startled squeaks in the clearing, a puff of wind at the right moment helping lift the little cloud of snow skyward. Four of the rabbits had died, only three managing to escape the black lightning striking among them.

Right on the spot she had devoured two of them, taking her kills while they were yet warm. Then, as a good mother would, she had shouldered the other pair and started the long gentle trot homeward.

The warning flicker of danger had flashed in her brain. It was nothing she could see or smell—just a stirring of the sixth sense. There was no wind this morning in the gorge. The high west wall rose seven or eight hundred feet above her, the east wall equally high. Not so much as the breath of a breeze stirred down there in the gorge. There was not a sound, not a pulse beat.

And yet danger lurked somewhere in the gorge this morning—danger that made the bristles on her back stand on end, a low growl coming up in her throat, instinctive caution holding it in.

She moved on, as sensitive now to every inch of her surroundings as a violin string so tightly drawn it might snap at the touch of a bow. The odor of the rabbits annoyed her. At the foot of the ledge she eased them down. Now she stepped to one side and sampled the air with her nose up, turning it this way and that.

The smell of the gorge went in and out, the odor of the forest high above coming down. Scores of smells came to her that would never have registered in the nose of a man. Each had its own particular meaning—dead clumps of grass left behind in the fall, a pile of rotting driftwood two hundred yards down the gorge, the hint of a stone marten that had passed up the ledges early in the night now dying in the awakening light in the sky.

Then danger, only a trace of it, but danger just the same. It was up the gorge, toward the den. She started toward it, then wheeled back, the rabbits almost forgotten. In a few moments she was across the floor of the gorge, hugging the deeper shadows.

DANGER. Danger. Danger. It thickened. As it thickened the coppery wolf eyes grew smaller, rounder, a cold, deadly fire appearing to stir in their depths. The hairs on her back grew taller, straighter. The strong jaws still gripped the legs of her kill, once making a bone crack. Lifted now were the forelips, her fighting fangs bared.

Again growls came up and were caught and held in her throat. Noiselessly, yet swiftly, she was covering the frozen ground, the icy rocks and patches of snow, a shadow hurrying among the shadows below the shelves and ledges— danger, herself, going into danger, the hunger for hot-blooded murder beginning to pump and pound in her wolf heart.

The sharpening smell ahead meant murder also, swift and terrible. The thing that gave it to the morning air was as unpredictable as life or death. Even man, the most cunning, ruthless and cruel of all hunters, was never able to know what a grizzly bear would do or how the bear would go about it.

And the smell ahead was grizzly. Spring was yet four weeks away. Other bears would remain in their dens, sleeping the long winter through, thoroughly unconscious of the outside cold, the snow and icy winds. A grizzly was different.

His nearest cousin was the raccoon. Like the 'coon he was apt to awaken at any time and be bitten with the notion to get out and prowl about a little, poking his nose into everybody's business, his terrific strength and indomitable fighting fury making him the rarely disputed bully of the high mountain valleys and the lofty crags of the peaks and cliffs.

It was a young male weighing about six hundred pounds. Apparently he had been out of his den somewhere for two or three days, having had time to disgorge balls of clay he had swallowed in the fall to keep his stomach extended during the long winter fast. Eating certain berries found along the banks of frozen streams and giving them a chance as a powerful purgative, he was now as hungry as a bear could be and ready to devour anything in sight.

He was about forty feet beyond the mouth of the hidden wolf den, his disposition sour and quarrelsome. Right at the moment he was busy pulling up flat stones from the frozen earth where a few gophers made their homes under the rocks. As Leloo stopped behind an old windfall

that had been washed down the gorge, she saw him rise to his hind feet and plop an exceptionally fat gopher in his mouth. There he stood chewing and smacking, little-pig eyes bright with satisfaction for the moment. Then he was dropping back to all-fours, clawing at the stones again.

A great pile of bone-white driftwood washed high and dry here by some spring flood was hiding the mouth of the den. Leloo sneaked on under the old logs, butts and limbs, twisting her way upward in the rocks. She paused twice to look at the bear.

Right at the moment a breeze had picked up, coming down the canyon, keeping her scent from the bear. Having a very excellent nose but poor eyesight he was going on at his business with the heavy flat rocks, cursing and quarreling in grizzly growls.

She slid on quickly into the den, her nose telling her the cubs were safe ahead. A low growl of her own silenced their whimpers. Leaving them to the frozen rabbits, she slipped back to the mouth of the den.

The bear was having more trouble with the frozen rocks. Never one to control his temper, he was slapping, scratching and telling them just what he thought of them. With the breeze still in her favor, Leloo went back down through the tangled bank of driftwood and sneaked in across the gorge.

Going in behind a low wall of ice and snow-covered brush over there, she heard the bear growl and saw him swing back to his hind feet.

He had caught a whiff of her. Now he swung out his young paws and rapidly began whipping the air to him, the nose sniffing, trying to locate her exact position, then make a sudden charge to end matters right here and now.

And to attract the bear's attention to herself was the reason Leloo had left her den. All things of the wild play these tricks to protect their homes and their young from danger. The wren comes down from her nest to tempt the snake, fluttering with apparently a broken wing just in front of it, coaxing, calling, crying, crippling a dangerous few inches beyond its reach, leading it away until it is at a safe distance—then suddenly it takes to the air to leave the foolish snake lying there.

SUDDENLY, in a light change of the wind, the bear made his charge. He hit the icy wall of brush with the noise of rocks crashing through plate glass windows. A full-grown horse would have gone down with one mighty blow crushing his head. But Leloo was not there to meet him, having shifted her position in a streak of blackness when the bear was well started on his rush.

Tongue lolling, eyes playfully bright, she sat on her rump now eighty feet away on a little rise of rocks, her bushy tail flapped forward and around her forefeet. She was laughing at the bear. She had seen him go through the brush like something cracking sheet-ice on a pool. With a surprised grunt he had landed against the rocks, a grizzly chuckful of fight and nothing to fight.

Leloo yawned at him, made a little half-whine of noise. He turned on his hind feet and glimmered at her through those pig-like eyes, wiping a paw across them. For two or three seconds he was like an exceptionally fat boy in a fuzzy-haired coat.

A growl warped itself out of one side of his mouth, a grin curling up the other side. The growl was the grizzly's way of laying down the law. This was not the way to play the game.

When she made her second yawn and half-whine it was too much for any self-respecting grizzly. This was insult added to injury. This was asking for trouble—this was come on, you! You poke-about lame brain! You bluffing coward! You're afraid of your own shadow. No grizzly needed a second invitation to fight. It was rare when he needed more than an opportunity.

The bear made his second charge.

Leloo played hard-to-get. She waited until it looked as if he was right on top of her and ready to slap her head off her shoulders, and then she flashed to her left, out of reach.

It must have amazed the bear. He stumbled, slipped on the icy rocks, and fell on his nose, one of the two really tender spots on a grizzly. Like a big boy in a fuzzy-hair coat, he got up and wailed, two small tears coming out of those piggy eyes, his fury knowing no bounds.

Leloo was waiting for him, perched on some ice-coated rocks ninety yards up the gorge. With a wail the bear was going for her again. This time the wolf was not waiting so long.

When he was ten yards away she wheeled off the rocks. When she struck lower rocks she let loose with a noise like a young dog. All at once she was limping as if the left foreleg had been broken or frightfully injured.

An older bear might have known that this was an old, old trick being played on him. He was a young bear. His dignity was hurt. No wolf could insult him and get away with it.

He kept going, snarling, bear-cursing, making a great show of himself, always just a few yards behind this crippled black she-devil, ready to break her back or smack the hind-parts off her.

Leloo kept up the good work, watching him back over her shoulder. When he showed hints of giving up the chase, the limp grew worse. A mile up the gorge from the den she turned to the east wall. Again he hesitated, probably some lingering taste of the fat gopher coming back to him. Possibly it occurred to him in some manner of bear-reasoning that he had been doing all right until this black wench came along. He stopped and looked back down the gorge.

IT WAS here that the end started coming to Leloo. She was up there on an icy shelf now and merely creeping. One whimper of sound after another came from her. Now she would have fooled any man except a smart hunter, and the bear lunged up and after her, knowing he would kill her before she could get to the rim.

And yet the wolf was on the rim just a few jumps ahead of him. He went after her now on level ground, tricked, humiliated. They raced on to the head of a little coulee filled with small pines, larger ones down the slope as they bent to southward.

Near the foot of it Leloo saw a glint in the air between two stout trees with their tops lashed together. The smart wolf made a sharp turn to her right. The bear plunged straight on. Something slipped, made a sharp hiss of noise, the bent tops of the trees straightening. At once the bear was jerked to a halt, slung off his feet and whirled around—caught in a hunter's snare.

Leloo ranged higher, getting herself out of the coulee, knowing something had stopped the enraged bear from following her, but having had no actual aim to lead him into that thing. She had seen the bent trees and caught the glint of metal just in time to avoid it herself. On the rim now she stopped, wheeling behind a snow-covered bush, dropping to her belly on the frozen ground.

The grizzly was making a mess of it down there. Another bear might have stood crying and whimpering, caught by only one paw and waiting for the inevitable. Never the grizzly. The grizzly fought anything, anywhere and anytime.

Caught around the neck and shoulders in the loop of a small but strong steel cable-wire—part of it snatched up under the pit of his right foreleg—he was whipping the tops of the trees. One of them cracked, broke, and come down. A minute later the overgrown boy in the fuzzy coat was clawing himself out of the loop and going on about his business up the other side of the coulee, free.

Now it was time to go home again, the morning light a danger in itself. A rifle might crack on some high place, and a wolf could find herself dropping dead in her tracks. Hunters and trappers of the two-legged kind were everywhere.

Death always stalked the high places where the wild creatures made their homes. The law up here was the law of the fang, the claw and the talon. Quick murder lurked everywhere. Only the strong, the shy and the swift-witted survived, and none of those had any real assurance.

The grizzly, now, would one day poke that nose too far, and the screaming two-legged hunter's bullet might find him to rob him of his fine coat and handsome claws.

Getting the bear out of the gorge was all that mattered for the moment to Leloo. Had he ranged closer, he might have smelled the den and the fat and saucy cubs inside. At once the young bully would have started raking and flinging the driftwood aside. Even if he could not have wedged himself inside, nothing would have stopped him from laying the mouth of the den bare. Smaller killers coming up or down the gorge would spell the end of it for the fuzzy cubs.

Back close to the den once more, coming down a ledge below it, she was suddenly stopped, every bristle going up. It seemed that everything had set itself to make trouble for her this morning. The breeze was still coming down the draw. There was no guess-work to anything now. The breeze was bringing her the most hateful smell that could come to a mother wolf's sharp nose. This was worse than the odor of man. Man was something to fear, to keep far away from.

The smell of a lynx was something else, the smell of the den-robber, the cold, slit-eyed cat—a mean, sneaking and thoroughly deadly enemy that often killed for what seemed no more than the sheer joy of seeing warm blood flowing.

ROUNDING a bend in the east wall she saw the waiting danger—three mottled devils studying the bone-white mass of driftwood that covered the mouth of the den. And she knew each one of them. There was old Crooked Paw, the big tufted-eared killer. To his left was Scar Face, a big female that looked as if she had been clawed by a grizzly or a wolverine.

Behind Crooked Paw and Scar Face sat the archangel of bloody murder. It was One Eye, stiff-legged, stub of tail pointed skyward, everything about her meaning fight. Her good left eye was like something riveted into the pile of driftwood, seeing right on through it.

What she was seeing was making the old cat drool. Boss of all situations where eviltry was concerned, she growled. It was the go-ahead, what-are-you-waiting-for? growl to Crooked Paw and Scar Face. Perhaps in lynx-fashion she was telling them they had been out all night, the hunt meatless, and here was the place to kill, to eat quickly, and to get along home quick.

Leloo moved on, every hair extended to make herself as large and ferocious looking as possible. As an empress of the devil she was facing death, going in to meet it. If she failed here it would not mean the mere end of herself. It would mean the going of the cubs also. Those smart cats had smelled them.

The only delay here was to make certain that the mother was not at home. Even a full-grown fighting wolf was up against a tough proposition when forced to battle with a single lynx. The cubs would be as helpless as babies in a play-pen.

Crooked Paw saw her out of the corners of his yellow eyes. He let go with the first snarling cat-spit, every hair flying, whipping down and flying up again, every muscle tensing. All three cats wheeled at the same instant, the smoke-like vapor of their hot breaths puffing little clouds in the frosty air.

At once the cats separated, swinging back and well apart, hell ready for a tune here and no diddling around about it. They knew their business, and this was business. Since their eyes were open in their dens, their mothers had taught them the bloody art of using their claws for attack.

Leloo came on. The intellect of a dozen big grizzlies would not equal the cunning in one mean lynx-cat's head. Leloo hugged the wall of the cliffs, keeping her right side against it. If she could only get herself backed into the mouth of the den she would have some chance of saving herself. Only by saving herself would she save the cubs.

There was no notion on the part of the wolf to charge the cats. Such a foolish move was exactly what the cats were waiting and sparring for. One Eye dared her. She made a wild rush, suddenly filling the gorge with a blood-chilling lynx-squall.

Leloo bent her head to meet her, but kept her place against the rocks. At six feet, One Eye wheeled aside. She made two wild jumps down the gorge, wheeled again, and came back as if for a lightning attack straight to the wolf's rear.

At this moment old Crooked Paw went into it like a thunderbolt of snarling, cat-spitting fury. Taking his cue from One Eye, he tried to wheel at the exact distance she had wheeled. Ice on a rock tricked him. The crooked paw slipped, the claws failing to grip and hold. He spun, a squall of terror coming from him as he slid rump-first to within reach of the wolf and her bared and ready fangs.

Leloo finished it. Her muzzle shot forward. Her open mouth filled and closed on the behind of the unlucky cat. She brought him up and back, slapping him a furious blow against the rocks. Then a hard sling right and left burst his belly wide open. Before One Eye could leap clear, a dead lynx flying through the air had hit her in the face, knocking her off her feet. When she came up, her forefeet and head were in a hot and bloody tangle of Crooked Paw's slung-out insides.

The rest was merciless murder. As she was, One Eye never had a ghost of a chance. It was like suddenly being caught in a bloody net and unable to swing free until it was too late.

Leloo had shifted with a lightning turnabout, letting all thoughts of old Scar Face go for the moment. In one straight black lightning shot she closed in on the tangle that was One Eye trying to fight out of the dead cat wrappings.

Before she could swing clear the black killer was on her. Wide jaws yawned. Killer fangs closed on her snarling head. Bones crunched. The fangs went in, ripping through the big cat's brains. One Eye was suddenly a dead lynx.

Scar Face saw what was coming. All the shady little tricks in a mean lynx-cat's head was not going to stop this. She had seen Crooked Paw and One Eye die in front of her, and she had never seen a wolf so quick, so merciless and so sure.

SCAR FACE turned to run for it, all the will to stay and try to finish this affair taken out of her. Leloo followed. Like two streaks they tore over the icy rocks. The wolf was gaining.

Crooked Paw came about on a little flat with a swirl of loose snow a quick puff in the air. Halting, legs stiff, every hair on end, she faced the wolf.

Leloo had stopped after a yard-long slide on her rump. Up and wheeling, she faced the cat. For a few moments she stood there, long tongue lolling. A lynx was a coward and had proved it.

She started slowly, governed by what she had just been through, giving the big cat a chance to make the first mistake. Scar Face yowled and set herself. Her eyes blazed. She was ready, watching that wolf face, watching those coppery eyes, going to make her first two strikes straight for them.

Scar Face made one rush. The wolf shifted her head at the exact instant to catch a slashing claw in her mouth. There was a snap, a crunch of bone, a cat-squall filling the gorge. In a wild sling the lynx went into the air, a whip-whap, whip-whap this way and that against the wolf's shoulders.

A leg suddenly tearing out of its socket, Scar Face flew free, turned a couple of times in the air, and smashed against an ice-coated rock. Slitted eyes opened an instant later. A big mouth closed in, long fangs crushing a second cat's skull in one morning.

Leloo sat back and looked at her, licked her chops. Her bushy tail flapped forward and around her forefeet. Her tongue came lolling out, making her look as if she was laughing about something. Cat meat was cat meat—three big ones self-delivered almost to the door of her den. Counting the two big rabbits, there would be enough meat to last two or three days.

She picked up the cat and went trotting leisurely down the now quiet and peaceful gorge. She was taking the last cat into the den—old Crooked Paw, the mess—when she looked up for a moment to see the first ray of morning sunlight swing over the tall hills.

Something told that perfectly quiet and peaceful wolf brain that springtime would soon be coming to the Rockies.

Cold Trail

"Drop that gun! Put up yer hands!"

By E. E. HALLERAN

Sometimes the best way to catch a hunted outlaw is to walk, cold-turkey, into the jaws of his waiting death-trap. . . .

SIGHT of the snow-covered line camp brought a vast relief to McKinney. After eight hours of battling the intense cold it was good to know that soon there would be warmth and food. And safety. Maybe that was more important than the other two.

He grimaced a little, his square-cut features feeling oddly useless in the cold. It was a little embarrassing to know that he had been afraid, but it was nerve-wracking business to hunt a notorious killer in these bitter mountains.

He picketed the shaggy sorrel in a protecting clump of firs and floundered through the knee-deep snow toward the little cabin, his ice-covered carbine cradled in the crook of a numb arm. Almost mechanically he noted that there had been but little additional snowfall since morning. He could still see the twin lines of footprints where he and Uncle Ben Sloan had left the shack to start the long search of the wintry hills. Good old Uncle Ben. Maybe the veteran lawman had been luckier than his newly commissioned deputy.

In his rueful mood McKinney could not even take solace from the fact that the blizzard had blown itself out. The snow had stopped and the bitter wind was not quite so stiff, but the mercury had been dropping all day. Even when a man knew that the enemy was sharing the discomfort he could find little to please him in such a situation.

McKinney hunched his big shoulders a little higher to keep his collar around his neck and plunged on toward the line camp. Cold was a funny sort of thing. It took something out of a man. It had been bad enough to ride through the hills expecting a bushwhack bullet at every turn but it had been completely unnerving to do the chore half blinded by sleet and snow.

It had been a combination of the two factors which had caused that hard fall during the morning. He had not seen the treacherous slide until it was too late. Nothing but luck, he knew, had saved him from complete disaster. If either the man or the horse had come out of that with a broken bone it would have been fatal.

He hurried a little as he approached the shack, thought of food and fire driving away the sluggishness which the bitter cold had put into his tired muscles. By the time Uncle Ben returned there ought to be something hot ready to eat. Maybe he could do a job as camp cook. Certainly he hadn't distinguished himself as a lawman.

He fumbled with a mittened fist at the wooden latch of the ill-fitting door, realizing his own numb clumsiness again. Maybe he had been lucky not to catch up with Slip Guinness today. That wily outlaw would probably have taken full advantage of a greenhorn's miseries.

HE STAGGERED a little as the door swung open, and heard a husky rasp. "Drop that gun! Put up yer hands!"

For just a split second the carbine swung in a motion of defiance but the voice came again, sharp and incisive. "Drop it, I tell yuh!"

In the gathering gloom McKinney could see the man in the big buffalo coat, a black whiskered man whose steady .44 was aimed straight at him. There was no point in arguing the matter. He let the carbine clatter to the frozen dirt floor, raising his aching arms.

Worse than the ache, however, was the realization of his helplessness. He had been trapped. The outlaw had outsmarted him and had gotten the drop on him. He could not quite figure how it had happened, but he knew that it would never have happened to Uncle Ben.

Guinness seemed to read his mind. "Kinda dumb, wasn't yuh?" he gloated. "A smart lawman woulda spotted how I walked backward in yer tracks to git in here."

McKinney fought hard to keep the anger and panic out of his voice. He had been stupid. He was willing to concede the point but he couldn't afford to let it get him. He had to keep his wits about him against Uncle Ben's arrival. Ben Sloan would know what to do but he might need help.

"I was kinda foggy," he agreed, steadily enough as he eyed the burly, crooked-nosed outlaw. "I reckon I was off guard because I didn't see any bronc around."

"Shot the critter this noon. He busted a laig." The whiskers parted in an expression of sour mirth as Guinness added, "That's why yer dumbness comes in so handy. I need a pony. Turn around—and keep them hands up!"

McKinney turned, hating himself for submitting so tamely but fully aware that he had no choice. He heard the scrape of a boot heel on the hard ground and tried to duck. It was too late. Black stabbing pain smashed at the base of his skull and he drifted off into space.

When he regained his senses he was

lying on the ground near the sagging door, an icy wind beating into his face from the gaping crack at the bottom. He rolled clumsily, trying to get away from the sub-zero blast before he could quite realize the full danger of his situation. He was trussed up hand and foot.

A warning growl came from the burly Guinness and McKinney saw that the outlaw was stoking the sheet iron stove. "Don't git gay, sucker," the killer advised. "Be on yer good behavior and I might even let yuh live. I'm thinkin' about it." There was something menacing even in his chuckle.

Guinness was evidently well pleased with himself. He went on talking as he spread thick hands above the stove. "I reckon we'll work this out right nice, you and me. This time I got Ben Sloan right where I want him—thanks to him bein' so dumb as to pick a greenhorn deputy."

He crossed to the door and peered out through the wide crack which kept the cabin cold even when the stove was roaring. "Ben oughta be along any minute now, and I got a right nice reception waitin' fer him. Wanta hear how it goes?"

"No," McKinney said shortly. He didn't want to appear curious because he was beginning to have the shadow of a plan in his mind. The exultant Guinness would tell him anyway.

"So I'll tell yuh," the outlaw grinned. "Never hurts to run over a plan ahead o' time. Sometimes it lets yuh spot the holes in it."

HE MOVED toward the carbine McKinney had dropped, picking it up to check its breech action and make certain that there was a live cartridge in the chamber. McKinney watched him for a second or two.

"How about rollin' me closer to the fire? It's as cold as brass monkeys down here on the floor."

Guinness laughed harshly and stood the carbine against the wall by the door. Then he used a heavy foot to roll the helpless deputy toward the stove.

"Always like to have my pards comfortable," he smirked. "And yuh're a pard, all right. Yuh've got a real part in the show. When Sloan comes back to camp he'll see a nice column o' smoke goin' up outa the chimney so he'll figger his bright boy is gittin' supper ready. Yer bronc will be picketed peaceful enough and Ben won't even imagine that his ol' friend Slip Guinness is on hand. He'll amble along, thinkin' about how some hot grub is goin' to taste—and I git a target which even a dumb jasper like yerself couldn't miss."

He took another observation from the door crack and chuckled. "Ol' Smarty Sloan. He's comin'. Ducks on the pond! Kinda funny when yuh think about it. Ben Sloan gittin' hisself drygulched because he got dumb enough to take on a yaller greenhorn fer a deputy—a yaller pup what wouldn't even put up a scrap."

He reached for the carbine again and McKinney let out a yell. "Sloan! Look out, Uncle Ben! Ambush!"

Guinness laughed aloud. "Ain't I the old joker though? Ben's still a half mile off and with this wind a-blowin' he couldn't hear that squawk a hundred feet. So it's Uncle Ben, hey? That makes it even funnier."

He put the carbine down again and came over to kick the prisoner a couple of hard jolts in the ribs. Then he bent over, still grinning, and used McKinney's own muffler to make a gag.

"As I was a-sayin'," he went on, pleased, "I'm plannin' to kill Sloan with yer carbine fer two danged good reasons. My gun ain't workin' since I had that spill this mornin'." He guffawed at McKinney as he went back to his observation post. "And yuh got yerself ketched by a busted gun. Too bad I can't tell Sloan about it."

HE RAISED the Sharps, eyeing it appraisingly. McKinney promptly swung his bound feet at the stove, trying to kick it. Guinness cursed and took a pair of quick strides to haul the bound man into the middle of the floor where he could make no noise. A vicious kick in the belly accented the order. "Keep quiet!"

Then he jumped back to the door, poking the carbine's muzzle tentatively into the bitter gale. "Mighty nigh close enough," he muttered. "A few steps more and—"

McKinney held his breath. There was a stamp of approaching feet as Uncle Ben tried to get circulation back into his numbed legs. Then the little shack seemed to explode. There was an ear-shattering roar and McKinney felt the tug of something cutting across the front of his buffalo coat. At the same instant a man's screams rose over the sound of the explosion.

He managed to roll over, avoiding the blind lunge of the frenzied outlaw. The killer's face was a bloody mass behind its beard while the stump of a right arm was a nasty, bleeding pulp. He uttered another animal-like scream and then smashed into the back wall to collapse in a quivering heap. Almost at the same moment Sheriff Ben Sloan came in.

The veteran lawman's eyes swept the shattered room, taking in the twisted piece of metal which had once been a fifty-two caliber Sharps carbine. Then he squinted hard at the bleeding form of what had been the territory's most brutal outlaw.

After that he moved across to cut McKinney loose. Only then did he offer a comment. Jerking his grizzled old head toward Guinness he observed dryly. "Looks like Slip had hisself a right tight little game worked up. How'd he manage to ketch yuh?"

McKinney straightened up a bit painfully. Those kicks hadn't done him any good. "I blundered in like a fool and walked smack into him."

"He got the drop on yuh?"

"That wasn't the worst of it. He did it with a busted gun. I didn't know his gun was busted but I did know that mine was plugged up tight with frozen mud. I didn't dare try a shot because I was pretty sure the carbine would explode." He grinned at the way understanding was beginning to come into the lined face of the older man. Then he added. "It did."

"Why didn't yuh clean it out when it got plugged?" Sloan demanded.

McKINNEY chuckled. It was like Uncle Ben to ask the right question, even at a time like this. "I was dumb, I reckon," he admitted. "I didn't look into the bore of the Sharps after I took my tumble. By the time I thought about it the slush had frozen hard in the muzzle. So I just headed back to camp with a dead gun—and Guinness was waiting for me."

Sloan glanced again at the bloody form against the rear wall. "Mebbe yuh wasn't the only dumb one," he commented. "I kin understand Slip wantin' to kill me with yer gun but I don't savvy a smart hombre like him not checkin' on the carbine's condition."

"That's the one point I'm claiming," McKinney told him with a grin. "Every time Guinness made a move to look at the carbine or to bring it near the stove I raised a ruckus and distracted his attention. I couldn't afford to let him find out about the plugged barrel—or to let the ice melt out. I got some nasty kicks for my trouble but it worked out all right."

"Serves yuh right fer bein' so danged stupid in the first place."

McKinney chuckled. He had caught a glimpse of the keen old gray eyes of the lawman and he knew that Sloan was grateful, almost approving. That was enough.

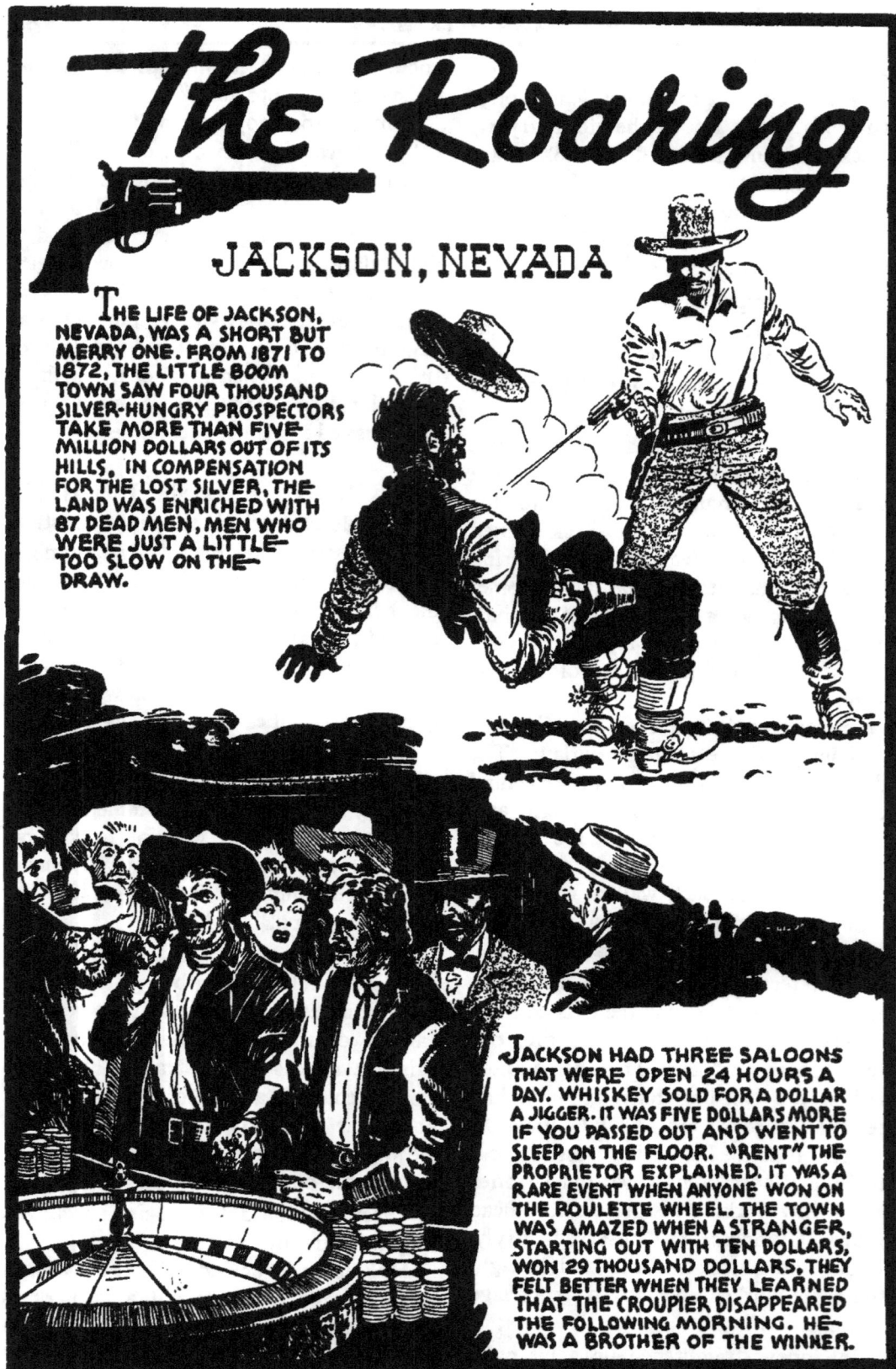

The Roaring

JACKSON, NEVADA

THE LIFE OF JACKSON, NEVADA, WAS A SHORT BUT MERRY ONE. FROM 1871 TO 1872, THE LITTLE BOOM TOWN SAW FOUR THOUSAND SILVER-HUNGRY PROSPECTORS TAKE MORE THAN FIVE MILLION DOLLARS OUT OF ITS HILLS. IN COMPENSATION FOR THE LOST SILVER, THE LAND WAS ENRICHED WITH 87 DEAD MEN, MEN WHO WERE JUST A LITTLE TOO SLOW ON THE DRAW.

JACKSON HAD THREE SALOONS THAT WERE OPEN 24 HOURS A DAY. WHISKEY SOLD FOR A DOLLAR A JIGGER. IT WAS FIVE DOLLARS MORE IF YOU PASSED OUT AND WENT TO SLEEP ON THE FLOOR. "RENT" THE PROPRIETOR EXPLAINED. IT WAS A RARE EVENT WHEN ANYONE WON ON THE ROULETTE WHEEL. THE TOWN WAS AMAZED WHEN A STRANGER, STARTING OUT WITH TEN DOLLARS, WON 29 THOUSAND DOLLARS. THEY FELT BETTER WHEN THEY LEARNED THAT THE CROUPIER DISAPPEARED THE FOLLOWING MORNING. HE WAS A BROTHER OF THE WINNER.

Towns

By **FREDERICK BLAKESLEE** and **JHAN ROBBINS**

JACKSON'S SHERIFF AND JUDGE WAS ED OLIVER. OLIVER PROMPTLY ARRESTED A MAN AFTER EACH SHOOTING. HE WOULD THEN TRY THE PRISONER IN HIS CAPACITY AS JUDGE. IT WAS A FIFTY DOLLAR FINE FOR THE FIRST KILLING, A HUNDRED FOR THE NEXT AND TWO HUNDRED FOR THE THIRD. ANYBODY WHO HAD OVER THREE KILLINGS TO HIS CREDIT WAS NEVER FINED. HE WAS TOO DANGEROUS TO BE TRIFLED WITH.

IN THE WINTER OF 1872, A TRAVELING PREACHER VISITED JACKSON AND TRIED TO SAVE SOME OF THE LOST SOULS. HE SPENT TWO WEEKS WITH THE MINERS AND THEN GAVE UP. "DEVILS ALL," HE MUTTERED AS HE LEFT THE ROARING HELLHOLE. IN THE SPRING OF THAT YEAR THE LAST OF THE SILVER ORE WAS MINED AND JACKSON'S STREETS WERE QUIET. THE "DEVILS" HAD GONE ON TO NEW BONANZAS.

1-174

Quaring was on the porch, his legs spread, his hand ready.

Night Call

By GIFF CHESHIRE

THE FIREPLACE rolled heat into the little room. In the shadows beyond its light Dorcas was undressing. She was still fastidious and shy, even after more than a year. She slipped her nightgown over her head, shrugging it down as she stepped out of her petticoats.

It was Pete Furness's fatal mistake to scare a coward into panicky, courageous action at precisely the wrong, deadly moment. . . .

Pete grinned and pulled at his pipe. Her shyness failed to conceal the fact that they would be parents in another month. It beat him why women tried to hide it. To his mind, Dorcas had never been prettier than now.

The rain made a steady drone on the shake roof of the cabin. Pete could hear the wind howling down from the high Teclas and gusting on the bare plateaus. It drove against the scraped deerskin that served as window panes, making them roll like distant drums. It had a wildness and fury a man liked in a hearth-lit evening, when he had a wife and a home.

The wind concealed the approach of the horse. Pete didn't hear anything until somebody hammered on the door. Dorcas squealed, grabbing up loose clothing as she scuttled through the curtain into the bedroom. Pete frowned. This was high range, sparsely settled by a few upland cattlemen. Visitors were uncommon, and night callers could mean bad news. He rose and went to the door in his stocking feet.

It was Ollie Dawson, half-drowned, shivering and alarmed. He wore no slicker but only a drenched coat too big for him and a hat that dropped to his eyebrows. Pete had heard he was sixteen, though he looked no more than twelve. The Dawsons' ragtag outfit lay five miles back in the foothills.

"What got you out, Ollie?" Pete asked. He motioned the boy in and thumbed him on toward the fire.

Ollie stayed by the door, water puddling about his worn boots. His eyes were bright with fear. "It's Jimmy. He's taken sick, and ma wants to know if you'd get the doctor."

Pete didn't like to look at this scared, starved kid. He must have scowled, for Ollie opened his mouth as if to plead. The request didn't sound like much, but it meant an eighty mile mountain ride to town.

"What's the matter with your dad?" Pete asked.

"He's—sick, too, Mister Furness. Ma said to tell you."

Pete's voice was rough. "Sick or drunk?"

Ollie swallowed and dropped his gaze. "He's been drinking. He's been worried. Jimmy's awful sick, Mr. Furness. Outta his head and pukin' fierce. Ma's tried everything. She's scared and—and—" Pete could see tears rise in Ollie's eyes. He was a lot like his father, furtive, shifty, whining. "Mister Furness, what'll I tell her?"

"I'll go," Pete said. "Better warm yourself before you start back, Ollie."

But Ollie had swung around, running for the door. He pulled it shut with a bang, moving for once with effect and purpose. This time Pete heard the horse as it clattered away.

He had a hunched tension in his shoulders, a mind turning in revolt. He thought, I'll have to change horses at Rocky Q. There's no way around it. Resentment rose in him, and it wasn't the first time he had wanted to whip Trink Dawson with his own hands.

DORCAS slipped through the curtain, her eyes disbelieving, her face pulled into strained lines.

"Did I hear you agree to that?"

"I reckon," Pete said.

Anger flashed in her eyes. "Ollie admitted Trink's drunk. He's scared to make that ride at night. But willing to send you in his place."

"It was Mrs. Dawson who sent Ollie over," Pete reminded her. "It's Jimmy who's sick."

She looked away, then flashed him an intent gaze.

"Pete, we've got to bring it out into the open. I know George Quaring's threatened to kill you. You'll have to change horses at their place."

Oh Lord, Pete thought. Don't say you know I've been scared to go to town. He swallowed, an icy cramp clutching his chest.

"How'd you find out?"

"Inez Prior told me. They heard the talk in town." Dorcas' voice had turned deeply tired. "I wish you'd told me, but I know why you didn't."

Pete made a light, dismissing motion. "It wasn't anything. What they're saying is just talk. Been trouble every summer when Rocky Q comes up to government grass. The Quaring boys like to run over us little fellows up here."

"What did you do to Lute Quaring?"

"Shot a gun out of his fist. Ruined his gun hand. He started to draw on me. Because I cussed him out, finally, for letting strays get on our grass. It's deliberate, and it's been going on for two-three years. His brother George took it up for Lute and spread his talk."

"I won't let you go," Dorcas said. "Not to do something Trink Dawson ought to. Will he ride for the doctor when I need one?"

"Reckon not." Pete was pulling on his boots. He stamped his feet into place, rose and went into the kitchen.

I never knew what it was like to be scared, not even after I married Dorcas, not till I knew a young 'un was on its way. It changes a man.

He took his gunbelt down from the peg, looked at the gun. He buckled on the belt and reached for his slicker. His fingers trembled. He had every right to dismiss it and go to bed. He wanted to, and the wish angered him.

Jimmy Dawson was about eight. Sometimes a scrub family produced one first-rate specimen. Jimmy had come down this way occasionally, fishing the creek. He had a quick, friendly grin, and something that must have come from his mother's side. She was a tired, patient woman with enough pride that she had never

called on Pete for help before. That was why he knew she needed it now.

Dorcas came out to the kitchen. She had pulled on a Mother Hubbard, was a distorted shape in the half light.

"Pete, you can't do it. What if the trail kills you, even if the Quarings don't? I can't stand to wait here wondering until you get back. I can't stand to face what I'll have to if you don't come back. And I shouldn't have to, not for an outfit like the Dawsons."

Pete straightened slowly to look at her. "Do you remember the time Jimmy brought us the trout? The admiring way he looked around when you asked him to come in, and how he tore in when we had him take supper? We'd been kind of blue thinking we were poor till then. We didn't think so afterward. And right soon we found out about the baby and figured we'd never give him reason to look the way Jimmy did that evening."

Dorcas dropped her glance and turned from him. "I remember, Pete. I guess you've got to go. But—but couldn't you go through without stopping at Rocky Q? It wouldn't be cowardly, Pete, with so much depending on you."

"Why, there's a good chance," Pete said. He knew from her quick relief that he hadn't sounded like a liar. She wasn't used enough to the cow country to know no horse alive could carry a man his weight the length of that storm-whipped mountain trail.

"You might run onto them in town. George Quaring's a show-off. He'd be more apt than ever to pick trouble there." Doubt again came into Dorcas' voice.

"Not likely," Pete answered. "Coming back the doc'll be with me, so George won't dare try anything." He had pulled on his hat, and lighted the lantern. He was steadier now that her worry had lightened, but he still felt hollow. He nearly lost his hold when she clung to him as they kissed. Then he stepped through the back door and pulled it shut. A shudder ran through him, and he headed for the barn.

H E HALTED his horse before the cabin and called Dorcas to the door. "I'll stop at Priors' and tell 'em to keep an eye on you. You mind the light chores and let the rest go till I'm back. And don't worry."

"All right, Pete."

It was a bitterly black trail. Pete had a lantern on his saddle horn but he didn't try to keep it lighted against the surging wind. Rain slashed his face. It pelted his hat and slicker until it sounded like rice pouring onto dry paper. He knew the trail, the country. He had known that in another month he would have to make this ride for Dorcas. But that would have had drive, sense, responsibility to it. This didn't.

Pete had a fair idea of what had taken place at Dawsons'. The woman would have been worried deeply over Jimmy, debating whether the doctor should be called out. Waiting, as with most back-country folks, until the last moment to decide. Pete could see Trink Dawson, the skinny, hangdog sire of seven.

Trink would have discounted the urgency, because no man hankered to make a hard ride at night. He had probably fortified himself against the possibility from the jug of corn whiskey he kept on hand and in the crisis refused to go. A man could sire more young ones, while it was a rough trail and a wild night.

It had brought a bad time to Dorcas, ahead of her natural ordeal. The unfairness of it made anger etch Pete's forehead as he jogged patiently through the rainswept night. Yet the firm honesty that lay deep in his mind kept asserting itself. You're afraid of George Quaring and you can't shift it onto anybody else.

Three miles out Pete saw the light at Priors' and turned in. The woman was in bed. Prior was stripped to his underwear and ready to retire, himself. Pete halted at the door.

"They need a doctor over at Dawsons', Henry. Can't be back with him before tomorrow night. You folks keep an eye on Dorcas?"

"Why, sure," Prior said. He was getting on in years, a bent and scrawny man. "Why don't Dawson get his own doctor?"

"Ollie says Trink's sick."

"You'd ride for a doctor for that thing?"

"It's Jimmy."

"The only one worth saving," Prior said. "Excepting the missus, maybe. She must have been hard up for a man. What's the matter with Ollie, then? He's half grown."

"Bad trail for a kid, Henry."

"I've known kids his size who'd of done it rather than call on a outsider. Pete, you'll have to change horses at Quarings', and they'll give you trouble. You go home and let me go for the doctor."

Pete turned angrily and strode down from the porch. The miles past Priors' were bitterly long, through a vast upland just yielding to settlement. He felt the strain of the saddle; his eyes probed the darkness for landmarks. Yet a harder part would be the Teclas, with their mountain torrents and twisting, high-ledged trails.

O N THE far plateau lay the winter range of Rocky Q. The good horse under Pete already showed punishment. There was no question about having to stop there for a change. Yet Pete did not regret the trouble with Lute Quaring, just before Rocky Q had taken out its summer herd. Sooner or later, if he had unfriendly neighbors, a man had to speak his piece.

They had argued over strays, called names, and Lute had tried to pull his gun. Both Quaring boys were unstable, disliked and distrusted. Pete could have killed Lute and maybe he should have. He broke the man's gun hand instead. Now, from what Prior had told Pete a couple of weeks back, the Quarings claimed Lute had never tried to draw. There had been a Rocky Q puncher with Lute, that day, who backed that statement. The story had spread.

It rained harder as Pete climbed into the mountains, with sleet mixed in. The canyons shielded him from the wind but on high points it caught him full, driving icy needles through his body. His hat no longer kept water from running down his neck. He was wet to his belt and again from his knees down. Eventually he walked a distance, resting the horse, restoring warmth. His nerves pulled tighter.

He had trouble at the Beaver. Dropping down a gully, he came to a creek where his horse balked. Pete swung down, got a match from his case and lighted the lantern. He whistled soundlessly. He had never seen the creek so high. There would be no crossing at the ford.

He paused, shame running through him at the awareness that he wanted to turn back. No one would blame him. Jimmy Dawson had an able-bodied father, a half-grown brother, while Pete Furness had worries enough of his own.

Pete turned upstream, leading the horse. The lantern was made from a lard-bucket, open-ended and using a candle. It threw a cone of light that helped Pete pick his way. He had to go a mile above the trail to find a place to get over, where a fallen pine stretched across. It took patience to get the horse to mount the log and follow him. Pete was a long while getting back to the trail.

He was reaching the ledges. The mucky high trail puckered his back when he slipped for a moment into thought. Once he heard a rumble on the mountainside as earth and rock loosened somewhere to

tumble down. He was aware long later that his horse was getting nervous. When it halted, Pete swung down, got a match going and lighted the lantern. He turned the yellow cone ahead, his eyes widening.

The trail was blocked with muck as far as he could see. He swung the lantern toward the rim and the enormous emptiness below. Though such lanterns could withstand much wind, a sudden blast extinguished his light. He stood still for a long moment. Why does it have to be so easy to turn back? He was no longer troubled by the cold, had in fact grown too warm. He unbuttoned his slicker at the neck, pulled off his hat heedlessly and let the rain beat full on his head.

At last he replaced the hat. He had to backtrack a thousand feet to find a place where he could get onto the slope above the trail. The horse held back, and Pete had to quirt him with the reins.

It was a bald slope, once burned over and now partly regrown with seedlings. Pete felt his way, climbing above the start of the slide. After what seemed hours he began a gradual descent. Without expecting it, he found himself on a clear trail.

It still climbed. There would be the same hazardous conditions beyond the summit, and on the plateau lay Rocky Q. Pete turned his thoughts away from that. The weariness, the tension, seemed to have left his muscles and settled as a steady ache in his bones. This was a new, more immediate worry. He had lived in rough country long enough to recognize the dangers of exhaustion. He knew he had been many hours on this ride.

HE WAS burning up when he came out of the mountains and dropped onto the high desert plateau. Yet it did one thing for him. He had no concern left, only the steady, stubborn drive that had kept him on the trail. His horse was lame, stumbling, about ready to balk. Winter's late daylight was breaking in the sky. Pete considered his horse. By risk of killing it, he might be able to flog it through town. He gave this no real consideration. He would change at Rocky Q.

The Quaring home ranch lay in a basin a couple of miles south of the trail. It was full light when Pete rode in. Though it was the time of year when ranch work was slack, the place seemed deserted. Pete saw no one when he came into the yard, but smoke lifted from the cookshack to disappear in the beating rain. He rode over and swung down in the pooled mud, and at that moment the door of the shack swung open.

A toothless, emaciated figure stood there, with a dirty flour sack tied around his waist. He showed surprise when he recognized Pete, and offered no greeting.

"Need a fresh horse," Pete said in a thick voice. "Where's George?"

"Been flooding down on the south end," the cook answered. "George took the boys out early this morning. Lute's over to the house sleeping off a jag. Want to see him?" The man made a pasty grin.

"Want a horse," Pete said. "They need a doctor out at Trink Dawson's."

"He'p yourself."

Pete rode down to the corral. The offering of remounts was established practice, the Quarings complying only because they frequently required such courtesy themselves. Pete snaked a horse from the saddleband, swapped saddles and turned his own jaded animal in. He swung up again, aching from long contact with the saddle. He felt no relief at having missed George. He would have to bring this horse back, and George would be warned and waiting. Pete rode out, drained and bleak. It had taken all he could muster to ride in here, and he had it all to do over again.

It was an easy trail after what he had put behind, and he had picked himself a good horse. He reached town in mid-afternoon, ready to flop from the saddle.

The rain still rattled down, keeping the streets empty and piling them with mud. He was lucky enough to find Doc Scanton in his office, which was a small lean-to structure affixed to the side of the express office.

Scanton took a brief look at the man who staggered in. "Pete, don't tell me the stork picked this weather to visit Coyote Creek."

"It's Dawsons," Pete said. "They got a sick kid."

The doctor gave him a close scrutiny. "Man, you're sick yourself."

"I'm all right, Doc. When can you start?"

Scanton rose from behind a littered desk. He was white-haired, ruddy, tired. "I got a woman in labor here in town, Pete. I'm pinned down till it's over. You pour a pint of whiskey down your throat and go to the hotel. Sleep till I call you."

"Maybe I should get back and tell 'em you're coming. You know that country well enough to ride it by yourself."

"Too damned well," the doctor said with a sigh. "Beats me why I make those rides, when I usually find a corpse on the far end. But I always do. Pete, I see you've got a Rocky Q horse out there. Patched up your trouble with George Quaring? I've heard the talk."

"George wasn't home."

"He will be when you take that horse back. That man's got a gun pride that's stupid but dangerous. He came along once when Lute was in to have me dress his hand. George can't stand to have it talked that anybody could shoot a gun out of a Quaring fist. The hell of it is he's twice as fast as Lute. He won't return your favor. He'll aim for your belly or chest."

"I won't run from him, Doc."

Scanton rubbed his chin. "No, but nobody would blame you if you did. It's plain as a mud fence George is lying to justify himself if he can kill you."

PETE had the shakes so bad he could hardly put his name in the hotel register. He managed to shuck out of his wet clothing, and he climbed into bed naked. He was asleep instantly. It was daylight when he wakened, and he didn't know at first whether a night had passed.

His head throbbed, and he was burning up again. He judged from the light presently that it was morning, so the doctor's case must have taken him more time than he thought. A baby case. It made him think of Dorcas and of George Quaring.

He threw off the covers and got out of bed. He nearly collapsed. His clothes were still damp, but he got into them, shivering in the room's scant heat. He was dizzy and weak, and his teeth began to chatter violently. Nausea hit him, and he staggered to the wash basin. Somebody rapped on the door.

Pete wiped his mouth as he looked at the visitor. It was the hotel man. He carried a tray displaying two bottles and a glass. He said, "Thought I heard you clumpin' around, Pete. Doc says you're to stay in bed. He left some medicine."

"What time is it?"

"Noon."

"Say when he'd be ready to go?"

The man put the tray down. "Already gone, bright and early. Said to tell you he'd let your missus know you're all right. For you to take this stuff and stay in the hay. Pete, get back in bed before you fall in."

When he wakened again it was dark. The hotel man had undressed him, got him back to bed. Apparently he had poured down some medicine, for there was a bitter taste in Pete's mouth. But his head was clearer. He had thrown it off.

He was in dry underwear. He got out of bed, located a match and lighted the lamp. Somebody had dried out his clothes and boots. There was whiskey on the tray. Pete took a pull on the bottle and began to dress.

The old clock behind the desk in the deserted lobby disclosed that it was just six, still an hour short of dawn. Pete dropped money for his room on the counter, passed into the street and walked on rubbery knees to the livery. It had cleared, though mud squashed heavily under his boots, and the wind brushed cold across his cheeks. He roused the hostler, who slept in the harness room.

The man was old and bent, and he stared at Pete through the waxy light of a lantern.

"Doc Scanton took out the Rocky Q horse, Pete. Said to tell you he'll pick yours up. Left his big stallion for you to bring out. Best cayuse in the country, the kind Doc sure needs. He'll take you through without stopping at Quarings'. And if you're smart you'll figure to pass there after dark."

Anger roweled Pete. "I'm duckin' no man, Ike."

"Course you ain't. It ain't yellow to step wide of a sidewinder. Them kind're the ones with a yellow streak. I seen 'em come, and I seen 'em go. Hidin' behind a gun rep, even ready to die to prove they ain't the cowards they actually are."

"Where's Doc's stallion?"

"I'll get him. How long since you et? Man, I'm going to rassle you some grub before I get you ary horse."

PETE came to the Rocky Q turn-off around noon. His slicker was lashed to the cantle, and he had his gunbelt strapped outside his heavy coat. The sickness had left him, and there was no hesitation when he swung the horse in. He knew what had steadied him—the awareness that he was no longer compelled to this thing at all. But it was for Dorcas and a clear trail that Pete needed when it came time to ride for Doc Scanton. It was for an unborn child, and a man's need to clear his name where talk has been made against him.

He didn't know if he would be expected, since Doc Scanton had returned the Rocky Q horse. But it was noon, and they would be in to eat. It could be settled. He saw activity from a distance. When he came into the ranch yard he saw that most of the crew was in the cookshack. A couple of punchers were down by the day corral. Pete pulled up in surprise.

The third man was Doc Scanton, and the riders were saddling a horse for him.

"You idiot," was the doctor's only greeting.

Pete grinned. "How's the Dawson boy?"

"Past the crisis. Pneumonia. He'll pull through. Tough as you, for you were sure building a case of it yourself."

"You can take your stud home," Pete said. He nodded to a Rocky Q rider. "If you'll let me take that horse to get home on, I'll see it gets back." But both punchers and the doctor were staring toward the house. Pete turned around.

George Quaring was on the porch, in his shirt sleeves but with his gunbelt strapped on. He stood motionless, staring out, and he had his legs spread apart. Pete swung down, taking his time. A puncher caught the reins he tossed. Pete turned and started toward the house.

He called, "George, we've got no quarrel. I spoke my piece about your strays, and Lute and me had our ruckus. Don't care what he told you, he tried to pull on me. That settled it as far as I'm concerned. You've made talk. I'm willing to forget that if you'll ask Doc and me in for a friendly drink."

"When I pour whiskey for you, Furness, it'll be on your grave."

Pete shrugged. The tension about him came to him on the stirring air, yet he was loose-muscled, steady-nerved, determined.

He said, "George, I got a notion you know the truth about the ruckus. But you're ready to die to prove a Quaring can't be outdrawn. Let me tell you some-thing. I'll try to bust your gun hand, the way I done Lute's. Think on that a minute. You won't be dead and a two-bit hero, if I'm the best man. You won't be able to hit the broad side of a barn, either, any more than Lute can right now. I won't kill you, George. That's all I'll try for."

George stirred, though he was careful not to make an exploding motion with his right hand. He kept up his flat, inimical stare, but for an instant his eyes seemed to recede. Then bluster gathered in his face, but it was hampered by something within him. He wet his lips.

George shifted his weight again. "He's making his talk for your benefit, Doc. Lute and Curly Adams both swear Furness pulled and shot Lute in the hand, then covered Curly till he'd got away."

"That's right as far as it goes," Pete agreed. "You want to fetch out Lute's gun and prove it wasn't in his fist at the time?"

"I don't have to prove nothin'. Their word's better'n yours."

"You know the truth, George," Pete said softly. "Or you wouldn't be wondering all at once whether I can fix you like I did Lute. I don't know, myself, but I'm telling you I'll do my damndest. Make your play, George. If you don't, it's admitting to Doc that you know the truth. And he swings weight enough in this country to clear my name."

There was an instant of intense quiet. Pete went cold when he saw George's shoulders pull slightly back, with his thin lips flattening against his teeth. Pete thought of Dorcas and prepared for the looming seconds that would settle everything.

A bleating protest rang out. "George—don't—!" It was Lute Quaring, a slightly younger counterpart of George, and he stirred out into the yard a few steps. "He'll do it! The man's greased

(Continued on page 130)

Down went the twelve hundred pound pony, and Hoss sailed through the air.

CHAPTER ONE

Jack Pot

ANY WAY you figure it, there is little doubt of this—however Hoss Greer walked or spoke or acted it was fated that he should attract trouble. About him was an aura that roused the worst in men—or the best. There was no in-between. Men either loved him or hated him fiercely.

Hating him, they were constrained to malicious and abusive slander. One of these libels was that his soul was a warped and galling cancer that gave him no peace unless he sought out a source of trouble and exploited it to the last bitter dregs.

To those who knew Hoss best and called him friend, this appraisal was maliciously untrue. But in all fairness to his traducers there were times when it seemed they were right. Such as the affair at Gunsight City.

Twenty-five years is a long time but to Hoss it was like a day when he read in the monthly bulletin of the Arizona Cattleman's Association that Sheriff Higdon

By HARRY F. OLMSTED

Hoss Greer—the Devil's Line-Rider

Hoss Greer was just the hard-hitting, bullet-slinging hombre to whip a tattered cow outfit into a mighty, fighting machine . . . or leave its range littered with a bumper crop of bloody, buckskin-clad corpses. . . .

Piebald Pete charged off through the brush, snorting defiantly.

An Action-Packed Range Hog Novel

Hiatt had been murdered in the Burrito Mountains by a renegade rancher and rustler—Doy Climmons.

Climmons was a grim, snarling badger of a man. He was the only man in half a hundred who had beaten Hoss to the pistol snatch, put him in the hospital for three months and gotten off without a scratch. And without any retaliation, either. Hoss hadn't bothered to resume the dispute. It had all been fair, and Climmons, knowing Hoss's reputation, was long gone from the Mogollon country by that time.

But now Climmons, up to his rustling tricks again, had killed a sheriff and gone on the dodge. Posses, it said, were combing the wild reaches of the Burritos for the killer and expected to have him in the net soon.

"Like hell," snorted Hoss. "He's a hundred mile off, right now, laughin' up his sleeve."

Two days, Hoss brooded over that article. Two days, the opposite poles of his character warred violently. His untamed ego counselled: "Go after him, boy. Go after the murdering polecat. The law has failed again and God knows you've got better cause than anybody to kill him." The better side of his nature rebelled. "Stand your hand, you fool. Nobody's more to blame than you for not settling his hash years ago. Let it ride. You don't owe nothing to the memory of Higdon Hiatt."

He recalled the days he and Hig had been saddle mates, riding line for the Hashknife, on the north slope of the Mogollons. They had planned to go partners when they got drunk in Payson and got into it with a crooked tinhorn.

In the ruckus, the gambler was killed and about all Hoss could recall of the matter was that he had fired the death shot. But when he was sober again, he found that Hig had confessed to the killing by letter and lit out for far places. Yes,

Hoss owed something to Hig's memory—maybe twenty-five years of life.

Hoss saddled his Traveler horse and hit the trail. First night he slept at Alamosita. Next day he rode into Gunsight City, county seat of Granite County. He found Hig Hiatt's funeral long over and the posses dispersed to their various communities.

A CHINLESS hostler acted frightened when Hoss showed inclination to talk about the Hiatt murder. He clammed up fast. It remained for a bartender in the Stockman's Saloon to advise Hoss, after carefully sizing up his tight-lipped mouth, chill eyes and professionally tied-down pistol.

"I ain't askin' why you're huntin' Climmons, stranger," he said, "'cause it's none of my business. I ain't passin' an opinion on the shootin'—I wasn't there. But if I wanted the honest low-down, I'd go to the sheriff for the Hiatt side an' I'd go to Climmons' DC Connected for Doy's side. Whichever way you lean, after hearin' both sides, I wish you luck in your hunt. You'll need it."

Hoss thanked him, had dinner at a lunch counter and spent several minutes studying the front of the sheriff's office. He hadn't asked who was sheriff now. That seemed unimportant. Whoever held the job was sure to be poisonously bitter against Doy Climmons. And, because that coincided with his own feelings and would add little to his problem, Hoss headed up Hardscrabble Creek toward the DC Connected, at the foot of the Burritos.

The day had grown increasingly hazed. Now the sun faded to a red ball and a bawdy wind came dancing across the flats, picking up clouds of dry silt, filling the eyes and sifting into the clothes. Hoss drew up his bandanna and fought against it. It grew colder and a thick layer of clouds came tumbling over the jagged peaks of the Burritos. The wind carried the smell of rain on creosote brush and the sound of thunder.

"Rain," muttered Hoss, disgustedly. "Bids fair to get almighty unpleasant. No you don't, Traveler. Head into it, critter. Can't be much further."

It wasn't. Hoss came upon the home layout of DC Connected quite suddenly, swinging about a sheltering point that formed one groin of the canyon mouth. He dipped in and out of a creek and plunged into the dust-whipped dooryard of the Climmons place.

There was nobody about and Hoss ducked into the big hay barn, unsaddled and put Traveler in a stall. He was forking down hay when a man entered the barn.

"Got business here, stranger, or was you just getting out of the wind?"

Hoss came down the ladder without answering and when he faced this young, good-looking puncher, he saw two not-so-good-looking men come in to back him up. Hoss stood there.

"I came lookin' for Doy Climmons," he said, and there was an arctic frost in his tone.

"I'm Doy's foreman, Mark Ament." The young cowman licked his lips. "Reckon I'll have to do."

"Better reckon that 'un over again, Ament." Hoss turned on an expression meant for a grin—a twisting of his weathered cheek muscles. "I've rode too far to be satisfied with some beardless cowcrammer drawin' his pay. Where is he at?"

"That's nobody's business but his own, stranger."

"Yeah?" Hoss's chuckle wasn't pretty. "You or no ten like you can stop me seein' him if he's around this spread."

"He ain't, Mister, so you may as well haul your freight."

Hoss laughed. The taunt in it sent their hands to their holsters. "Better be good, boys, if you unlimber. Take me to who-ever's bossin' this spread—an' don't tell me you shorthorns are runnin' it."

MARK AMENT'S face grew studious. After a minute it lightened. "You can come up to the house, Mister," he said, grudgingly. "We'll go along to see that you watch your tongue while you talk to a lady."

At the house a girl opened to them—a very pretty girl. They filed in and she closed the door. In the big living room, with its Indian rugs on the floor, its mounted deer heads and its roaring fire on the great hearth, she faced them.

"Well, Mark, what is it?"

"Libby, this gent says he's going to see your father in spite of hell or highwater."

The girl's eyes came to Hoss—big, round eyes with a touch of violet in them. "Why?" she asked, the color ebbing from her cheeks. "What do you want of my dad?"

"Is Doy Climmons your dad, Miss?"

"Yes. I'm Libby Climmons."

"I didn't know Doy had a family," muttered Hoss. "Him an' me, we was neighbors once. A long time ago. I'm Hoss Greer."

The girl inclined her head. "My father isn't here."

"Where is he?"

She looked into his chill eyes. "My dad is in the hospital, never mind where, Greer. He's fighting for his life."

"Bullet wound?"

"His spine is injured. He cannot walk and never will again."

"Why not, Miss? Doctors perform miracles these days."

Her lips tightened. "As far as I'm concerned, there might as well be no surgeons. No money. If we could get him to Doctor Cassel, in Chicago, there's a good chance he'd walk again, but—"

"You've got a big outfit here. Sell off some beef and send your dad to Chicago. Or put a loan on the place."

Libby shook her head vigorously. "We're rustled poor, Mr. Greer. You see, we've got a good neighbor—Beals Golliher, who wanted this spread. When dad refused to sell, Golliher threatened to ruin us. He has. The sheriff came out here on a frame up. But Sheriff Higdon Hiatt wasn't stupid. He was smart—and very crooked."

"Some lollypaloozer of a cow crew you've got, Lady," Hoss growled, eyeing the hands. "What do they do to earn their pay?"

"They're good and they're loyal, Greer," she snapped. "They stuck by us when the bullets flew, and when others quit."

"Why'd they stay?" rapped Hoss, turning on them. "What held you useless hairpins here?"

"None of your damned business," said Ament. "We're useless because we stuck —is that it? A big, strong hellbender like you would have left Libby to her doom and called himself brave, eh?"

"What good were you to her?" Hoss snapped. "You led me in here, not knowin' if I was a Golliher killer or not. The girl needs money to send her dad away. Do you great-hearted bunkhouse brush-poppers go out an' get it for her? Not in a million years."

THEY were muttering angrily. Libby flushed. "They couldn't have done a thing. Nobody could. There were no cattle."

"Not any, Miss? Seems like these red hot horsebackers could have checked any rustling."

"Golliher is lousy with killers. He got all our tame stuff, but there's still wild cattle in the hills. Outlaw steers, eighteen years old, that haven't felt a rope since they were calves. Next spring, when the snow's off, we'll take more men and—"

"More like these, ma'am? What's the matter with these hearties—now?"

A clap of thunder shook the house and the girl pointed at the roof, noisy with the first rain. "Can't work the Burritos in weather like this."

"Child's play," exploded Hoss. "I know cow work upside down. If the stakes are high enough, you can work anywhere, anytime. I came to see Doy Climmons, my old neighbor. Instead of trying to learn where he's at, I'll ramrod this hen-yard outfit to hell and back, if it'll get money to buy surgery for your dad, Miss."

"You'll not ramrod me, Mister!" Ament backed, his hand on his gun. Hoss stood hard.

"Yes I will, for you'll go down the hill to make room for some willing cowhand. Make up your mind—quick!"

"I got it made up." Rage blazed in Ament's eyes.

Libby's sharp rebuke jarred them all. "Mark! Boys! Please. Go wash for supper. We'll talk this over like folks—not like caged animals."

CHAPTER TWO

Piebald Pete

THEY threshed it out, Hoss and Libby doing the talking. The girl, concerned with defending his three hands, gradually came under the spell of Hoss. It was her judgment to stand with him.

Her decision was a blow to Ament, whose eyes held a rankling dislike for Hoss. When the young ramrod tried to argue, Hoss left the table and went out into the rain. Darkness had fallen and the air was cold. After looking to his Traveler horse, Hoss went to the bunkhouse for the night.

Long before daybreak, Hoss wakened the sleeping punchers.

"Crawl out, you hibernatin' sheep lice!" he bawled. "Sluff off them soogans an' pile out!"

They turned out in the chill darkness. Rain pounded the roof and the wind moaned a dirge. They cursed him as they donned their wet clothes.

"Whip into it, gents. You're soft from luxury loafin', but I'll fix that pronto. From here on out, pack you a lantern for light an' ketch your sleep on the fly. Come on! We ain't got all day, you know."

Mark Ament was bitter. "You musta hypnotized Libby. But I'll prove to her this is all damned foolishness, before half a day is done."

"What you'll prove, Ament, is that you an' these boys is strictly mail order. Pull on them boots an' let's get to breakfast. Libby's been up a good half hour."

Through the rain they trudged to breakfast. It was a silent, uncomfortable meal, and soon finished. The men made no further complaint. Libby made only one brief appeal as they filed out. "Don't be too tough on them, will you, Mister Greer?"

"I'll sort the men from the boys, ma'am. I aim to put the DC Connected onto its feet or die a-tryin'. Don't you worry about Ament, Libby. If he lives up to your idea of him, he'll make you proud. If not, he'll bunch it."

The horses were wet, chilled and mean. The slickered men had to knock the humps off. Even Traveler acted up and Hoss had a time uncocking him. Up the canyon trail they galloped, collars up, hats jerked down, heads lowered against the wind.

Five miles up Hoss called a halt, running his glance up steep, cloud-hazed slopes—murderous slants that were all scrub oak, manzanita and chamisa. Footings were treacherous with loose rock and shale, oozing water. Suicide stuff.

Hoss knew this kind of a range forward and backward, its dangers, the habits of its denizens, the proper answer to its challenge. He was not as confident as he acted.

"Stuff will bush up close in this soup," he declared. "We'll have to kick out what we get. Waterhole, you take out up that gulch, makin' all the noise you can, plumb to the ridge. Pike, you do the same up the next draw. Ament, you an' Coberly will flank me as we scour what's in between."

THEY split, each putting his animal up the brushy slope. It was undiluted hell. Brush was heavy with water, drenching them. Horses lunged, plunged, ears laid back. Wind shook torrents from the trees. Low clouds cut visibility to a rod. Brush tore at their slickers. And the rain continued to fall, soddenly.

Now Waterhole Charlie's voice came filtering up from the canyon on the left. "Hi-ee-e-e-ee! Comin' straight at yuh, boys! A blue ox as big as a cattle car!"

The big brute came from Mark Ament's side and Hoss reined toward him, building a loop with his customary lazy swing. Through the swirling mist, he saw Ament spurring toward the break, standing in the stirrups, his loop trailing lax in his outstretched hand. Some of the best ropers Hoss had ever known worked that way. Hoss was admiring Ament's horsemanship and was caught by surprise when a big brindle steer got out from under his feet, bawling and ringy as he shed Hoss's hurried cast.

Hoss yelled: "Yip-e-e-e! Look lively, Coberly, or he'll run right over you!"

Hoss was coiling his rope when Waterhole Charlie's blue steer piled over the brink, thick legs churning, split hoofs throwing gouts of mud. Here was a ton of dynamite on the hoof, and Ament was right in its way. As the beast swerved left, Ament sent his rope out with a flip, the loop standing vertically until it ate up the slack, then snapping before the thundering renegade's face and over his horns.

Hoss yelled for Ament to unload as the great beast pivoted and hurtled back into the canyon. Horse and rider took off like birds, soaring into space. Hoss's fear for the young DC Connected ramrod died a-borning. A big wild cow with twin calves popped up over the rim right before him.

Hoss laid his rope on her, thankful she wheeled up the hill. Traveler braced and the cow pitchpoled, bawling. Hoss was on her, whipping on the strings.

Coberly was battling with the brindle steer. He'd roped and busted it, but slipped and fell and was slow getting to it. The steer got up and the lanky cowpoke was trying to bulldog it to earth. The brute was mopping up the canyon bottom with him when Hoss forefooted it and jerked it down.

A few minutes later, Ament came riding down, skinned up and bleeding some, but grinning. Action had warmed him up, thawing out all the sullen bitterness.

"Nice going," he cried. "Them three beefs won't average less'n sixteen-fifty. Lame Johnny's tied to something up yonder. I'll go give him a hand." Not a word about the misery of cold, wet clothes. No mention of his near escape from death, when jerked into the canyon. Only exultation at their success.

THIS initial haul—two big steers, a heavy cow and a yearling heifer—was a bright promise. But they rode hard until mid-afternoon without further luck. But just as they were about to head for home, Waterhole Charlie flushed and tied his steer, to his great delight.

They were a tough-looking lot when they checked in at the DC Connected, bloody, begrimed, their slickers in shreds. Hoss got out the bottle he'd fetched from Gunsight City and a pull all around made the gray skies seem brighter.

Libby had supper ready and as they sat at the table, Hoss had to smile. He was the silent one now. The other four outdid themselves embellishing the day's results for the girl. Better than four hundred dollars necked down to trees, out yonder. A few more days like this, Mark Ament

opined, and the Old Man could have his operation.

Hoss sneered. "You talk like a shorthorn, Ament. It ain't ketchin' beefs, but gettin' 'em to rail an' turnin' 'em into cash that count. An' what'll this Beals Golliher be doin' when he hears DC Connected is drivin'? He'll come at us with hired gunsmoke an' you rabbits will stampede for your holes, leaving me to face 'em alone."

"You sure do hate yourself, Greer. I give you credit for selling us the idea of working slippery slants for renegade beef. Sure. But I say you are as fast on the run from Golliher's bullets as we are, and I dare you to prove different."

When they went out through slackening rainfall they were so mad at Hoss they snubbed him. Rain quit during the night but dawn broke gray, bleak. Clouds blanketed the dripping hills and the wind was cold. Hoss routed the boys out, deflating them cruelly, shaming them.

Though Hoss drove them from dawn till dark, the tally never quite equalled that of the first day. But it wasn't bad and, after a week, there were smiles on the gaunt, bearded faces. Twenty big steers were cooling out.

Clearing weather brought new problems. Bushed renegades, made wary by the chousing, sunned themselves on the points, ducking into heavily brushed canyons at the approach of riders. It demanded new strategy and Hoss, terribly short-handed, rose to it.

"Yonder's the Devil's Fingers, where we've seen big beefs sunnin'," he explained. "We'll each work a draw, bein' cautious. A lone hand is out of luck if he gets hurt where we can't find him. Besides, I won't waste time huntin' bushed-up carcasses."

"That ain't so smart," growled old Lame Johnny. "There's big stuff in them finger draws. Yestidday, I saw Ol' Piebald Pete yonder. Cripes, what a critter.

When I drawed close, he thumbed his nose an' dove into Rattlesnake. That 'un will go a ton. I wouldn't dab a rope onto him if beefs was a dollar a pound."

"Naturally not," sneered Hoss. "Takes a tophand to bust them biggies. I'll take Rattlesnake an' if your Piebald Pete's still there, I'll show you shorthorns something."

Ament bridled. "I've had two ropes on that devil, Greer, an' couldn't hold him. I never had a chance. I've got fifty dollars that says you got even less chance."

"You've made yourself a fool bet, cowboy."

"Me, I'd like a fifty dollar hunk of that, Greer," said Lame Johnny, and Waterhole Charlie and Lanky Sam Coberly put in for the same. Hoss accepted the bets, smiling thinly.

"Hate to take your money, boys, but easy come, easy go. Let's wipe off the chin slobber an' fly at it." He was talking hard, but he wasn't feeling it. The grind was exhausting him. And the younger men—Waterhole Charlie, Lanky Sam and Mark Ament—were thriving on it. Lame Johnny, failing after the third day, had been put to unnecking the tamed steers and driving them to a fenced trap at the mouth of Lynx Creek.

But Hoss ached all over. He was getting too old for this. As they rode to comb the Fingers, Mark Ament expressed concern.

"Greer, you look like a bull that's been whipped from the herd. Suppose we wrap up the deal and light out for Gunsight City, some soothing syrup and assorted fun."

"Like hell," snorted Hoss. "I know, you'd like to be sparkin' pretty Libby, but that can wait. Every man gets a big beef out of the Fingers. C'mon."

They approached the Fingers uncomplainingly, almost gleefully. It would be worth it to see Old Hoss humbled, especially if he tied to Piebald Pete. Hoss found no such mental solace as he gouged along the north slope of Rattlesnake.

CHAPTER THREE

Dry-Gulched!

LAME of body, Hoss rode with a heavy heart, hoping Piebald Pete and all his tribe were long out of Rattlesnake. It was Rocky going, rough and steep.

Traveler shied from the sound of a rattlesnake, snorting. But brush was crashing below, and then Hoss was staring at the biggest hunk of beefsteak rolled into one hide. Red eyes struck fire. Wide horns tossed defiantly. Ragged breath gusted from flaring nostrils.

The giant piebald whirled, hurdled a thicket and smashed into the canyon bottom. It was Piebald Pete. He'd heard the yarns—a giant animal mostly seen from afar. He'd shed many a loop. He'd broken many a rope. His tally of dead cowboys was five. A streak of varicolored hell, fleet as a deer, savage as a puma.

Traveler was after the steer, Hoss clawing at his rope strap while trying to shield his face from the catclaw. They soared over the brush in swift, perilous pursuit. Flying debris from Piebald's churning hoofs pelted horse and rider. Experience told Hoss that this was suicide, but suddenly he didn't care. The fever was in his veins and his loop was ready.

The steer hit the bottom and wheeled downstream. Hoss slanted as Traveler took the turn and kept his feet. Fifty yards of open, sandy going, and Hoss was gaining. He swung his rope in swift circles and sent it out—straight and true across those spreading horns.

The rope sang taut. The big beef catapulted through a flying half circle, heels over head, to a crashing fall. Breath jarred from its body and Hoss, beaming at his perfect hoollihan, was stepping from the saddle with the strings.

But he figured too soon. The steer came up instantly. Maybe it was stunned. Maybe it was roused. *Quien sabe?* Instead of lunging against the tied rope and braced pony, it spun and charged, horns lowered, bawling angrily.

Hoss straddled leather again and pivoted Traveler. A needle-like horn scraped Hoss's leg as the steer flashed past. Traveler dutifully braced, but nothing could hold such an impact. Down went the twelve hundred pound pony, with Hoss hurled clear. Piebald Pete dragged the horse a full, rod before the cinches—weakened by the gruelling strain—parted. Lying there, Hoss watched the big wild critter vanish around a brushy bend, the saddle—its rope tied hard and fast—whipping along behind.

Bruised and bleeding, Old Hoss sat up, his face lugubrious as he watched Traveler gain its feet. The horse stood there dejectedly, its head sagging, tail drooping, knees sprung, spent and spiritless.

"Licked," Hoss groaned. "Licked by a damned ox. Traveler, looks that Piebally devil cut us into the canners. We're headed slappity-bang for the last pasture."

The pony whickered and Hoss got up slowly, painfully, swiping moisture from his eyes. He cursed the loss of his two hundred dollar full stamped, rim fire, Silver City saddle. Somewhere along that careening critter's trail, the kak would catch on something and snap the rope.

SOMEWHERE up the gulch, blue jays were sqawking. Hoss figured maybe they were screeching at his saddle. It was worth a look. Before he started, Hoss laid a hand between Traveler's ears, scratching.

"A damn fool play of mine, pony-horse. By rights you should have a broke neck an' me a broke spine. Only the sand saved us. Any numbskull should know better than to tie to a yak like that without britchin' front an' back. It would have

bin nice to have bragged a little an' collected them bets, wouldn't it, huh, Traveler?"

The pony nuzzled him. Hoss hadn't more than a hundred yards to go to the spot where the jays yelped. He found his saddle. He found Piebald Pete too—something he wouldn't have dared hope.

The steer had started up the hillside, threading a thicket. The saddle hung up. The rope held. Taking slack, the steer bore to the left, wrapping up the thicket. Somewhere in his struggles, he'd leaped over the rope and there he was, snubbed close in the heart of the thicket, scarcely able to move.

Hoss had little trouble whipping the hogging strings around Piebald Pete's hind legs. It was more difficult and infinitely more dangerous to bulldog the tangled creature to earth and tie the front and hind legs together.

Removing the rope, Hoss carried his saddle back and, after a makeshift cinch repair, mounted and rode to the steer, dragging it onto the sand flat with his loop around the horns. He had scarcely recoiled his rope, preparatory to necking the brute to a pliant cottonwood, when he straightened.

The sound were hoof echoes dropping from the rim. Before Hoss had located the rider, the hail came tumbling. "Aieee-e-e, Greer!"

"Hullo!" yelled Hoss. "Who's that?"

"It's Mark Ament! Come up here —quick!"

"If you want me, come down here." Hoss wanted to see Ament's face when he looked at Piebald Pete. Dabbing his loop on the big steer had somehow revived him. "Come on down, Ament, with your money in your hand."

He heard the slow curse and Mark Ament put his pony down the rimrock and quartered down the footslope, sliding. Silent and plainly flabbergasted, he drew rein in the bottom, staring at the giant beef critter he'd worked so hard to capture. He hardly knew Hoss was there. Finally, like a man stunned, he said:

"Old Piebald! You—you roped him, Greer?"

"He didn't lay down for me, Ament. I cannot tell a lie. I done it with my stout Manila." Hoss felt no need of telling the whole truth—why should he? He felt fine now. He felt wonderful. "The easy way the critter handled, Ament, I had my doubts this was Piebald Pete. You ease my mind, sayin' it's really him."

AMENT took off his hat, scratching his head as if puzzling some knotty problem. Then he looked at Hoss.

"I can't imagine it, Greer, but I hand it to you. I've never doubted you were good, but never could believe you were that good. Yep, you win all the marbles. Will the boys ever be surprised!" He paused, clapping on his hat and flinging a scared look toward the rim. "Holy smoke! This almost made me forget why I came."

He drew a long breath, hesitating, licking his lips. Hoss said, impatiently: "Out with it, man? What's the matter? One of the men hurt?"

Ament gulped. "Hurt, yes, but not working beef like you're thinking. It's Lame Johnny. When I left him he was dying."

"Dying of what?"

"Lead poisoning. Three slugs in him and plenty of blood drained out. Seems when he left us, he went for them two steers in Squaw Creek, loosed 'em an' hazed 'em toward the Lion Creek trap, slow. Then he ran into Beals Golliher an' his gunnies."

"Yeah?" Hoss stiffened. "What they doin' in here?"

Ament spat. "Golliher 'lowed he'd heard DC Connected was rustling his beef in these hills. Came up to investigate and, sure enough, he found a lot of his stuff panned at Lion Creek, turned it loose and sent two men with it towards the loading pens at Cartright Station. Then they came looking for us."

"Too bad they didn't find us," grinned Hoss. "Then what?"

"Well, Golliher wanted to know where I had the boys working. Lame Johnny wouldn't tell so they manhandled him some. The old warhog got mad and went for his gun. They shot him off his pony and rode away. But he takes lots of killing. He got up, whistled his pony and rode to me in Ice House Canyon, all the while bleeding like a stuck hog. I left him with Waterhole Charlie and rode to find you. I doubt if Lame Johnny's breathing when I get back."

"Rode to find me, eh?" If the young ramrod had known Hoss better, he wouldn't have wrongly interpreted Hoss's smile and strange softness. "That's thoughty of you, son. Warp your rope around this yak's horns an' snub him up—not too tight. I'll cast off the hoggin' strings an' then we'll light out an' see what can be done to get that beef back."

"You're an optimist, Greer," said Ament as he snubbed Piebald Pete. "You ain't got the chance of a snowball in a fryin' pan of getting anything off of Golliher."

"We don't care who buys our steers, Ament. We want the money an' Golliher's money's as good as the next."

"Getting money from Golliher?" Ament sneered. "Don't make me laugh, Greer."

"Laughin's good for the belly, Ament." Hoss cast off the strings and stood back to watch the steer get up. "You laugh an' I'll get the mazuma for Doy Climmons. Let's go."

LEAVING Piebald Pete to fight his snub, Hoss and Mark Ament sent their ponies across the rim and around the rincons in the longest but easiest way to Ice House Canyon. Arriving there, they found Waterhole Charlie sponging the stricken man's fevered face and answering his pleas for water with cool drippings from a squeezed bandanna. Waterhole had ripped up his shirt to bind Lame Johnny's wounds.

Hoss took one look at that graying face and knew Lame Johnny was doomed. "Gotta get him to the medico quick," he told them. "Hand him up to me, careful. Mark, you ride to Gunsight City with me. Waterhole, you locate the other boys and ride to the ranch to be with Libby. Easy now. Boost him a little higher. That's it. I've got him. Come on, Mark. We're on our way."

Hoss pressed Traveler, yet held the gait to an easy singlefoot that was not too hard on the wounded man. At times Lame Johnny was dead to the world and Hoss would believe him gone. Then, rallying, he would wake up, grin at Hoss and wax jocular.

"Sorry I can't stick around to collect that Piebald Pete bet, Greer."

"Collect, you tough bait of jerked bull meat! Why you think I'm totin' you to the sawbones? I win that bet, fella, an' I aim to keep you healthy till you've paid me off."

"Quit joshin'. Don't tell me a glandered up ol' coffin model like you could tie to Piebally an' come off best."

"That's just what he done, Johnny," spoke up Ament. "And 'lowed he had his doubts about it being Piebally on account of how easy it was to bust him. Yep, Greer's got the critter necked down on the Rattlesnake sand flats."

Lame Johnny smiled and shook his head. "That does it," he murmured. "Now I'm content to die. I've seen everything." And he was unconscious.

Time and again, Lame Johnny wakened and Ament, watching the quiet exchange of words between Hoss and the wounded man, wondered what they talked about. Actually, the talk was about the Z Cross boss—Beals Golliher, his persecution of nesters, small cowmen and farmers, destruction of defiant politicians, fear of him by lawmen and juries.

According to Lame Johnny, Hiatt had rebelled against the orders of the man to whom he owed his job. The old-timer, bedded in the feed barn, had overheard the quarrel. Golliher handed Hiatt a warrant for Doy Climmons' arrest—charge, rustling. "Hiatt's posse come to the DC Connected," recounted Lame Johnny, "an' browbeat Libby to tell where her dad was. I saddled and took the shortcut to upper Hardscrabble. They beat me to him.

"I seen Doy shot down without warnin'. In the millin' confusion, somebody shot Hiatt. Doy didn't do it, 'cause he was out cold an' stayed thataway till I got him to the Cartright Station medico."

The two horsemen with their unconscious gunshot victim drew curious men from their dinners in Gunsight City. Hoss carried Lame Johnny into the doctor's office. Doc Knott wasn't in and Ament went to find him. While he waited, Hoss uncorked one of the medico's bottles and trickled whiskey down Lame Johnny's throat.

Then the sawbones came—a small, unkempt man. As the door closed behind him, Knott froze. A voice boomed from the street:

"Don't doctor that man, Knott! You hear me?"

Knott hollered: "I hear you, Hank," and flinched under Hoss's glare. "I'm sorry, sir, but a doctor mustn't play dirty, rotten politics."

CHAPTER FOUR

Death at the Cowskin

HOSS was stumped. "Where's another doctor, Mark?" he asked.

"None closer than Cartright Station,

on the railroad. Long ways out there."

"Horse doctor," scoffed Knott, moving to Lame Johnny and feeling for a pulse. "Unfit to minister to human ailments." Hoss tried again.

"We'll forget politics, Doc, but for God's sake fix this man's hurts."

"Sir," said Knott, icily, "you heard what the gentleman said."

"You'll be coffin freight in about a minute." Hoss jabbed him with his gun. "If Lame Johnny dies, so do you. Wash up and get busy."

Knott showed none of his vaunted fear, smiling, nodding. "It will be best, sir, if you fire." Hoss was flabbergasted. Outside, that booming voice cried, "Come out, Doc! You patch that Pike hombre an' I'll cut off your whiskey."

Knott shuddered. "Coming, Hank. Coming!" Then a latent revolt flamed in him. "No, by the gods!" he swore. "That's not fair, playing on my weakness!" He drank deep from the bottle Hoss had opened, shucked his coat, washed noisily and took sterilized instruments from a pan on the stove.

Hoss and Ament watched a miracle. Knott, fighting the shakes moments ago, was suddenly calm, steady, sober. He told Ament how to administer the ether and then extracted bullets, closed sundered blood vessels and sewed up minor incisions.

After bandaging Lame Johnny, he prepared and injected a saline into his half-emptied veins and covered him with a blanket.

"He will sleep," he said, wearily, "and so will I. His chances of going on living are infinitely better than mine." He killed the bottle, drinking the whiskey neat like water. He stumbled into an adjoining bedroom, fell across the bed and was instantly asleep.

Hoss, grimly silent now, removed Knott's clothes, tucked him into bed, looked to the window fastenings and tip-toed from the room, closing the door.

"Well, Mark," he said, "we got more than we had any reason to expect, didn't we?"

THE YOUNG ramrod turned from the window, where he'd been drawn by hoof echoes on the street. "That," Ament sneered, "was Beals Golliher and his gun cuties. Probably just getting back from Cartright Station, after selling our big steers. Damn his soul all to hell!"

Hoss said, casually, "Where does the great man hang his hat, Mark?"

"Upstairs, over his Cowskin Saloon. They say he's got quite a lush place up there."

"You stay with Lame Johnny," said Hoss. "I'm going out the back way. Lock up after me. Don't let anybody in till you've made damn sure who it is. Doy Cimmons' gal will feel purty bad if anything happens to you, Mark."

"You're joshin', Greer."

"Son—" there was something pitiful in the sudden wistful look on Hoss Greer's face—"I never married, mostly because I never found just the right one—or thought I hadn't. I ain't half the man I'd have been workin' beside a good woman. Nor will you be. The gal loves you, even if you're too blind to see it. She needs you an' if you don't speak to her, by crimus, I'll do it myself. If I was thirty year younger, you wouldn't stand a chance. Think it over."

Hoss let himself out the rear door, moved casually into the alley so as to attract little attention.

Nonchalantly, he rolled and lit a cigarette. Along the cross streets, left and right, he saw normal movement, but the alley was clear. He moved leisurely to the two-story building housing the Cowskin Saloon. At the rear door, only a step from the alley, he paused, listening.

Testing his gun pull, Hoss let himself inside, closing the door. He took a long minute, accustoming his eyes to the gloom. This short passageway gave to the card room hall, and to the upper floor by a staircase slanting above a litter of brooms, mops and slop buckets. Hoss climbed the stairs.

At the stairhead, Hoss paused. Low voices came through an open doorway. He tiptoed down the hall and entered. Hoss was surprised. Golliher, at a table, was equally so. He was big, handsome, swift with the lazy lightning of a snake.

Across the table sat Hank Burley, powerfully muscled, fiery haired, pock-marked. He bent a pig-like glare at Hoss, his great hands flexing as they poised over his guns.

"Who's this, Beals?"

"Search me. How come you bust into a man's rooms without a go-to-hell, fella? Clear out."

Hoss grinned, scratching a ten-day stubble. "You gents don't know me from Aunt Addie, but I'll bet you ain't in no doubt as to why I'm here."

Golliher scowled. "What's this, a hold-up?" He gestured to the gold on the table. "You won't get away with it. Gunsight's a Golliher town and this is Golliher gold."

Hoss closed the door grinning. "Not a dime of that money is yours."

Burley said, "He come here with Ament—carrying Lame Johnny."

"Miss Libby's hiring gunhands and she sent her prize gunnie to collect for her," Golliher grinned. "What a shock that gal's in for."

"Wrong, Cochise." Hoss paused, letting the name bring pallor to the great man's cheeks. "You've fooled plenty people, Cochise, including me. Way too late, I'm piecing the busted pattern. You've changed. And these gray hairs and stubby whiskers change me, don't they? Me— Hoss Greer."

"Hoss Greer?" The boss was sweating. "It—can't be! But—"

"No? You made it tough, feller. When Doy Climmons and I killed that Faro Briggs tinhorn in Payson, we went into your black book. Neither of us suspicioned you was Cochise Briggs. Nice how you framed Doy and steered us into a gunfight to finish us both. You was sure I'd kill Doy, so when he drawed on me, you shot me from the brush."

"Hoss, you got me all wrong."

"You were born wrong, Cochise. One of my men found cigarette stubs and an empty shell where you'd bushed up. I came hunting him as Hig Hiatt's killer, only to find that you worked the same game on Doy and Hig that you worked on me an' Doy. You said you'd ruin Doy. And when Hig tried to do what he thought his honest duty, you shot him from ambush. Don't bother to lie about it. Lame Johnny follered the sign. Now that you know why I'm here, Cochise."

"Shall I beef him, boss?" asked Burley. "Say the word."

Golliher's yellow eyes glittered. "Can't see how he can get us both before one of us gets him." He moved, widening the angle between him and Burley. "He's too old to be very fast, Hank. Try him out careful. If he draws his gun on you, I'll notch him. If he chooses me, you pot him. How can he win?" Now his voice rose frantically. "Draw, Hank. Fill his lousy carcass with lead! Kill him."

CHAPTER FIVE

Rest in Peace

GOLLIHER sailed to his right, leaping, drawing. Burley, a stupid killer used to obeying Golliher, came out of his chair with a guttering roar. Hoss chose him, drawing with blinding speed.

His .45 spat as it cleared the holster lip and Burley grunted like a man flung to earth. He shuddered, rose, his broad face convulsed with terror. Then he dropped.

Without jarring the smooth rhythm of his drawing motion, Hoss pivoted toward Golliher, knowing he was far behind and —by any yardstick—a dead pigeon. The Gunsight boss's pistol flamed and the room was again jarred.

Bringing his weapon to bear up that staring face, Hoss saw it disintegrate.

The ear-splitting report had come from behind and to Hoss's right. He spun about and there stood Doc Knott.

"Couldn't sleep," he said, pensively. "Nerves. When Ament told me what you were up to, I decided to attend to some unfinished business. Thanks a lot for choosing Hank Burley and leaving Golliher for me."

Hoss strode to the window.

What he saw gave him a start. Down the street came Waterhole Charlie on one side, Lanky Sam Coberly on the other. Between them, and a rod back, rode Libby Climmons, her trim body clothed in levis, her blond hair flying. As they rode, the three of them were throwing lead, spearing back Golliher hirelings who had attacked them as they entered town.

Down at the medico's office, Mark Ament came out, and dropped to one knee, sending lead toward the front of the Cowskin.

HOSS saw Libby quit her pony and race toward Mark. He heard her call his name, saw the young ramrod catch her in his arms. They went inside. At that moment, Hoss' attention came back to Harper Knott. The doctor had not obeyed Hoss. His voice now rang through the upper story, gladly, wildly.

"Gentlemen, gentlemen! Stand back and let's talk."

"Here's talk." A gun blared, shaking the hall. Hoss heard the brutal impact of lead striking Knott, heard the gust of his breath. The roar of the scattergun dominated all other sounds and that, in

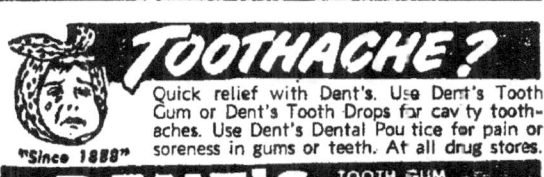

turn, was succeeded by the vengeful screaming and cursing of men wounded by flying buckshot. Harper Knott reeled into the room and fell, his weapon thudding against the floor. Hoss knew he was dead before he measured his length.

At the stairhead, Hoss could hear men talking.

Someone called: "Hey, Beals!"

Hoss faked Golliher's voice. "Help! Hey—" Hoss gargled the words, ending them by cracking his palm against his thigh.

"By cripes, they're holdin' Beals in there. Gotta get him loose. Ease along the walls, boys, an' when I give the word, rush that door."

Hoss picked up Beals Golliher's gory carcass and, holding it by the collar and the seat of the pants, moved toward the door.

"Two can play that rushing game, boys," he roared. "Comin' out after you, you lawless sons of dogs!"

He heaved Golliher's body through the portal. The response was instant and violent. The hall was filled with the shuddering concussion of guns. Bullets smacked solidly into Golliher's unfeeling flesh as he fell. For a second all was silent, Hoss standing poised and ready, his gun palmed. An agonized gasp broke the hall hush.

"My God, boys! It's Beals—dead!"

"The hell," rapped another. "Well, how was we to know? Ain't much light up here an'—"

"Me, I ain't waitin' to do no explainin'," yelped one, his feet beating a swift tattoo down the hall. "I'm gettin' scarce."

The retreat became a panic and then a rout. Hoss had to laugh softly as he heard them tumbling down the stairs and out of the lobby.

Hoss, moving slowly down the stairs, breathed normally again. He had run a long bluff on a pair of dirty deuces. And there had not been one man with the nerve to call.

THE TOWN buried its dead and erased the scars of battle. Then, as men suddenly realized they were out from under the shadow of terror, they were free again to speak and act and vote according to their consciences.

The merchants kicked in for a big celebration, fiesta, rodeo and carnival. The whole countryside attended to pay tribute to Hoss Greer and Doy Climmons, and Harper Knott.

That celebration was quite an affair, lasting three full days. They had a great granite boulder hauled down from the hill and planted in the center of the main intersection. Under it they buried the Body of Doc Knott. On the boulder was written:

> HARPER MAXWELL KNOTT
> WE CRUELLY CALLED HIM SOT
> TILL A HERO'S WREATH HE GOT
> WHEN THE TYRANT TOOK HIS SHOT
> 1859-1907
>
> **Rest in Peace**

Next day, at the same intersection, Mark Ament and Libby Climmons were married by the Padre of the Trails, a circuit-riding sky pilot. Waterhole Charlie stood up with Mark and the daughter of the acting sheriff attended Libby. Hoss gave away the bride, in the absence of Doy Climmons whom he had come here to kill.

About all that's left of Gunsight City is Doc Knott's massive tombstone. The pull of the railroad sounded Gunsight's death knell. But each spring, when the warm winds melt the snows and bring out the profusion of wild flowers, Mark and Libby, their three boys and Old Doy, rendezvous with Hoss Greer at the grave of the drunken medico, there on the grassy flats.

THE END

(Continued from page 113)

lightnin'! Damn it, George, don't take the chance!"

Doc Scanton's voice was like a clap of thunder. "Lute, you're admitting it was like Pete claimed."

"Maybe it was! George, don't let him cripple the both of us!"

Scanton laughed and stepped forward, placing himself between George and Pete. But George had subsided, his moment of proud drive gone. He studied the muddy ground, then flung a scowl at Lute.

"You damned yellow dog."

The doctor's voice was cheerful. "That's right, George, and you're his only defense now against a neighborhood that hates him. He can't stand the thought that you might lose your gun hand, too. Nor can you, and it shows all over you. George, supposing I tell it around that the three of us got the truth out of Lute, and that you've retracted your talk against Pete Furness?"

It was a long moment before George replied, then his voice was barely audible. "Go ahead, Doc. Furness and me ain't got any quarrel since Lute's blatted."

"We'll drink on it, George," Scanton said.

Pete was on the point of refusing until he saw the doctor's strategy. Throughout the West the sharing of a friendly drink rendered all previous differences null and void.

"Come on in, boys," George said.

Pete left the doctor at the main road. "You've cleared yourself a trail, Pete," Scanton said. "Now get on home. I reckon Dorcas can do more for your aches and pains than I could."

Scanton turned his horse, a tired old figure with the weight of his frontier practice on his shoulders. But they were square shoulders. Pete grinned at them, squared his own and headed home.

www.ingramcontent.com/pod-product-compliance
Lightning Source LLC
Chambersburg PA
CBHW080912020726
47502CB00008B/2437